PRAISE FOR
EARTH FORCE RISING

"A richly detailed, highly imaginative world and a cast
of clever, creative kids. Readers will be eager to bound
into the next book."—Shannon Messenger, author of
the Keeper of the Lost Cities series

"A joyful space adventure full of humor,
friendships, and action . . . This is a great sci-fi adventure
for boys and girls alike. I had so much fun reading it!"
—S. J. Kincaid, author of the Insignia series and *The Diabolic*

"Fans of *Ender's Game* will feel right at home in this
fast-paced debut. . . . I read it in a day, unable to put it
down, and look forward to more from this promising
new author!"—Wesley King, author of *The Incredible
Space Raiders from Space!* and *OCDaniel*

Also by Monica Tesler

Bounders, Book 2: *The Tundra Trials*

BOUNDERS
BOOK 1

EARTH
FORCE
RISING

Previously titled *Bounders*

MONICA TESLER

ALADDIN

New York London Toronto Sydney New Delhi

ALADDIN

An imprint of Simon & Schuster Children's Publishing Division
1230 Avenue of the Americas, New York, New York 10020
First Aladdin paperback edition December 2016
Text copyright © 2016 by Monica Tesler
Previously titled *Bounders*
Cover illustration copyright © 2016 by Owen Richardson
Also available in an Aladdin hardcover edition titled *Bounders*.
All rights reserved, including the right of reproduction in whole or in part in any form.
ALADDIN and related logo are registered trademarks of Simon & Schuster, Inc.
For information about special discounts for bulk purchases, please contact
Simon & Schuster Special Sales at 1-866-506-1949 or business@simonandschuster.com.
The Simon & Schuster Speakers Bureau can bring authors to your live event.
For more information or to book an event contact the Simon & Schuster Speakers Bureau
at 1-866-248-3049 or visit our website at www.simonspeakers.com.
Cover designed by Karin Paprocki
Interior designed by Mike Rosamilia
The text of this book was set in Adobe Garamond Pro.
Manufactured in the United States of America 1116 OFF
2 4 6 8 10 9 7 5 3 1
Library of Congress Control Number 2016955683
ISBN 978-1-4814-4593-1 (*Bounders* hc)
ISBN 978-1-4814-4594-8 (pbk)
ISBN 978-1-5344-0092-4 (eBook)

For Nathan

EARTH
FORCE
RISING

I

I KNOW IT'S RUDE TO STARE. HOW MANY times has Mom told me that? A million? But I've never seen an alien before. Not up close, at least. Sure, we've all seen the *Global Geographic* specials that air on the webs in a constant loop, 24-7. Anyone who hasn't seen pics and vids of the Tunnelers must have been hiding out in a dingy hover garage for the last twenty years.

But there he is. Sitting across from me on the air rail car. Me, Jasper Adams, riding the rails with an alien—a real live Tunneler—on my way home from school.

It must be a sign. I mean, what are the odds I'd have a

close encounter with an alien the day before I ship out to the space station?

The alien's lips pucker in a perfect circle and then whip back. A snarl bubbles out of his throat. *Errr. Arrr. Kleek. Kleek. Arrr. Kit. Ahhh.*

I'm staring at his mouth, when a mechanical voice makes me jump. "Can I help you?"

I spin around in my seat, looking for its source.

Kleek. Arrr. Kit. Arrr. "Yes, you. The boy who keeps staring like you've never seen an alien before. Can I help you?"

Busted.

I didn't notice the translator box hanging around the alien's neck. "Sorry. I shouldn't have stared."

"It's not a problem," he says through the box. "I'm sure I would stare, too, if I encountered an Earthling on our home planet."

That must mean it's okay to look. The alien is small. It's not like I'm one of the short kids, but I'm not that big for twelve, either. And I'm a lot taller than the alien. He has a long, rodentlike snout, bristly brown hair sprouting from every patch of skin, and is wearing dark glasses that curve around on the sides. The light probably bugs him, since Tunnelers live underground. He's wearing the standard officer's uniform—gray jumpsuit with slanted orange lettering: *EF* for Earth Force.

Soon I'll be suiting up in my own Earth Force uniform. I

leave for the space station in the morning. Maybe the alien will be on my flight.

"Do you work at the space station?" I ask.

"I do," he says. "A group of us came down to help at the aeroport. The first batch of Bounders is shipping out to the new EarthBound Space Academy tomorrow. While I'm here, I thought I'd do some sightseeing. It's my first trip to the planet."

He's here to help out for the Academy? Maybe I should tell him I'm a Bounder. I've never told anyone in my life. I mean, my parents know. And Addy knows, of course. She's a Bounder, too. And all the doctors and scientists who I visit every year for testing know. But I've never told anyone. I'm not supposed to tell anyone. Mom has seared that into my brain. She won't care if I tell the alien, though. I'll probably see him at the space station. Plus, tomorrow the whole world will know anyway.

The alien hops off the bench. His upper half hunches forward. The Tunnelers have a different center of gravity than humans. They probably have to stoop to make the clearance in all those tunnels. "Nice chatting with you, Earth boy. This is my stop."

"See ya." I missed my chance to tell him. Oh well.

I scoot across the aisle to grab his window seat, and press my hand against the glass. Out the window, beyond the two hundred blocks of skyscrapers webbed together by the air rail, I glimpse the edge of the retaining wall. On the other side of that wall is the ocean. And ten miles out to sea is the Earth Force Aeronautical Port. Tomorrow I'll board a passenger craft headed to the EarthBound Academy with the other Bounders. I'll finally be with kids like me. I won't feel like the alien on the air rail anymore.

Mom and Dad wanted Addy and me to grow up without the Bounder badge slapped across our chests, to lead a normal life. I might be clueless sometimes, but it's not like I don't know Bounders equal "not normal." Bounders are so weird, scientists basically bred our genes out of the population decades ago. Kids like me were "undesirable"— whatever that means. From what I can tell, it just means different. Or, okay, I guess different with a few challenges. So I've spent my whole life—all twelve years of it—trying hard to act normal. Not like a B-wad.

But Mom and Dad don't get that I wear the Bounder badge whether I tell or not. And it's not all bad. I mean, being a Bounder means going into space. How cool is that? Scientists discovered people with genes like mine have the best brains for quantum space travel, or bounding, as everyone calls it. Even though the aeronauts have been piloting the quantum ships for years, they're still not as good as they say the Bounders will be. That's why they bred us. That's why I was born.

The air rail jerks to a stop at the next platform, right

in front of a wall-size billboard of the Paleo Planet. The huge landscape looks eerily like early Earth. Herds of mammothlike mammals range on fields bordered by spiky mountain peaks. Trips to the planet are supposed to start this summer as part of Earth Force's new tourism plan. But lucky for me, a field trip to the Paleo Planet is the final event of the first Bounder tour of duty. In six weeks I'll be right there, strolling through the high grass, hanging with the wildeboars.

I lean my head against the window and fix my gaze on the ocean. The skyscrapers blur together as we race by, and my mind drifts a whole day into the future. I'm standing on the aeroport flight deck with my family, watching the passenger craft lower slowly down in a straight vertical line. Smoke billows up in big shoots from its two front engines. Then the ramp lowers and Admiral Eames descends. She crosses directly to me with an outstretched hand.

Welcome to the EarthBound Academy, Jasper.

"Jasper?"

"Jasper!"

I spin around in my seat. Two kids from class stand in front of me—Dilly Epstein and Will Stevens. That's weird. I didn't even know they were on the rail.

"Jasper," Dilly says, "wasn't that your stop?"

My mind feels cluttered. Part of me is still thinking about

Admiral Eames and the EarthBound Academy; the other part is trying to process what Dilly said.

"What?"

"Your stop," she says. "Don't you live in Building 537? We just passed it."

Oh no, not again. Now I'll have to transfer to an inbound rail, which means I'll be super late. As I jump out of my seat, half the stuff in my backpack scatters across the floor. I must've left it unzipped. Again.

"Really, Jasper," Will says, "are you ever gonna get it together?"

Am I supposed to answer that?

Dilly crouches and helps me gather my things. When she passes me my clarinet case, Will bursts out laughing.

"Dill, we've gotta go," he says. "It's our stop. Let the freak fix his own problems."

Dilly lifts her eyes to mine. I dive beneath the bench to retrieve an *Evolution* figure that escaped my bag. Why can't I just look at her? Say something normal for once.

"B-wad," Will mumbles as he steps out of the rail car.

Shut up, Will. I want to yell, scream, get in his face. But he's gone.

Dilly slips between the doors as they close. I probably should've said thanks.

When they hear I'm headed to the EarthBound Academy, they'll understand. They'll know why I'm such a spaced-out klutz. A spaced-out klutz who was born to bound across the universe.

· *EF* ·

"Mom! Jasper's home!" Addy yells as soon as I open the door. "Nice of you to show up, J. Mom's battery is a bit overcharged, even for her. Don't say I didn't warn you."

Mom jets from the kitchen. She still wears her whites from the pediatric ward. "Hi, honey. Thank goodness you're home. I was getting worried. How was school? Can I get you a snack? How are you feeling? Ready for your big day tomorrow? Are you holding it together?"

I never really know if I'm supposed to answer all those questions. They pile on top of one another in my mind. I rearrange them in their order of importance, or at least what I think is the right order of importance. But they just sit there, stacked up and dangling, so all I say is, "Hi, Mom."

She dashes to the kitchen. Mom always moves fast, like she's being timed. Like she's competing in some secret race none of us are fast enough to run in. I follow her, figuring there's something good in there. The smell of chocolate wafts through the apartment. "What are you making?"

"Your favorite, J-sweetie. Chocolate chip cookies." She lifts a pan with a batch of cookies fresh from the oven.

"Cool. Thanks, Mom." I grab a cookie and head to Addy's room.

"Ever heard of knocking, B-wad?" Addy shoves her journal into her drawer and glares at me. I don't blame her for not wanting to write on the webs. No privacy. She taught herself to print last year and keeps her journal hidden in her desk.

"Whatever." I hop onto her bed and curl up my legs. Maximilian Sheek, one of the famous quantum aeronauts, stares back at me from the poster above Addy's desk. She's obsessed with Sheek. Addy and all her friends stream EFAN—the Earth Force Affairs Network—on the webs constantly, hoping for a glimpse of him.

We don't talk at first, which is weird. For her. Addy is used to me being quiet, but she usually talks enough for both of us.

"I saw a Tunneler on the air rail today," I say.

Addy doesn't respond. Okay, that's really weird. You don't just run into a Tunneler every day. Chatty Addy should be all over it.

"What's up?" I ask.

She shrugs. Her face sags until her mouth pinches down. "It's just so unfair, Jasper. How come you get to do everything first?" She twirls her gold-brown hair around her pinky finger. We have the same hair, except on her it's long and wavy, and mine is lopped off at my ears and always falling in my eyes.

"Sorry," I say. And I really am sorry. I wish Addy were coming with me. "Next year, when you're twelve, we'll get to go to the EarthBound Academy together."

Once the kids at school find out I'm a Bounder, they'll know Addy must be a Bounder, too. They'll know our parents are part of the Bounder Baby Breeding Program. Just like you need the right combination of genes to have a baby with blue eyes or red hair, our parents carry the dormant genes needed to have a Bounder baby.

Being a Bounder is definitely a mixed bag. All the kids I know wish they could be an aeronaut—the next Maximilian Sheek or Edgar Han or Malaina Suarez. That's why they think it's totally unfair only Bounders can train to be aeronauts from now on.

Dad says other kids are jealous. That's why they say we're freaks with abnormal genes. That's why they call us B-wads. And trust me, it stinks. The kids at school call me a B-wad, and they don't even know for sure I'm a Bounder.

Yeah, they're probably jealous. But they're not wrong. I *am* different. A lot of the time I'm lost in space. Even when I do pay attention, I can't translate half of what my teachers say into my schoolwork. And don't get me started on my klutz factor. The other kids don't seem to have any trouble. It's like they were all there when the handbook for life was passed out, and no one saved me a copy.

Does Addy feel the same way? I'm not sure. She always seems to have it together. A lot more than I do, anyway. Still, it might be rough for her once the other kids find out the truth. Addy has another year before she ships out to the space station. She has to wait through my first two tours of duty.

I try to think of something to make her feel better, but I blank. Addy's the one who always knows what to say.

Dad peers in with a half-eaten cookie in his hand, letting me off the hook. "Okay, kids. Time for dinner. We need to get to bed early tonight. Jasper's got a big day tomorrow."

· E_F ·

Dinner is awesome. Mom wins the kitchen gold medal. We have spaghetti and meatballs with sauce made from scratch, garlic bread slathered with butter and weighed down with greasy cheese, and more chocolate chip cookies, of course.

No one says much. Dad offers up some compliments about Mom's cooking, and Addy and I shout out our agreement in between chews. I mean, the food really is good. We're mostly just busy eating. But the silence curls at the edges, like something is trying to get out. Something thick and dark and heavy, like the shadow that hung over Addy earlier. Tomorrow everyone will know we're Bounders. Tomorrow I'll be gone.

The first tour of duty is only six weeks. I won't be away that long. But when I come back, everything will have changed. I want to go. Really. I do. It's just, things are pretty good the way they are. And everything about the space station will be new and different. What if the food is terrible?

After I get ready for bed, Mom, Dad, and Addy show up

at my door. Even though I vetoed tuck-in sessions two years ago, I give a special, one-time exception. Addy slides in beside me, and my parents sit at the end of my bed. Dad tells one of his classic made-up tales about Horace the House Mouse and his silly space adventures that Addy and I used to be obsessed with when we were little. After the story, Mom shoos Addy out of the room, settles me under the covers, and plants a kiss on my forehead. Dad kisses me, too, then lingers in the doorframe for a moment after flipping my light switch.

Finally the door shuts, and I'm left alone. Three layers of blankets pile on top of me. It's not cold, but I need the weight to fall asleep. I close my eyes, and I'm back on the flight deck. The sun's glare off Admiral Eames's medals is blinding.

I can hear Mom and Dad talking in the living room. Too loud. I try to shut out the noise. Will it be this loud in the space station dorms? Will I ever be able to sleep?

Mom's voice swells as Dad urges her to whisper.

Mom: But I don't get it. What on earth are a bunch of kids going to do?

Dad: We've been through this, Emma. Their minds are perfect for performing the quantum calculations. They'll be better than the aeronauts at piloting the quantum ships.

Mom: Come on, Richard. That doesn't make sense. They use computers for the quantum calculations.

Dad: Why can't you let this go? We have two healthy, happy children. And Earth Force has assured us they'll be safe. What more could we want?

Mom: Healthy, yes. Happy, I hope so. But they're not typical kids. You don't understand about these conditions. The old medical journals talk about attention problems, sensory difficulties, social challenges, impulsiveness, and many other potential issues.

Dad: I thought you told me Jasper and Addy didn't have those conditions.

Mom: I've said there's a lot of variation. And Bounders aren't typically the most severe. But one thing is sure: it's a big deal to reintroduce these genes.

Dad: How many times are we going to have this conversation?

Mom: You know there's something they're not telling us! What are we sending our baby into?

Baby? Please. Mom can be so dramatic. I pull the covers over my head and press my hands against my ears.

That kind of talk has been going on for years, and usually, I just ignore them. But really? On the night before I leave for the space station? Are they trying to make me nervous?

It doesn't really touch me, though. Sure, part of me wants to stay here—safe at home with Mom and Dad, and especially Addy. But a bigger part of me wants to go. I'm a Bounder. I've always been a Bounder. I belong in space, bounding between the galaxies.

I close my eyes. See the passenger craft lowering onto

the flight deck. Grab Admiral Eames's outstretched hand.

There's a knock at the door. What now? I ignore it. I figure it's Mom, all emotional and wanting to give me another kiss my last night at home. The door isn't locked. If she really has to see me, she can walk right in.

The mattress sags near my feet. I pull the blankets off my face and scoot back on my elbows. Addy sits at the foot of my bed. Her purple pajamas have a rip at the left knee. She sniffs, and I can tell she's been crying. Then I see what she's holding. Her rosewood violin lies across her thin legs.

"Wanna play?" she asks.

Something wells up in me, too. Geez. I haven't cried in forever. I can't remember the last time we played together. I thought Addy was done with the violin.

I pull my clarinet case from my closet and place it on the bed. I fit the pieces together and raise the reed to my lips. Addy draws her bow. She pulls, and a piercing hum fills the room. I join, finding a natural harmony, and we feel our way together through a haunting, melancholy tune.

Addy leaves as silently as she came. I lay my clarinet in its velvet case and close the lid. I step toward my closet to put it away, then change my mind. I set the case on top of the duffel bags Mom packed for the EarthBound Academy.

MOM GASPS WHEN SHE SEES ME. "YOU LOOK
so handsome."

I peek at my reflection in the info screen mounted above
our mantel, and adjust my mosh cap. I have to admit, she's
right. No one would guess I'm twelve. I look fourteen, at
least.

The Earth Force cadet uniform isn't comfortable, but it's
crisp. The cotton is heavy, and the color is rich, a thick navy
with a hint of purple. The Earth Force officer uniforms are
dark gray, but they decided on a deep indigo for the cadets.
The insignia is the same: a russet orange circle with a ring of

smaller circles along the outside edge, the slanted letters *EF* in the center. Most people think the insignia represents our solar system—the planets revolving around the center sun—but I read in *Earth Force: Rise of the New Frontier* that the center circle is the Earth and the outer circles symbolize all the planets we'll explore. So according to Earth Force, our planet really is the center of the universe.

Addy slouches on the couch. I can't believe Mom won the battle and forced Addy into such a flowery, poufy dress. It's about as anti-Addy as possible. As soon as Mom turns around, Addy pumps her armpit, sending fart sounds through the room.

Priceless.

I fall onto the couch, laughing. Mom spins around. Addy points at me, and I jab her in the ribs. Mom just shakes her head.

Well played, Addy. What's Mom going to do? Send me to my room and make me late for my own launch?

Addy flicks the webs remote, and the info screen snaps on. She flips to EFAN. They're running old footage of a bounding mission, but the ticker at the bottom reads: *Tune in today at noon for live coverage as the first class of Bounders ships out for the new EarthBound Academy.*

"Look at that," Addy says. "You're a celebrity."

"Right," I say, "just like Sheek."

"You wish."

Dad walks in and claps his hands. "It's time." He picks up my duffels and walks to the door. I grab my clarinet case. Addy hops off the couch.

Mom freezes in the middle of our kitchen. She always buzzes about like she has a built-in motor, so her stillness is strange. Plus, her face is super pale, and her hands are shaking. I think maybe I'm imagining things, but then Addy laces her fingers through Mom's hand. That's even more un-Addy-like than the dress. She wouldn't do it unless she thought Mom needed help.

Maybe she does. Today everyone will know about Addy and me. It's a big deal. Maybe for Mom the most. She's been the one always making sure we kept the secret.

Dad holds the door, and we shuffle into the hall. We make it to the lift without running into any of our neighbors. The bell chimes, and the lift doors open. It isn't crowded, but there are probably thirty or forty people inside. As we step on, the passengers move back, creating a huge hole for us to fill. Dad has both of my duffels in one hand. He places his other one on the curve of Mom's back and pushes her in.

"Jasper, whoa!" someone shouts. A seventh grader I know from school steps forward.

Heat creeps into my face like a spotlight is shining on me and my Earth Force uniform. I brace, expecting him to call me a B-wad right here in front of my family.

"A Bounder?" he says. "Cool. Good luck."

"Thanks." I stand as straight as I can and stare out the window. Lifts like the one we're on cling to the skyscrapers like mythical beasts scaling the crossbeams.

Mrs. Garfield, my mother's friend, slides to the front. I didn't notice her when we first got on. Her gaze trails from my mother, to me, to Addy.

My mother stares at her shoes. She doesn't look up, not even when Mrs. Garfield touches her forearm. "How come you never told us, Emma?"

The silence stretches out, and the same lump that crept into my throat last night while I was with Addy comes back. I try to stand tall, but I slump.

My father drops his arm from my mother's back and drapes it across my shoulders. "We didn't want Jasper to be distracted," he says. "We wanted him to build a solid academic foundation before serving with Earth Force. Now he's ready. We couldn't be more proud."

I lean against Dad. He's right. I get pretty distracted as it is. If everyone knew about me, school would be doubly distracting. Plus, the novelty of a Bounder on the lift seems to be wearing off. The chatter is up, and only a few pairs of eyes stare in our direction.

Still, Addy has Mom's hand again.

· *EF* ·

When we board the sea shuttle to the aeroport, I want to grab Mom's hand, but I don't. My eyes almost pop out of my skull as we approach. The Earth Force Aeronautical Port. The place is even more enormous than I imagined. It rises like Atlantis, a city in the sea.

I pull at my collar. The starched cotton scratches my skin. Mom says I'll get used to it, but right now the cadet uniform feels like a straitjacket. The fifteen-minute ride from the retaining wall dock to the aeroport feels like fifteen hours. I step closer to Addy so our shoulders touch, but just barely.

Buildings of all shapes and sizes spring from the aeroport platform, everything painted the dark blue-gray of the sea. A dozen rocket launch sites, ten passenger craft landing zones, a mega-size zero-gravity training center. And now adding to its list of hugeness: the biggest bunch of Bounders ever brought together in one spot.

The guard boats surround us and escort our shuttle to the dock. The systolic pump lifts the shuttle level with the platform. As we cross onto the tarmac, the ocean rages beneath us, shooting spray onto the deck and dousing my uniform. A large placard with an arrow reads WELCOME BOUNDERS in black block print. My family moves with the herd in the direction of the arrow.

There's a weird thickness in my chest that makes it hard to breathe. This is what being a Bounder's all about, right? The

MONICA TESLER

upside. My nerves are cutting off my oxygen supply, but I'm actually pretty excited. Really. I am.

Dad's got my duffels, and I carry my clarinet case. I hold it low against my leg. Clarinets don't exactly equal cool. I better stuff it into my duffel before we launch.

Media crews from EFAN and other networks border the walkway. Mom covers her face with her purse. Reporters shove microphones at me, one after the next:

"How does it feel to be in the first class of Bounders to attend the EarthBound Academy?"

"Have you always known you were bred to be a Bounder?"

"Are you excited to visit the Paleo Planet?"

"Is neurodiversity really the answer to expanding the space program?"

Neuro-what? I stumble and swing out my hand clutching the clarinet case to break my landing. Dad grabs my arm and yanks before I fall on my face. Geez, Jasper, I thought you were leaving the clumsiness here on Earth. I look around, hoping none of the other cadets saw me trip.

Dad hurries us past the row of reporters. Earth Force officers line the path, too. Their gray uniforms blend into the gray buildings behind them. They usher the crowds, passing us along to the next officer in line.

"Welcome to the Earth Force Aeronautical Port."

"Bounders, proceed this way."

"Please keep moving."

As we bump along with the crowd, I end up next to another cadet, a small blond boy. Addy kicks my shoe. When I look at her, she rolls her eyes and nods at the cadet.

Oh yeah. "Hi," I say.

"Hello."

"I'm Jasper Adams."

"Cole Thompson."

The officers herd us to a roped-off area near the passenger crafts, where dozens of Bounders in their cadet uniforms stand with their families. I stick with Cole. "Pretty cool, huh?" I ask.

He doesn't look at me when he says, "I estimate there are already three hundred and twenty-eight people in this roped-off area, roughly sixty-two of whom are Bounders."

So he's good with numbers. "Yep," I say, "you're probably right."

He still doesn't look at me, but he smiles. Okay, then, I have a friend. A Bounder friend. I smile, too. The vise grip on my throat loosens a little. This is going to be okay. No, this is going to be great. I've been waiting my whole life for today. And I'm ready to do this.

A tall woman dressed in black, wearing big round sunglasses and spiky high heels, click-clacks over to a podium set up in front of the center passenger craft. The news crews close in with their cameras.

Addy jabs me in the ribs and whispers, "That's Florine."

As head of public relations for Earth Force, Florine Statton would be hard not to recognize. Her face is plastered all over EFAN every day. Not to mention, she stars in all the Bounder info vids they make us watch every year when Addy and I go for testing.

Florine's hair is white, the same bright white as her big teeth, which she's flashing at us through a forced smile. She taps the microphone with a long fingernail, sending coughlike sounds through the speakers placed across the tarmac. "May I have your attention, puh-*leeeze*? Good morning. Ladies, gentlemen, men and women of the press corps, esteemed and honored guests, Bounders . . ."

She sounds bored. Come to think of it, she always sounds bored, like she could be doing something so much better.

"Who's excited?" she asks in a voice that clearly says she's not. She brings her fingertips together in a butterfly clap.

Why did they send her, anyway? Why did they pick the world's snootiest person to run their public relations? If the gawk sites are right, all she cares about is getting her pic snapped with celebrities. I bet that's why she wanted the Earth Force gig. She gets to hang out with the famous aeronauts all the time.

Addy kicks my foot again. Florine kept talking, and I completely zoned out.

"Twelve-year-old Bounders from every metropolitan area on Earth will be initiated as the first class of cadets at the EarthBound Academy," Florine says with absolutely zero enthusiasm.

"You'll be bounding soon enough, kids," she continues. "But don't get ahead of yourselves. First you'll be trained by the best quantum aeronauts, some of whom were bounding before you Bounders were even born. Your genes might give you superior aptitude for bounding, but aptitude is meaningless without hard work. And our ranks of quantum aeronauts have already put in years of hard work. You'll do well to remember that."

Thanks for the lecture, Florine.

"Now, what else was I supposed to tell you?" she says.

Whispers flutter around me. A hunched hairy form in an Earth Force uniform approaches the podium. Oh wow, I'm pretty sure . . . Yep, it's the Tunneler from the air rail. I'm glad he's wearing his sunglasses, or the glare off the sea sure would be bugging him. He says something to Florine. Or I guess he grunts, and his translator box fills in the blanks.

She waves him off, but he persists. Finally she covers the microphone with a long-nailed hand and spins to face him. She towers over the poor guy. I can't hear her words, but I can tell the Tunneler is getting reamed. I wouldn't want to be on the receiving end of that.

A few tense seconds pass before she turns back to the microphone and smooths her black business suit. "I've been asked to announce that bags and belongings should be stacked behind the rope. Now say your farewells and prepare to board."

Dad joins the stream of parents flowing to the luggage dump. Around us, Bounders huddle with family, giving hugs and good-byes.

Mom stares out to sea and bites her lip. When she faces me, her cheeks are damp. "Six weeks," she says. "Then you'll be home."

Who is she reminding? Me or her? "I love you, Mom."

Dad returns from depositing my bags. He grips my shoulder and bends down so his eyes line up with mine. "We're proud of you, Jasper. Be safe."

"I will, Dad."

I turn to Addy. "So this is it."

She paints her face with a determined smile. "That Cole kid seems all right," she whispers. "A good first friend. Stick with him. And pay attention! You better remember everything about the Academy and your tour of duty. I need to get ready for next year, okay?"

"Sure," I say. "And, Addy, you always tell me not to care what other people think, right? Well, you shouldn't either. Being a Bounder doesn't change who you are. Remember that."

She tips her eyes to mine, and I hear her voice in my mind. *You remember, too, Jasper. You, too.*

· *E_F* ·

A straight-faced officer trades places with Florine Statton. "Welcome, families. I'm Lieutenant James Ridders. I need all the cadets to join me in front of the podium. We'll be boarding momentarily."

Cole and I cross to the roped-off area along with the other Bounders. A few parents escort their children, but officers step in and wave them back as soon as they reach the ropes. A couple of kids cling to their parents. A few cry. I can't watch. The massive lump in my throat returned as soon as I stepped away from my family, but I refuse to crumble. I've dreamed of this moment too many times not to be brave when it matters. I suck the salt-tinged air into my lungs and fix my eyes on the waves behind the passenger crafts, watching the spray jump onto the flight deck and roll back into the sea.

Still, it's hard not to look. A tall girl with a golden braid down her back jostles Cole and me as she darts for the front of the group, chased by her mother, who wedges past the officers.

The girl moves lightly, like a scrap of paper in a breeze. She wears a pale-blue tank top and a silver chain. She holds her thin arms out by her sides, gently brushing her fingers against everything she passes. Every few strides, she twirls.

"Mira. Mira!" her mother yells. She holds the girl's indigo

shirt in her hands. The shirt billows out behind her like a flag as she runs.

Lieutenant Ridders stares at the girl. He has the same expression as most of the kids. The same expression as I have, probably, because I ache with frustration and a familiar shame for the girl. We watch in slow motion, no one knowing what to do.

The seconds stretch until Lieutenant Ridders leans close to the microphone. "Miss, you need to be in uniform."

She doesn't look at him. She doesn't even seem to hear him. But her mother closes in and seizes her. The girl goes rigid as her mother drapes her with the indigo cloth, slips her arms into the sleeves, and fastens the buttons. I can tell by her mother's expert fingers it's not the first time she's wrestled the girl into her clothes.

The mother guides her by the shoulders and places her in the line. She leans in and kisses the girl's cheeks before returning to the family area. The girl—Mira—stares straight ahead, but her eyes are vacant. Whatever spirit possessed her was tamed by the Earth Force uniform. I'd never admit it, but I liked her better the other way.

AS WE STAND IN LINE BENEATH THE
mammoth silver disk of the passenger craft, we're shielded
from the sun and the glare off the sea. As I wait my turn
to board the craft, I check out the other Bounders. Even
though we come from all over Earth—the Americanas,
Eurasia, Amazonas, everywhere, really—we're the same.
We're dressed the same. We're going to the same place. We
share the same future. Finally I can blend in. I can stop
trying to force myself into a space I don't fit.

When I make it to the top of the boarding ramp, I turn
back and scan the crowd for my family. Dad folds Mom into

his chest. Neither of them notices me. But Addy does. Across the sea of people, Addy locks eyes with me and stretches her arm straight in the air. I raise my palm. "Good-bye," I whisper. I swear I hear her whisper back. Addy will be coming with me next year on my third tour. Then I'll be able to connect my two right spots in the world—home and space.

As I board the craft, Cole tugs my sleeve. "Quick. There are seats near the back. We'll have the best view out the rear windows when we exit the atmosphere."

We dash past the sealed cockpit and the side sections reserved for Earth Force officers. I tail after Cole across the sturdy brown carpet, past the rows of seats covered in tweed and tan pleather. We dodge a dozen Bounders milling around in the aisle, and jet for the back. We choose two seats in the center zone, last row.

I flop down on the oversize seat and sink into the tweed. The seat backs in front of us have built-in touch screens. Cole activates his screen and pages through the safety instructions for the craft. I get up on my knees and look out the back window. The maintenance crew is checking the craft, making sure we're ready for flight. Beyond them is the edge of the tarmac and the open ocean. The sea is a dark steely gray with tips of white and shadows of black.

Something slams into the back of my head. *Ouch!*

A standard-issue brown lace-up shoe lies on the ground

beside my seat. As I reach for it, a short freckly kid dives in front of me and tackles the shoe.

"It's mine!" he yells.

I stare at him. Obviously, I didn't steal his shoe. Geez, it nearly knocked me unconscious.

The freckly kid spins around in the aisle and freezes. A meaty boy with sloppy hair and bad skin saunters down the aisle. He takes his time. The huge grin on his face is mesmerizing and nauseating at the same time.

The freckly kid squares his shoulders. He raises the shoe in the air and shakes it in the meaty boy's face. "You shouldn't have stolen my shoe, B-wad! It wasn't funny." He makes a decent show of confidence, but his hand trembles as he holds the shoe.

The smile on the meaty boy's face grows until it floats in space like the Cheshire Cat's. "Yes, it was. It was really funny. We're all here to have fun, right?"

That seems to confuse the freckly kid. "Uh, sure."

Another guy I didn't notice at first steps up. He has an unbelievably relaxed posture, like you could pummel him with a dozen apple pies and he'd just shrug them off. He stares down at the freckly kid. "Why'd you call him that?"

"What?" the freckly kid asks.

"B-wad." The guy has dark hair and brown skin and is almost a head taller than the rest of us. "You know what it means, don't you? What the *B* stands for?"

"Sure, but, you know, everyone says it."

"Do you do everything everyone else does?" the tall guy asks. "Last time I checked, every kid on this craft is one of the *B*s in B-wad. So figure out a better way to swear, okay? Let's start treating ourselves with a little more respect. And have some fun, like the guy says."

The freckly kid looks at me. I shrug. He shoves his foot into his shoe and walks up the aisle.

The tall guy turns to the meaty boy. "Hey, Regis. Go back where you came from."

I brace for Regis to flip out or maybe even throw something, but he doesn't. His shoulders roll forward, and he mumbles, "Whatever," before heading to the front of the craft.

The tall guy offers his hand to me. "Sorry about your head, dude. The name's Marco. Marco Romero. I'm from Amazonas."

I shake his hand. "I'm Jasper. Americana East. And this is Cole."

Marco extends his hand to Cole, but Cole doesn't take it.

"We're not here to have fun," Cole says. "We're here for an important Earth Force assignment."

Marco laughs. "Yeah, whatever you say, Buzz Kill. Later." He turns and disappears into an aisle a few rows up.

I plop onto my chair. "Why didn't you shake his hand?"

"I don't like him," Cole says. "You didn't see what happened.

He was with that guy Regis. They stole the kid's shoe, played catch across the craft, and then nailed you in the head with it."

"Oh." Marco seemed okay to me, although the whole scene was a little odd. If Addy were around, she'd remind me I stink at reading people.

· *EF* ·

The engines jump to life, sending vibrations through the craft. Cole's face brightens. I'm sure mine does, too. In a matter of minutes we'll be airborne. Destination: space station.

"May I have your attention, puh-*leeeze*," Florine Statton says, dragging the word please out so long, she sounds like she's in pain. She stands at the top of the aisle, still wearing her giant sunglasses even though there's nothing sunny about the passenger craft. "The captain has informed me the atmospheric push is rough. You need to fasten your harnesses."

A chorus of clicks runs through the rows.

"Once we engage Faster Than Light Speed, or FTL, we'll shift into autopilot," she continues. "Then you can move about if you choose. We'll arrive at the space station in a few hours."

Cole and I flip around in our seats to see the final gear check. As I watch the flight crew communicate through hand signals, I inhale a huge whiff of . . . roses? A long pink nail taps me on the forearm.

Florine stares down at me through her sunglasses. "Ex-*cuuuse* me. I said it was time to fasten your harness." I'm doused with another wave of her rose perfume as she flashes her bright cold smile. Honestly, I've never seen anyone with whiter teeth. They're even whiter in person than they are on the webs.

"Sorry," I say. Cole and I snap into our five-point harnesses. Florine moves down the aisle, checking the other Bounders.

"What's her deal?" I whisper to Cole. "Why is she wearing those sunglasses? And why is she on the craft anyway?" Cole seems to know a lot. I figure he'll know why she's here.

Just as Cole shrugs, a head pops up over the seats in front of us. A girl with wide-spaced eyes and warm brown skin stares at us. Her braided hair is tied with red and yellow ribbons.

"Florine Statton's been appointed Director of Bounder Affairs at the EarthBound Academy," the girl says. She stares at me like I asked the most ridiculous question she heard all day.

"How do you know?"

"I asked."

Okay. Pretty good way to get an answer.

"Who are you?" she asks. Her high voice tickles my ears.

"Jasper Adams. This is Cole Thompson."

"What? Can't he speak for himself?"

Cole stares at the girl vacantly. I kick his shoe. "Oh. Hello," he says, looking away.

"Hello, yourself. I'm Lucy Dugan. I had to give up drama club to come, you know. This better be good. I'm sure it will be. Florine told me all about the dorms and the teachers and the end-of-tour field trip to the Paleo Planet. Have you heard anything about how they'll group us at the Academy?"

"Wait a minute," I say. "How do you know Florine? When did she tell you all this stuff?"

"I don't really know her. I met her this morning."

Florine's voice blasts over the intercom. "The captain has been cleared for takeoff. Do not make me come through the cabin again." And, as an afterthought, "Puh-*leeeze*."

I peek behind me through the window. Smoke billows out around the craft, blocking the view of the sea. When I turn back, Lucy has disappeared into her seat. I'll have to talk to her once we clear the atmosphere. Lucy has a lot of info, and she knows where to get more. When Cole's head of facts draws a blank, I bet Lucy can fill it in.

· *Ef* ·

"This is your captain. Prepare for lift-off."

The floor rumbles, and I lean my head against the back-rest. An odd pulling sensation seizes my body, and then an enormous weight compresses me, constricts me, holds me in place. The noise grows until it sounds like a freight train chugging through my brain. I fix my eyes on the front windows and try not to hyperventilate.

The world falls away as we rush up past the skyscrapers, the lifts, the air rail.

MONICA TESLER

Up.

Up.

Up.

I lose all sense of direction. All I can see out the window is whiteness. I don't know if the whiteness is smoke or clouds or the thin air that crowds the atmospheric orbital line. The craft shakes and the engines roar. I'd do anything just to stop the noise.

The pressure creeps into my lungs and squeezes. I strain to raise my head from the seat back. I try to lift my hand from the armrest. Nothing budges. My body is a prison. My breath comes in short bursts. I'm not sure how much more I can take.

Boom! The noise is so loud, my brain almost explodes.

Then . . . *ahhh.* Every single cell in my body relaxes.

My arms float up from the armrests. My body lifts off the chair and pulls against the harness. The vise grip that holds my lungs lets go.

"I am now stabilizing gravity," the captain says over the intercom.

A few seconds later I feel like myself again, in control of my mind and body. I close my eyes and take a deep breath.

"You have to see this," Cole whispers.

Cole has unbuttoned his harness and is facing backward in his seat. Who knows if we're allowed to do that, but

Cole seems fine. He hasn't floated away or anything.

I unbuckle and turn. The entire rear window of the craft is filled with the image of Earth just as it looks in the web pics. The creamy white swirls of clouds mix with the royal blue of the oceans. Clusters of green mark the vegetation lands. The scorch zones stretch flat and brown. And the silver circles show our cities. It's beautiful. My throat gets tight, and my eyes fill up. I shake my head to snap out of it. No way do I want to look like a sap.

"That's Americana East," Cole says, pointing to the silver circle on the edge of the American continent. "It's one of the twenty-two cities visible from space."

I nod. Cole likes to state facts, and I don't think he does it just to sound smart. I think facts keep him grounded. And we're definitely not grounded.

"Is that where you're from?" I ask.

"Yes. District 17."

"I'm District 8," I say. How many minutes before we engage FTL?"

"Less than ten. The crew conducts a second systems check, but it won't take long."

"Scoot over." Lucy stands in the aisle and shoves my shoulder.

"Shouldn't you be in your seat?" Cole says.

"Who's asking?" Lucy steps over my legs, pushes up the

armrest separating Cole's and my seats, and wiggles her way between us.

"It's simply gorgeous, isn't it?" she says.

"That's Americana East," I say. Geez, I'm starting to sound like Cole.

"Yeah, uh, no kidding," Lucy says. "Is that where you're from?"

"Yep. You?"

"No, thank goodness. You Easties are way too stressed-out. I'm a Westie."

"Really?" I've never met anyone from Americana West. I've never met anyone who has been to Americana West. Come to think of it, until today, I'd never met anyone who had been anywhere other than East—ever.

"There's West," Lucy says, pointing out the window. "What are all those smaller circles in between?"

"Those are the farm plots. All the food for the American continent is grown in those three zones," Cole says. "You can't see from here, but all the transport lines connect at those plots."

Lucy studies Cole. "Are you, like, one of those trivia magnets?"

"What do you mean?" Cole asks.

"You know, a lot of Bounder kids have a head for facts. They love to sort and categorize and memorize them. But that's definitely not how it's expressed in me. I'm more of a high-energy, low-focus type."

"Me too," I say. I really have no idea what Lucy is talking about, and I'm not sure about the high-energy part, but I definitely don't have a head for trivia like Cole does.

"How do you know?" Cole asks Lucy. "I've read all the published literature on Bounders, and I've never seen any mention of that."

Lucy shrugs. "I asked. You *do* go for annual testing, don't you? Those docs see hundreds of us. They're gold mines when it comes to Bounder scoop."

Addy and I went every year for examinations, but I never thought to drill the doctors and scientists about other Bounders. Until I turned ten, I didn't even know if the examination team would clear me for the space station. I've heard a lot of kids in the Bounder Baby Breeding Program don't make the cut. Actually, I never really thought I'd make it. There's nothing particularly special about me. Addy's hyperaware and always tuned in to people, but I'm basically the opposite. Now here's Cole with all the facts and numbers, and Lucy seems kind of like Addy. Maybe they made a mistake. Maybe I'm not supposed to be here after all.

A bell chimes, and the captain announces we're about to engage FTL. Lucy returns to her seat and buckles in.

"Have you ever traveled at FTL?" Cole asks.

I laugh. "I've never left Earth."

"Me neither," Cole says. A loud thud shakes the craft. "Did you feel that? They just folded back the sides."

I crane my neck to look out the front window, but all I can see is an endless field of stars.

The craft buzzes like my apartment building's backup generator. Then, for a split second, I feel like I've been flung against a wall and smashed with a flyswatter. Before I can even process the feeling, it's gone. And we're just as we were before, except the front window is blurred with brightness. We engaged FTL.

Lucy pops back over the seat. "So, like I asked before, do either of you Easties know anything about how they're going to group us at the Academy?"

"Why don't you tell us what you know?" I say. "Because you obviously want to."

"Thanks, I will," she says. "I don't know much, but they're going to divide the cadets into pods. Florine told me."

"Pods like quantum pods?" Cole asks. A pod usually refers to the group of five quantum aeronauts who crew each quantum ship.

"Kind of like quantum pods. There will be groups of five kids. Some of the teaching happens all together, but most of the lessons will take place in pods. Each pod will be paired with an instructor. And I heard a rumor that some of the quantum aeronauts are going to be instructors."

Pods. That will be weird. So much depends on who's in your pod.

"I have my fingers crossed Maximilian Sheek will be my instructor." Lucy smiles and makes a dreamy face. "Have you seen his latest EFAN interview? I can't believe he studied opera. A natural baritone! *And* he's looking for that special someone who appreciates the arts!"

"Yeah, the art of being annoying," I say. "You sound just like my sister. I can't wait to meet Edgar Han. Do you know he trains for ultramarathons while on duty by running in place in an equal-gravity chamber? And he's an accomplished photographer—there's some arts for you. He's the coolest aeronaut by a mile."

"Yeah, right," Lucy says. "Sheek's clearly the best, but I wouldn't mind being paired with Malaina Suarez. She has advanced degrees in Sustainability, Logic, and Military History, and I think she's the youngest female officer ever promoted to aeronaut. She may be kind of new, but she seems fierce."

"Fierce?" Cole says. "Suarez is far from fierce. . . ." Cole launches into an endless monologue about every aeronaut who ever lived and their relative fierceness as determined by their rank in the bounding training protocol.

"I wonder if we'll be ranked," I say. "How do they determine the pod assignments?"

"Is it random?" Cole asks. "Or do they assess personality and skills compatibility like they do with the aeronauts?"

"Florine said they based the assignments on the data they collected during our years of testing, to make sure each pod has well-rounded skill sets," Lucy answers. "But she also said they're still finalizing things and may make changes after seeing how we mesh. They want to create the best balance within the pods."

"What do you think the chance is we end up in the same pod?" I ask. "Pretty slim, right?"

"Maybe not," Lucy says. "If they see we click, maybe they'll want to put the three of us together."

"You want to be in our pod?" Cole asks.

Lucy shrugs, but I think that means yes.

"Why?" I ask.

"I figure you guys are pretty smart. After all, you grabbed the best seats on the craft."

I look around at the other Bounders. Most kids are sitting quietly, staring at the info screens or gazing blankly out the windows. A boy in the next row rocks back and forth. His lips move without sound. At least a dozen kids pace through the aisles. A girl with short black hair huddles beneath a blanket she scared up from who knows where. Some kid I can't see hums really loudly. A big group of kids up front hover around Regis, and they all crack up at the same time. I spy Marco slipping into the hallway reserved for officers. Cole's right. He's trouble.

Lucy and Cole watch the others, too. I'm sure they're doing the same thing I am—gliding over each face, sizing everyone up, wondering who will be in their pods. I hope the officers are watching. I hope they see how well we get along. I really want to be in the same pod as Cole, and I'd even be fine with Lucy.

"I'd be okay with most of these dopes," Lucy says, "as long as I'm not stuck with Dancing Queen."

"Who?" Cole asks.

"Oh, you know, that batty girl at the aeroport. I'm shocked she even got through. One of the doctors told me tons of Bounder-bred kids are loony like that."

There's obviously a lot I don't know about Bounders. In my mind, all I can see is the pale thin girl dancing through the crowd, her arms outstretched, her head lifted to the sun. And her mother's voice—*Mira! Mira!*—calling her back to Earth.

"Look! Snacks!" Lucy says.

Sure enough, two low-ranking Earth Force officers— plebes—push a large cart down the aisle. They dole out snacks to the Bounders. Their cart is full, but that won't last long. Regis and his crew pounce on the bounty.

"This is what stinks about these seats," I say. "We get last pick at snacks."

"Don't count on it." Lucy slips out of her seat and skips off to the snack cart. I almost dash after her, when I notice a small figure clad in chain mail in Cole's hand.

"Whoa. What is that?" I ask. "The Crusades token?"

Cole nods. Every time you level up in *Evolution of Combat*, they send you a new figure with a scan key to open the next level on your tablet. The figure Cole holds is retired. The current Crusades token has a battle-ax, not a scimitar.

"Do you know why I think they retired him?" Cole says. "Scimitars weren't used in the Crusades. It's a sword that originated in Southwest Asia."

"Why do you know that?" I ask. Cole stares at me with blank eyes. "Never mind."

"Do you play?" Cole asks.

"*Evolution*? Yeah. Who doesn't?" I can't wrap my head around his retired token. "How long ago did you clear Crusades? I don't know anyone who has the scimitar."

"Two years ago."

Two years ago? How is that possible? *Evolution* just came out a couple of years ago. "What level are you now?"

"World War Two."

"Yeah, right." I probably should know Cole wouldn't lie about something like that. I don't think he brags. He just tells you how it is.

Cole stares at me, expressionless.

"Okay, so you're World War Two," I continue. "Show me your figure."

Cole reaches inside his Earth Force jacket and fishes something out of the interior pocket. He hands me a small figure dressed in green fatigues and a bucket helmet.

"Dude," I say, "that's unbelievable. And I thought I was good. I've never met anyone who's even reached World War Two."

"What level are you?"

"American Revolution." I'm stunned. I've always been the best at *Evolution*. I suck at basically everything else remotely cool, but the kids at school come to *me* as the *Evolution* expert.

"That's pretty good," Cole says. I can tell he's trying to be nice. "Do you think they'll let us play at the space station?"

"I'm not sure." They're cutting us off from most media access, but maybe *Evolution* is outside the restrictions.

"Scootch." Lucy stands in the aisle. She took off her Earth Force jacket and is using it as a sling to carry snacks. "Please don't tell me we're talking about that awful game." She must have spotted Cole's figures. "I refuse to share these snacks until you put those things away. No *Evolution*. No exceptions."

That's annoying, but I'm starved. And, honestly, I don't want to hear any more about how awesome Cole is at *Evolution*. I wave a hand at him, and he shoves his figures back into his pocket.

Lucy squeezes by me in a yellow T-shirt that says PACIFIC PLAYERS DRAMA CLUB on the front and CAST on the back in bright red letters. She dumps the snacks on the seats and crouches in the row to sort the loot.

Freeze-dried yogurt chunks, carob-coated fruit balls, veggie puffs, and an assortment of protein bars. I was hoping for something cool, a space station exclusive. No luck. Just the standard Americana fare. They must have stocked up at the aeroport.

That doesn't stop me from attacking the snacks. Cole and Lucy have to fight me for the last pack of fruit balls. And, yes, Lucy wins. After all, she was the one who sweet-talked the plebes into giving her a whole uniform full of snacks.

"THIS IS YOUR CAPTAIN. WE ARE DISEN-
gaging FTL. We'll be arriving at the Earth Force Space Station
in approximately twenty-three minutes. Return to your seats,
and fasten your harnesses."

"Later," Lucy says as she climbs over the seat.

"What a relief," Cole says. "She thinks she knows everything."

I choke back a laugh. I guess it takes one to know one. "I
like her. Although she really talks a lot."

Cole mumbles something under his breath.

A loud boom shakes the craft. My body pulls against the

harness again, just as it did after we cleared Earth's orbit. A few seconds pass, and I fall back against the seat like I was yanked down. Gravity? Stabilized.

Through the front windows, the space station is suspended like an enormous spider web, and we're the unlucky bug about to be caught. As we close in, I can see how truly huge the station is. There are at least fifty structures. Most of them look like gigantic metal shoe boxes, the size of futbol fields, all tipped at different angles. They're connected by metal tubes that twist through space like the wires and hoses that connect the parts inside a hover engine.

Small crafts take off and land from two dozen docks, some mounted on top of structures, some with interior launch sites. The top deck of the space station belongs to the quantum fleet. The sphere-shaped ships made of liquid metal stand in a line. Beyond them, space flickers and waves. I blink. I know it's the quantum field, but it feels like my eyes are playing tricks on me.

"I've received a message from the control tower," the captain says over the intercom. "A quantum ship is bounding through in about thirty seconds. Keep your eyes focused on the quantum field, and you can watch."

Cole and I loosen our harnesses and sit up on our knees so we can see out the front windows. The strange wavy space makes me lose focus, zone out. I blink hard and press my fingers on my temples to stay alert. Am I imagining things? No. The space bends outward like a balloon filling with air. Then . . . *pop!* The quantum ship pushes through the field. I can hardly believe that a second ago that ship was in a different galaxy.

The ship's liquid metal skin glistens with the light of a million rainbows as starlight and the floods from the space station dance across its surface. I've studied the technology behind bounding and the quantum ships, but it's hard to get my head around the physicality of the thing. It looks like a giant silver ball of water that should drop to the ground like rain and form a puddle on the bounding deck. Instead the liquid clings together in its spherical form. Inside, the atoms race around the sphere at FTL Plus, holding the structure together in some sort of Einsteined–up centrifugal force.

Spider Crawler robots surround the ship and bring up the occludium membrane to shield and stabilize the outer core. The boarding platform bridges the top of the ship, and one of the Crawlers peels back the hatch. Within seconds the aeronauts emerge. Five of them. All geared up in the silver aeronaut suit of Earth Force.

"Five," Cole says. "A pod."

"Yep." I was thinking the same thing.

"Oh my goodness!" shouts a girl a few rows ahead. "That's Maximilian Sheek!"

An echo of screams follows. *Shrieks for Sheek.* I think that's the slogan. I should know. It's scrawled across the poster hanging above Addy's desk. I can't believe Earth Force lets him pose like that—muscles all flexed in his skintight aeronaut suit. He has a silly half grin and a big pouf of wavy brown hair. Addy always says I could do my hair like Sheek if I wanted. Right. Give me a razor, and I'd shave my head before I'd leave the house looking like Sheek. Good thing most of the other aeronauts seem decent and not all caught up in their celebrity. What will happen when the Bounders learn to pilot the ships? Will the people love us the way they've always loved the aeronauts?

A few rows ahead, a group of girls won't shut up about Sheek. I roll my eyes and whisper to Cole, "If this is gonna turn into a love fest for Sheek, I would have stayed back on Earth." I scan the other aeronauts on the bounding deck. "Do you think that could be Han?"

Cole isn't paying attention. "Look," he says, "someone else is coming out of the ship."

A small hunched form hauls himself onto the boarding platform.

"That aeronaut's so short," Lucy says from the row ahead. "Is he a kid? A Bounder?"

The aeronaut tips forward at an odd angle. "Nope," I say, "that's a Tunneler."

"I didn't know they could pilot the ships," she says.

"That was the deal," Cole says. "They gave us their occludium mining technology, and we taught them how to bound."

We dip beneath the bounding deck, clear the space field, and coast into the hangar. At least four passenger crafts could fit within its walls. And the hangar is almost as high as it is wide. Something about it reminds me of the hospital where Mom works. Maybe it's because everything looks ultrasterile. The floor, ceiling, and walls are all painted grayish-green, the color of spearmint toothpaste. Rows of fluorescent lights cross the hangar's roof, throwing a glare across the cavernous space.

"Did you see that?" Cole whispers.

"What?"

"At the front of the hangar. There were at least a dozen active gun stations. And look, there's another dozen in here."

Sure enough, manned gun stations line the perimeter of the hangar. "Up there, too." I point to a gunner stationed at an upper post. "What's that all about?"

"I don't know," Cole says. "I've never seen any reference to it."

"Attention, puh-*leeeze*," Florine says over the intercom once the hangar crew has signaled for the hatch opening. "We have arrived. Line up to leave the craft and follow the officers' instructions. The Earth Force induction ceremony will commence as soon as we are assembled. Admiral Eames will administer the officers' oath. Try to demonstrate some measure of military decorum."

As we stand in line to leave the craft, Cole tells Lucy and me the history of the Earth Force induction ceremony. I tune him out. I'm not really capable of listening. Since we landed in the hangar, my heart's been beating so hard, my blood's pumping double time in my eardrums. We're just moments away from meeting Admiral Eames and taking the oath to serve as officers of Earth Force.

We follow the other kids off the craft. By the time we reach the ramp, most of the cadets are already lined up at the center of the hangar. The plebes usher us to our positions. At least three hundred officers stand at attention behind a podium placed five meters ahead of our group. Lieutenant Ridders stands behind the podium. His arm jerks in salute. "Admiral on deck."

I don't know what to do. Should I salute? We aren't technically Earth Force yet. I sneak a glance at Cole. He stands tall, his right hand lifted in a line against his forehead. I bring my hand up in a swift snap.

Admiral Eames enters the hangar. She looks just like she does on the webs. She's tiny, probably only a few inches taller than Addy, and she has thick brown hair she wears twisted up beneath her cap. She was the best FTL pilot in the regimen, the youngest officer in the senior ranks. And, of course, the first and only admiral of Earth Force.

As she walks our line, her gaze lights on each face. I will myself not to turn away when her eyes settle on me.

"At ease," she says when she reaches the podium.

We drop our hands to our sides but still stand straight. It's hard to be at ease in front of the admiral.

"This is a momentous day. A day thirteen years in the making." She takes a deep breath and scans the crowd. "Welcome, Bounders. You've heard your whole life you are the future of Earth Force. Let me tell you again. You are the future of Earth Force. And the future starts now."

Lucy bumps me with her hip. When I glance at her, she beams. This is it. I'm about to be inducted into Earth Force. I squeeze my hands into fists and take a deep breath. Next to me, Cole bounces on his toes. I'm right there with him. So much adrenaline pumps through my body, I think I might burst.

"Fifteen years ago," the admiral continues, "I was privileged to be part of the diplomatic mission to P37. That day heralded a new era for Earth Force, an era we share with our friends."

Admiral Eames led the diplomatic envoy to Planet 37, the Tunneler planet, when she was still a junior officer. She wasn't only a skilled pilot; she was an excellent negotiator. She brokered a deal between Earth and P37 that paid off for both planets.

The admiral scans the line of officers and nods each time her gaze touches a Tunneler in the exchange program. When her eyes graze over the Tunneler from the air rail, he swings up his hairy hand in salute.

The admiral lowers her voice. "Sadly, that era was quickly shadowed by the tragic Incident at Bounding Base 51. While those who gave their lives in service of their planet are on our minds today, we think of them in glory and tribute."

The admiral bows her head, our cue to do the same. The Incident at Bounding Base 51 happened the year before I was born. A famous quantum ship failed to materialize during a routine bound. The entire crew was lost. All those aeronauts—gone—their atoms adrift somewhere in the cosmos, never to reassemble.

After the Incident, Eames was appointed admiral, and Earth's space agencies and military were all brought under the Earth Force umbrella. Within a year Earth Force started screening for Bounder genes. Positive couples like my parents had to have their babies premade in a petri dish to make sure their recessive genes danced in the right way to produce a Bounder baby.

Somehow the Incident at Bounding Base 51 and the Bounder Baby Breeding Program were connected. Somehow we—the Bounders—are the insurance policy that such a tragedy never happens again.

"For today we take our era of advancement to the next level."

Oh no, not again. The admiral kept on talking, and I completely spaced out. Focus, Jasper.

"For you," she continues, "you, Bounders, are the future of our space program. We've been waiting for you. We are honored to serve with you. With your aptitude for quantum space travel, there is no limit to where we will go in the universe."

The lump in my throat is back. The oath is next. In seconds we'll be officers in Earth Force. I wish Addy were with me. I wish we could take the oath together.

Admiral Eames lifts her right arm, palm forward. "Please raise your hand and repeat after me."

Line by line, as she states the oath, we repeat it back:

I promise to protect and defend Earth,
to be faithful to our planet,
to obey the orders of the Admiral,
and to serve at all times with honor in Earth Force.

As we speak the last words, Admiral Eames spreads her arms wide.

"Congratulations, Bounders. We welcome you as fellow officers of Earth Force and our very first class of cadets at the EarthBound Academy. May the torch of quantum space travel, so gracefully carried by our strong ranks of aeronauts, soon pass to you and ascend to a level of which we have only dared to dream."

The hangar erupts in applause. I clap, too, but I'm kind of stunned. I can't believe it. I'm an Earth Force officer. Lucy tosses her arms around me. A little dramatic, but it helps bring me back to the moment. The clapping continues, and the hangar echoes with the thunderous sound. I cringe. A couple of the cadets cover their ears. Yeah, we're pumped, but can we cut the noise?

The admiral gestures to Florine to take the podium. Something silently passes between the two of them. Even though Florine stands a head taller than Admiral Eames, she seems to shrink in size. She bows her head and removes her sunglasses. The admiral nods and steps aside, flanked by Ridders and another officer.

"Congratulations," Florine says, flashing her white teeth. She looks strange without the sunglasses. Her face is kind of droopy. "Enjoy the moment, because it won't last. No more thinking you're special. That's in the past. You are cadets—the lowest on the totem pole, even lower than the plebes. Our quantum aeronauts are the heroes here—not you, Bounders. Don't forget that."

Geez. I guess boosting Bounder morale is not part of the job description for the Director of Bounder Affairs.

"It's past midnight back on Earth," Florine continues. "The flight crew is getting your luggage off the craft. We'll show you to the dormitories, and tomorrow . . ."

Florine keeps glancing to the right. She's distracted. I follow her gaze. Most of us do. One of the Bounders has left the line. She is gliding toward a gun station. A long blond braid swings behind her. Mira.

"Ex-*cuuuse* me," Florine says, directing her words to Mira. "You cannot go over there. That space is off-limits. Mira, stop!"

The girl responds to her name, but not in the normal way. She turns slowly, and a serene smile creeps across her face. She doesn't react at all to being called out. It's like she has no clue what she's doing is wrong or strange.

By then two officers have left their positions and approached Mira. When they touch her, she falls to the floor and curls into a ball. A man in civilian clothes darts across the hangar in long fluid strides. He is tall and kind of old, maybe my parents' age, with dark hair and thick stubble on his cheeks. He waves off the officers and kneels on the floor next to Mira. He whispers something too quiet to hear. Then he stretches out his hand. A long moment passes. Mira lifts her head and her eyes dart around the hangar. Then as quickly as the drama came on, she settles. She takes the man's hand and lets him walk her back to the line. He doesn't leave Mira's side for the rest of Florine's talk. He grips her firmly on her shoulder, holding her in place, holding her together.

· EF ·

Florine leads the girls to their dormitory. Lucy waves before dashing to the front of her group to talk with Florine. Lieutenant Ridders rounds us up for the trek to the boys' dorm. We leave the hanger and start down the hall. Everything is decorated in the dull sameness: gray-green paint, florescent lighting, chrome trim. The lights make my head hurt. The ceiling is low, and the halls are narrow. And everything smells funny. Like a nasty combination of lemon cleanser and day-old hot dogs.

Cole and I are stuck in the back of the line again, which is fine by me. I feel dizzy, queasy, and claustrophobic.

"You guys got it all figured out, huh?" comes a voice from behind.

I turn. It's Marco. He must have hung back on purpose.

"What is that supposed to mean?" Cole asks.

"Nothing, Wiki, just making conversation."

"My name is Cole."

"Yeah, yeah. But Wiki suits you. You're like a walking fact machine."

"How would you know?"

"I heard you on the craft. Dude, take it as a compliment."

"My name is Cole."

"Got it." Marco rolls his eyes at me. I'm kind of with him. Cole is acting lame. But I've already picked sides. I'm stuck with Cole. And I doubt Cole would appreciate my joining in a little friendly ribbing.

Up ahead, the other boys stop. Good. Maybe we can shake Marco.

Lieutenant Ridders stands in front of a clear enclosure about three meters square. One side has a long metal trough. The other has a huge vent hanging from the ceiling, and a metal grated floor. Between the two sides, computer panels are mounted to the wall. The top screen flickers with red and green lights. It's a blueprint of the space station.

Cole has a huge smile on his face. He knows what's up. I wish I did.

"Cadets," Ridders says. "This is the primary way we get around here. Some of you may know about the suction chutes—"

A loud buzz interrupts Ridders, and a green light blinks above the metal trough.

"Incoming," Ridders says. "Perfect timing."

Just then another officer shoots out of the wall and slams into the trough. When she looks up, she freezes, clearly surprised she arrived to an audience. Ridders stands at attention, his hand raised in salute. Around me, hands fly to foreheads. I jump to attention. We haven't gotten the protocol thing down yet, but we're working on it.

She hoists herself out of the trough, brushes off her uniform, and steps out of the cube. "At ease," she says.

Whoa. Is that . . . ?

The freckly kid from the craft sidles up next to Cole. "She's one of the aeronauts, right?"

Cole nods. "Malaina Suarez."

"Boys, this is Captain Suarez," Ridders says. "I'm giving them a tutorial on the chutes," he explains to her.

She nods and heads down the corridor, calling over her shoulder, "You're in for a wild ride!"

I can't believe it. Malaina Suarez stood right there, three meters in front of me. And she actually spoke to us! She looks exactly the same as she does on EFAN. I watch her hurry down the hallway and disappear around a corner.

"Even the aeronauts use these to get around," Ridders says.

I stopped paying attention and missed what Ridders said. Get with it, Jasper. Focus!

"In house, we call these chutes and ladders after the kids' game," Ridders continues. "It's how we travel from structure to structure. Once you activate the suction chute, the vent will open, and you'll be sucked up by the vacuum. The chute pulls you out of this structure, through open space, and into another structure. You'll end up in a trough like that one at the other end. You get numb to it after a while, but the first few rides are quite a rush."

Sucked into open space? You've got to be kidding. My stomach takes a few flip turns. I study the blueprint of the space station—dozens of freestanding structures connected by a web of shiny metal tubes. I had no idea those tubes were used for transport. Some of them are pretty long. And windy. And scary, like the world's most intense water slide without the water.

How did I not know about the suction chutes? I should have done more research before coming to the EarthBound Academy. And Cole should have cued me in on our flight from Earth.

"Who wants to go first?" Ridders asks.

Two dozen arms shoot up, but Marco skips that step. He grabs the door handle and steps inside the chute cube. "Which button do I push, Lieutenant?"

After Marco, I watch at least twenty cadets activate the chute. It's slow going. Most cadets can't wait for their turn, but some of the kids refuse to go into the chute until Ridders talks them off the panic ledge. The guy standing next to me is practically hyperventilating. And I get it. Most of the ride is outside the structure, as in flying through space. What if something goes wrong? What if the chute gets disconnected? You could be launched into space without a suit.

I psych myself up for the chute, but my heart still beats its way into my throat when Ridders points to me. Stay calm, Jasper. You've got this. I enter the chute cube and plant my feet on the grate. I check the screen. Geez. There have to be more than a hundred chutes connecting the space station structures. The blinking green light shows where we are on the blueprint. Oh no. The chute isn't a direct shot to the landing cube. It bends sharply in the middle, which means I'll be vertical for half the ride and horizontal for the other half. I remember what Cole told me as we waited our turn. Spatial orientation is simply a matter of perspective on the space station. The floor is a floor and not a ceiling only because of the gravity stabilizer. Since the chutes are zero gravity, it shouldn't matter if I'm right side up or upside down, as long as the suction works.

I take a deep breath, pull the vacuum seal, and press the chute activation button. The vent above me opens. Here goes.

Every muscle in my body tenses as I brace for the suction. Wind fills my ears as an indescribable force grabs me, like a giant sucking me through his straw.

All is black as I rush upward, the force pulling, my body flying.

Faster.

Faster.

Wind tickling, taming, sealing my uniform tight against my body, pinning my limbs down.

Around the corner, picking up speed.

Faster still.

This is awesome.

Up ahead, a faint glow grows brighter and brighter. I brace again before slamming into the exit trough.

The air hisses and is quiet. I can move again. I push up on my elbows. All the Bounders who rode before me watch. Some of them laugh. Yep, I probably look pretty scared. After all, seconds ago, the thin walls of the chute were the only things keeping me from being launched across the galaxy.

As I exit the chute cube, Marco steps up beside me and raises his hand in the air for a high five. "Quite a ride, huh?" he asks.

I slap his palm. "Oh yeah."

"Hey," he says. "Let's explore."

"Do you think that's allowed?"

Marco gives me a *What the heck's your problem?* look. "Uh, it's definitely not allowed, but why should we let that stop us?"

I DON'T THINK BREAKING RULES ON DAY
one is the brightest idea, but I don't want to look like a complete wimp in front of Marco. Something tells me keeping cred with him is important. When no one's looking, Marco ducks out of the corridor, and I follow.

So yeah, this place is cool—I mean, it's a space station and all—but the hallways are narrow, and the lights are way too bright. And knowing the crushing weight of open space is pressing against the walls doesn't exactly calm my nerves. There's a platinum stripe running down the middle of the floor. I focus on the stripe, place one foot in front of the other, and ignore my growing dizziness. But there's no ignoring that nasty hot dog smell.

"Hey! Spaceman! Snap out of it!" Marco stops short, and I nearly crash into him.

"Huh?" I say.

"What gives? You're, like, completely zoned. Aren't you even checking things out?"

"Right. It's just, I have a headache. And this place stinks something awful!"

Marco spins in a circle, arms outstretched. "We're on a space station! So it isn't homey. . . . So what? Get over it and pay attention!"

I frown at Marco, but his words sink in. Once I push past the claustrophobia, there actually is a lot to see.

The platinum stripe may not be just a stripe. There's some sort of sensor embedded in the floor. I wonder . . .

Beep! Beep! Beeeeeeeep!

Oh no! We're busted! I spin at the same second Marco grabs my shirt and yanks. I stumble to the floor just as a shiny black box the width of a dinner plate barrels past us.

"What the heck is that?" I say.

"Must be a robot. Let's follow it!" Marco is already darting after the speeding box by the time I'm back on my feet.

I dash after him, ignoring the growing dread that we're racing right into a whole heap of trouble.

At the corner, the robot takes a ninety-degree turn, following a new branch of the platinum stripe. So that's what the sensors are for, apparently.

Marco is fast on the robot's tail. At the next hallway, the robot turns, and Marco skids to a stop. "Whoa. That was close. There's a bunch of guards around the corner."

Great. I knew this was a bad idea. An acidy taste gurgles up from my gut. We definitely aren't supposed to be doing this. "We should head back."

"Not so fast." Marco peers around the corner. "Cool. That robot's like a mini Spider Crawler. Check it out."

We came this far, I might as well take a peek. I switch spots with Marco and carefully lean out. Up ahead about twenty meters and down a steep ramp, four guards stand at a door. The robot has raised itself up on skinny legs, just like the Spider Crawlers that man the quantum ships. One of its legs is lifted to the door, jabbing at a console. Then it ticks forward on its spindly legs and disappears.

"I think the robot must have gone in that door," I whisper to Marco. He doesn't respond. I turn around to an empty hallway.

Great. Just great. I can't believe he bailed. I hope I can find my way back.

I start off following the platinum stripe, but before I've gone more than a few meters, a door flies open beside me.

I nearly jump out of my skin, but it's only Marco.

"Hey, Zone-Out," he says, "in here."

I step inside an empty room that looks like a mini auditorium, except instead of facing a stage, the three tiered rows of seats face a glass window on the opposite wall.

"Great, Marco. Big thrills in here. Thanks for showing me. I'm heading back before we're busted on this clearly off-limits discovery mission."

"Wait a sec, Mr. Cool. You think I'd drag you in here just to show you a bunch of chairs? I'm pretty sure the room they were guarding is through that glass. Check out the window. And be subtle, okay?"

Shaking off my nerves, I walk around the chairs, dragging my hand along their plastic backs until I reach the edge of the window on the opposite wall.

A story below, a crowd hovers around a table in the middle of the room. It looks like a medical facility. Most of the people wear long white coats. Monitors and carts and all kinds of equipment flank the table and line the walls. The robot we followed scurries up to the crowd. A compartment pops open, and it uses three of its long limbs to extract a large vial filled with a neon-green substance. One of the white coats takes the vial from the robot and turns toward the table.

"What are they doing?" I ask.

Marco creeps up behind me. He steps alongside and leans against the glass.

"Hey, step back!" I hiss. "They'll see you."

"Nah," he says. "I'm pretty sure this is one-way glass. You know, we can see them, but they can't see us." He waves his hands over his head in wide arcs.

I tackle him. As I hold him to the floor, Marco cackles. Yeah, this will be really funny right up until the moment we get busted.

Sure someone is going to come through the door any second, I turn back to the window. A few of the people in white coats work at carts in our direct sightline. If they could see through, they would have noticed us.

"Keep your eyes on the action," Marco says. "And get your hands off me while you're at it, Tough Guy."

Two of the white coats step away, opening up a partial view of something thick and slimy writhing on the table. My stomach heaves, and a great flood of bile rises to my mouth. My gaze is glued to the window.

"You okay? You wouldn't want to lose your lunch," Marco says.

"What on earth is that?" I ask.

Another white coat steps aside, leaving a clear view of the table. On top of it is a man. No, not a man. A thing. A slimy green thing with an enormous head that's lit up like a flickering light bulb. His hands and his heart beat to the same rhythm, lighting him from the inside with each pulse.

His skin looks wet, like washed-up algae. A long incision crosses his abdomen. Wormlike tendrils wave in the air above, spurting mucous everywhere. The green thing struggles with the dozen white coats who try to bind it down.

Again my stomach heaves, but I can't turn away. "That's an alien." I say it matter-of-factly, but I'm hoping Marco will weigh in.

"No kidding. But not like any alien I've ever heard of."

Right. That thing definitely isn't a Tunneler.

"Hey, Mr. Cool," Marco says, "check the corners."

I don't know how I missed it before. Guards stand in every corner. Eight are stationed in front of the closed door that glows with a strange silver light. They all have their guns out, cocked, pointed at the table.

"I don't get it," I say.

"Neither do I," Marco says. "But I have a weird feeling it has something to do with why we're here."

"Nah. It couldn't possibly . . ." Even as the words slip from my mouth, they sound wrong.

In a flash the alien surges from the table. He whips his arm in a wide arc. The nearest white coat flies across the room, landing in a heap in the corner.

"Whoa!" I grab Marco's arm. "How did he do that? Did he even touch him?"

"I'm not sure. He must have." The color has seeped from Marco's olive skin.

The guards race to press the alien down. White coats strap the alien's wrists to the table and cover his hands with thick mitts. All around us, lights flash and alarms sound.

"We need to get out of here," I say, already dashing for the door.

"No joke, Flash. Keep running."

· E_F ·

When we reach the corner before the chute cube, Marco and I slow to a normal pace. None of the alarms or lights are signaling in this section of the space station. No one has a clue what's happening just a few turns away. In fact, no one even seems to have noticed we were gone. Well, no one except Cole.

"Where were you?" Cole asks. He speaks to me, but his eyes keep darting to Marco, and let's just say his face doesn't exactly radiate happiness. Marco doesn't care. He doesn't even notice, actually. He's off talking to some other cadets.

"Nowhere, really." I hope Cole doesn't notice I'm still trying to catch my breath. "We just wanted to see if we could find the dorm." I don't know why I'm lying. I guess I'm not ready to talk about the alien on the table. And I'm definitely not ready to hear any of Cole's fact-heavy theories or—worse—lectures for wandering off.

"Marco's trouble, Jasper. Don't say I didn't warn you."

That annoys me. Who is Cole, anyway? My dad? I shrug. Whatever. I don't feel like fighting. Not when my heart is still pounding from what Marco and I just saw.

"How'd you like the chute?" I say, changing the subject.

"The feeling of zero gravity combined with the suction pull was exhilarating."

"Right," I say. "It was awesome."

We follow Ridders to the boys' dormitory. The room stretches way back, with bunks stacked four high on either side. The bunks are built in to the walls like racks on a ship. Beneath the bunks are pullout storage bins.

"Listen up," Ridders says. "Everybody gets a bunk, all seventy-six of you. Look at the bunk number, and find your matching bin underneath. That's where you store your stuff. Out of sight, all the time. The plebes will be here soon with your luggage. Grab your bag. Claim your bunk. Understood?"

We grunt our agreement as eyes turn toward the line of bunks. Scoping.

"What do you think?" I ask Cole.

"Definitely the front," he says.

"Really?" The front bunks are the last place I would have

picked. I may not be that sharp at social stuff, but I'm pretty sure front bunks are for losers.

Marco waltzes over and jabs me in the ribs. "What's up, Jasper? Wiki? We're gonna claim the back row of bunks. You in?"

Cole's eyes narrow. "Jasper and I are claiming the front bunks."

A lopsided smile spreads across Marco's face. "The front. Hmmm. That's your plan, Jasper?"

I look from Cole to Marco and back again. It's a critical moment. The way I figure it, Marco couldn't care less if I say yes to him. In fact, he may just be toying with me to annoy Cole. But Cole's a different story. To Cole, this moment is a true test of our new friendship.

I take a deep breath. I really don't want to be pegged a dork. Still, I like Cole. He's smart and serious and seems to know more about Earth Force than most of the other cadets. And Addy said he was a good first friend. Addy always has it right about people.

"Yep. The front. That's my plan."

Marco nods. Then he laughs. "See ya, suckers."

The plebes march in with our bags. Cole runs ahead to claim the front bunks. He squats on the third bunk up and tosses his shoes on the high bunk. The funny thing is, at least two-thirds of the cadets dash for the front.

The plebes heft the luggage on top of the long tables that stretch down the center of the dorm, separating the two rows of bunks. As I scan the pile for my bags, a couple of cadets hassle Cole over the top bunk. He holds firm. Once I grab my duffels and my clarinet case, I head over.

"Your turn," I say. "I'll hold the bunks."

"Thanks." Cole nods at the top bunk. "It's all yours."

As I climb the side ladder to my bunk, I'm confused. The top is clearly the best. You can see the entire dorm from the high perch, and there's a lot more head room than the other bunks. At first I can't figure out why Cole gave it to me. Then I realize it's his way of saying thanks for choosing him over Marco. Okay, sure. He owed me the top bunk. And in this group, it looks like the front is the best anyhow. As long I keep my klutzy ways in check, things should shape up nicely at the EarthBound Academy.

Most of the cadets set to work, unpacking their bags and stowing their belongings. A guy a few bunks down keeps yelling out letters. I think he's alphabetizing his stuff. I shove everything into my bin as fast as I can and then retreat to my bunk. It will be a pain to dig things out later, but I can't keep anything organized anyhow. As I scan the dorm from above, I see I'm not the only cadet who took that approach.

The freckly kid, whose name turns out to be Ryan, snagged the rack next to ours and is unloading his geode collection.

Weird. Why would anyone waste his weight allowance on rocks? Cole doesn't think it's odd. He hops off the bunk and launches into a never-ending talk with Ryan about crystals and gems and meteor fragments.

As soon as I made it back to the bunk with my bags, I stuffed my clarinet case under my pillow. I'm kind of jealous of Ryan, the rock guy. At least he has no problem being right out there with his dorky hobby. I spent the last three years hiding the fact I still love to play an instrument. Clarinet does not equal cool at East, District Eight, Grade Six. Why do I care what other people think? Addy always asks me. I don't know. Being out there with the clarinet was inviting others one step closer to the truth. I'm different. I'm a Bounder.

But at the EarthBound Academy, I'm not different at all. That will take some getting used to.

Marco, Regis, and a big group of cadets from the back bunks cluster around the center tables. Regis jumps on top and pulls up another cadet. They wrestle until one of them falls off. After five matches, Regis is still the victor. When no one else will fight, he skips down the length of the tables until he reaches the front.

"Hey!" Regis shouts. He looks right at me. I duck my head and hope he's talking to someone else.

"Hey, you! Top bunk!" he yells. Reluctantly, I lift my head. "Get up here. Show these clowns how to chicken fight."

I don't see a way out. And there's no way in the world I can beat that guy. I can barely make it off the air rail without tripping over my own feet. I'll be laughed right out of a fight.

Still, I have to save face. I slowly slide off the bunk and cross to the table. The metal chair leg screeches against the floor as I pull it out. I lift my foot, still stuffed in its indigo sock, onto the chair seat and hoist myself up. Regis's crowd claps, egging me on. Regis beckons me with his hands. He looks wild, hungry, like he wants to devour me.

A whistle pierces right through the ruckus.

I turn. We all do. Lieutenant Ridders stands at the door. I leap to the ground.

"Stand and salute your senior officer!" he shouts.

Everyone snaps to attention.

"Obviously, you need to be reminded you are Earth Force officers. I expect you to show respect for your rank at all times. Am I clear?"

A hodgepodge of "yeahs," "yeps," and "uh-huhs" answer back.

Ridders walks right up to Regis, who jumped off the table when the whistle blew. "There is only one way to address a senior officer when he asks you a question, and that is 'sir.' Understand, cadet?"

"Yes, sir," Regis says.

"And what about the rest of you? Am I clear?"

"Yes, sir!" we reply.

"Good," Ridders says. "Lights out, cadets." He crosses to the door and presses the control panel, leaving the room lit only by floor runners. "Wake-up call is at six hundred hours. Stay in your bunk. Leaving the dormitory at night is against the rules."

When Ridders leaves, everyone slumps. Some of the cadets— mostly Regis's crew—complain about the rules. Others are annoyed Ridders pulled rank. And from what it looks like, a lot of kids are just plain anxious—pacing, mumbling, rocking, whimpering, all of the above. Me? I'm just relieved I don't have to fight Regis and make a fool out of myself in front of the entire dorm.

After climbing up to my bunk, I pull out my clarinet case. The supple leather gives beneath my fingers. I pop the clasp and fit the pieces together. As I grip the black-and-silver instrument in my hands, I recall each detail of last night. The whisper of Addy's movements in the dark. The sad melody that slipped from the strings of her violin.

There's still some chatter in the dorm, especially in the back where Marco and Regis set up camp, but most of the kids are silent except for the rustling of sheets and swish of blankets. I put my clarinet away and shove the case in the crack between the mattress and the bed frame.

It's cool in the dormitory. And even though I'm surrounded by dozens of boys—dozens of Bounder boys like me—I feel completely alone.

"Cole," I whisper into the darkness, willing my voice not to crack.

"Yeah?" he replies.

"Good night."

"Good night, Jasper."

Maybe I'm imagining things, but I think he sounds grateful. I close my eyes and drift to sleep.

· *EF* ·

The next morning brings a true taste of life in the Force. Lieutenant Ridders shows up at six a.m. He's nice enough, but he has five other officers with him. Each is meaner than the next. They shout at us to get out of bed, and drag out the cadets who aren't fast enough. Anything we forgot to stow away—shoes, hats, even one cadet's framed picture of his pet hamster—they kick across the dorm floor. They bark orders to get into daily uniform.

I'm not even sure which clothes make up the daily. I dig into the duffel filled with Academy gear Mom packed. Earth Force shipped the stuff direct to us a few months back. Predictably, Cole knows exactly what to wear. I copy him as best I can, and once he's dressed, he rummages through my storage bin and pulls out the rest of what I need.

"How were we supposed to know?" I say. "I figured daily uniform was what we wore yesterday."

"No," Cole says. "Those were dress formals."

"It would have been nice to get a little direction. I mean, we're just kids."

An officer with black hair and bad breath steps close. "You got something to say, plebe?"

"No." What on earth is his problem?

"No, what?" the officer says.

"Uhhh . . . I don't get it," I say. "Just no."

The officer bends down and yells in my face. "No, sir!"

I try not to turn away as his bad breath rolls over me. "Got it," I say. "Sir. I mean, no, sir." I hold my breath, hoping that's enough to get him off my back.

The officer stretches up to his full height. He looms over Cole and me, and he's thick. "That's more like it, plebe. Don't step out of line. I'll be watching." He shoves my shoulder, knocking me straight into my storage bin.

He lingers for a moment, a sick grin on his face, and then moves on to the next rack to harass some other cadets.

I scamper out of the bin and struggle to catch my breath. Pull it together, Jasper. Don't let that bully scare you. That's all he is. A bully. After all, what could that clown do? You're the Bounder, not him.

Cole tugs my sleeve. The cadets are lining up. The officers position us by the door and march us out.

"He's probably just jealous," Cole says.

"Who?" I ask.

"The officer with the bad breath."

Yeah, right. "Why on Earth would he be jealous of me?"

"Did you see his rank?" Cole asks. "He's an auxiliary officer. That means he was skipped over for quantum aeronaut."

Hmmm . . . he couldn't even make the cut? I smile. Cole with all the knowledge. He's definitely a good first friend. "Yeah, he's probably annoyed he has to chaperone a bunch of Bounders."

Ridders leads us out of the dormitory and into the long narrow corridor. Something about the dorm felt a bit more homey—probably just because my stuff was there—but the hall is like a slap to the face. Wake up, Jasper, you're not in Americana anymore. My dull headache returns the second I step under the bright lights, and the walls close in around me. The only thing that breaks the monochromatic sameness of the spearmint walls is the occasional door with its brushed metal handle and a flashing keypad mounted alongside.

And the place still stinks. Did they forget to circulate the air in here?

We follow Ridders, all dressed in our dailies, in a single-file line down the center stripe. If you ignored our out-of-sync steps and our short stature, you might actually think we were Earth Force officers.

Wait a second—we *are* Earth Force officers. Geez, that is awesome. Mind-blowingly awesome.

MONICA TESLER

"What do you think the sensor is for?" Ryan asks as he places his foot on the platinum stripe.

"Definitely some kind of automated transport device," Cole says.

"Oh!" I say. "It's for these mini Spider Crawlers. They look like plain black boxes when they're zipping along the sensor, but then they have these long spiky limbs for walking just like the big Crawlers."

"How do you know that?" Cole asks.

Uh-oh. The only reason I know about the robots is because of my escapade with Marco. The last thing I want to think about right now is that mystery alien, and I'm definitely not ready to tell Cole. I shrug. "I must have read it somewhere."

Cole frowns. I worry he's going to interrogate me, but I'm saved by our arrival at the mess hall.

The hall is filled with a couple dozen circular tables, all a funky orange color. The walls are the same dull green, but the orange brightens the place up. There are even portholes along the wall where you can look out into space.

When we walk in, our formation falls apart. The girls are already here, and there's a lot of chatter. If I close my eyes, I can almost believe I'm in the school cafeteria back home.

Most of the boys beeline for the food. I'm hungry, but I can't shake the horrid smell of stale hot dogs. It kills my appetite.

Lucy rushes over and steers me to a table in the back. Cole follows. She frowns at him, but she doesn't shoo him away.

"Guess what I found out," she says.

I raise my eyebrows. She's going to tell me no matter what I say.

Sure enough, she keeps right on talking. "After breakfast they're announcing the pods."

"Really?" Cole says. "Have you learned any more about how they assess compatibility?"

She shakes her heard. "No. Total silence on that front. But Florine says they're not going to finalize assignments until this morning."

Hmmm. What are they waiting for? What grand insight into our character did they expect to get in less than twenty-four hours?

At the next table, Ryan and some other cadets inhale plates of something yellow and spongy that might be scrambled eggs. As I watch them, I try to make sense of what Lucy said.

"Well?" Lucy asks. She must have kept talking. I zoned out.

"Sorry. Ask me again." I fix my eyes on Lucy. She's changed her hair. Her ribbons match the daily uniform—indigo and orange. Like the tables.

"How was your night?" she asks.

"Fine," I say. Cole embellishes my answer with a technical description of the racks and storage areas and the morning wake-up committee.

"That sounds just like the girls' dorm," Lucy says. "But you guys didn't have the late-night excitement we did."

"What happened?" I ask.

"I bet you could guess. Oh, don't bother. I'll tell you. Dancing Queen decided to take a stroll in the middle of the night and set off all kinds of alarms. Let's just say, no one could have slept through it."

"Mira?" I ask.

Lucy nods. I follow her gaze across the mess hall. Mira sits alone by a porthole, her hand pressed against the glass. Her shirt is untucked, and some of her hair has pulled loose from her braid.

"Wait a minute," Cole says. "The dorm doors are linked to an alarm?"

"To put it mildly," Lucy says. "It was like a five-alarm fire when Mira wandered off. Before we knew it, a dozen armed officers showed up. They checked each bed, taking a head count."

"I don't understand," Cole says. "Why would they need that kind of security?"

Lucy shrugs. "Let's eat."

As I follow Lucy and Cole to the chow line, I'm struck by the memory of what Marco and I saw in the med room. I have no clue why they need so much security either, but I can't shake the feeling it has something to do with the alien.

.

ONCE WE GET OUR FOOD, LUCY DITCHES
us for a table with a group of girls. Cole and I set our trays
down next to Ryan and some other guys who have bunks
near us in the dorm. They seem all right, although one guy
constantly interrupts, and another can't seem to get off the
topic of astroharvesting as the future of agriculture. A thrill-
ing topic for absolutely no one.

I shovel an enormous bite of scrambled eggs into my
mouth.

"Blahhh!" I spit the eggs back onto the tray. "What is that
nastiness?"

"Fluffed tofu," Ryan says. "They ship it here freeze-dried and then pump it with hot air in the kitchens. I kind of like it." His mouth is overflowing with the stuff as he talks.

"Take mine if you want it." I push my plate away and nibble on some fruit sticks I grabbed in line. Maybe lunch will be better.

I talk to the other cadets and try to ignore my grumbling stomach. Two guys at our table are from Americana West. One of the guys is from Eurasia. And another is from Australia. I guess there really are Bounders everywhere.

The Westie next to me keeps checking his watch.

"You gotta be somewhere?" I ask.

"What?" he says.

"You keep looking at your watch. What gives?"

He shrugs. "It's time for lunch. On Earth, I mean. After lunch on Saturdays, I watch *Stellar Rangers*. Always. I know I have to miss it, but it sucks."

"Yeah." What else can I say? I'm not upset about lunch and web shows, but this is all pretty overwhelming.

"I'll get used to it," he says. "The new schedule, I mean."

As we finish eating, Florine Statton enters the mess hall, flanked by Earth Force officers. One of the officers I've never seen before, but the other one is the guy with the bad breath who knocked me down this morning. Florine wears black sunglasses and a black business suit that look identical to the sunglasses and suit she wore yesterday.

Giggles erupt at Lucy's table, and the energy in the room swells. Heads swivel to the rear entrance where a group of Earth Force officers is filling in.

Cole bumps me on the shoulder. "Those are the quantum aeronauts."

I can barely believe it. We're in the same room with the actual aeronauts. There's Edgar Han. And Malaina Suarez. It's like watching EFAN, but it's happening right in front of us. Soon a whole line of aeronauts stretches across the back of the mess hall. They're young and lean and fierce-looking. Well, except for the older guy at the end who isn't wearing a uniform. I recognize him from last night. He's the man who calmed Mira down.

Another officer strides in alone. Sharp intakes of breath ripple through the mess hall. A girl at the next table says, "Ohmygoodness-ohmygoodness-ohmygoodness."

Please. Spare me. Maximilian Sheek has arrived, fashionably late, of course. His hair is even higher in person. Lucy whispers to the girls at her table, and they all burst out laughing.

"Good morning, Bounders," Florine says. For the first time in maybe ever, she actually sounds enthused. She continues talking in an odd, lilting voice as she hurries across the mess hall. "It is my greatest pleasure to introduce to you the true stars of Earth Force, starting with this gentleman right here, Maximilian Sheek." She grabs Sheek's hand and drags him back through the crowd of Bounder-filled tables to the front of the mess hall.

Screams and applause echo through the room. Even Florine squeals. Maybe that's why she bonded with Lucy. They both shriek for Sheek.

"It is very exciting, I know," Florine says. "Our aeronauts are the true face of Earth Force." She beams at Sheek. "I mean, will you look at that face?"

More shrieks. I catch Marco's eyes across the room. He shakes his head in disgust.

"Okay, now breathe," Florine says. "Let's review, Bounders. Your Earth Force tour of duty lasts six weeks. It will end with a field trip to the Paleo Planet. We expect you to be great ambassadors for our tourism program starting this summer. And of course, you'll need to be on your best behavior, because EFAN might just be filming during the field trip."

More squeals. Lots of clapping. My head is going to explode.

"Pay attention, puh-*leeeze*," Florine continues. "Here at the EarthBound Academy, some of your classes will be full-attendance lectures, others will be in small groups, and—you've probably heard this already—some of your learning will be in pods." She raises Sheek's hand in the air and shakes it. "Yes, that's right! You'll be assigned a pod just like the real quantum aeronauts!"

Florine keeps talking, but I only half listen. She describes the teaching format. Every day we'll have a full Academy lecture taught by one of the quantum aeronauts or a special guest. Ridders is teaching a Technology class. Malaina Suarez is teaching Subsistence. All the bounding instruction will take place in pods.

I scan the aeronauts at the back of the mess hall. Which one will lead my pod?

One thing that really stinks is that Bad Breath, whose name we learn is Chief Auxiliary Officer Wade Johnson, is teaching Mobility. At least it's only one class. And it doesn't sound like a very important one. I mean, how much can we possibly need to learn about being mobile?

"Later this week I'll give you details about the pod competition. . . ." Florine says.

Competition? Now that will be interesting.

"But let's not waste another minute. Pod assignments!"

The cadets clap. Lucy winks at me and raises her hand to show her crossed fingers. I don't want anyone to see, so I cross my fingers under the table.

"This is how we'll proceed," Florine says. "I'll introduce these fine aeronauts"—pause to flash her toothy smile at Sheek—"and then they'll read off which five of you have been assigned to his or her pod. There will be twenty-six pods in total, twenty-five led by aeronauts and one led by a . . . civilian." She spits out the word *civilian* like it tastes bad. "Once you're called, you can leave with your instructor to go find your special pod room. First up, Captain Malaina Suarez."

Yet more clapping as Malaina Suarez, the officer we met last night at the chutes, steps next to Florine. Her dark brown hair is cut short, and she looks like she could pummel Florine—or any of us—at a whim.

"Captain Suarez is our newest aeronaut," Florine reads from a tablet. "She hails from the mountain region in Amazonas. She received several advanced degrees from the Combined Ivies University in Americana East before being directly recruited into the Earth Force quantum aeronaut officer training protocol. In the fall, she'll be featured in her first prime-time EFAN documentary, which will focus on her research into off-planet food production. . . ."

Suarez places her hand on Florine's forearm. "I'm sure that's enough on the bio. They'll learn plenty about off-planet food production in my Subsistence class."

"Very well," Florine says, clearly irked by the interruption. "Read the names for your pod."

"Okay. If I call your name, follow me." Malaina reads off five names, and the cadets jump up and exit the mess hall with her.

Florine clears her throat. "Attention, puh-*leeeze*. Next we have Captain Edgar Han, a real Renaissance man. He's fresh back from a personal sabbatical at Oxford in his home region of Eurasia, where he spent a year studying classic photography. Perhaps some of you caught my exclusive interview about his return to Earth Force."

I clap along as Han crosses to the front of the mess hall. He seems cool, and his photography is pretty great. I'm really hoping he calls my name.

When Han reads off the cadets in his pod, Regis and two of the guys from the back bunks join some girls from Lucy's table at the front. They leave the mess hall as a group.

Well, that stinks.

Florine introduces a few more aeronauts, who read through their pod lists. The *Stellar Rangers* guy shuffles out along with another cadet at my table.

"Here's a name you all know," Florine says. "Captain Maximilian Sheek!" Screams again. Lucy's lips are moving. I can't be sure, but I think she's mouthing *please, please, please*.

"Quiet down, now," Sheek says. "Why don't we let Miss Statton do her job?" When he throws a dazzling smile back at Florine, she fans her face.

"What can I tell you that you don't already know about this true Earth hero?" Florine says. "After a childhood in front of the spotlight as a web actor, Sheek left Americana West and studied opera at the renowned Metropolitan Institute of the Arts in Americana East. There, he showed extraordinary prowess for the unique intellectual and physical demands of the quantum bounding protocol and was hand-selected by Admiral Eames and other senior leaders to represent our great planet in Earth Force."

"Florine, you flatter me. . . ."

"Truth is not flattery." Florine slides her pink-nailed hand around Sheek's waist. "Despite his unmatched success in Earth Force, he's kept his finger on the pulse of style and trend. I'm sure you all watch his weekly EFAN show, *Chic with Sheek*. Am I right?"

Screams. Squeals. Please. Make them stop.

Cole taps my shoulder. "What does she mean 'unmatched success in Earth Force'?" he whispers. "I don't think he's actually done anything more than the other aeronauts, at least in terms of bounding."

"Well, he managed to keep his hair in a pouf during the atom replication process," I say. "So there's that."

"Without further ado," Florine continues, "I give you the one true face of Earth Force, Captain Maximilian Sheek."

Sheek pauses—or more like, poses—for a dramatic moment before reading the names on his list. I don't know if Ryan is excited or mortified when he's called for Sheek's pod. Frankly, it's a relief when Sheek and his cadets leave the mess hall.

"Less exciting, but no less important," Florine says, "let me

MONICA TESLER

introduce the acclaimed scientist, Jon Waters." Florine's words sound nice, but her tone says she's entirely underwhelmed as the guy in civilian clothes—the one who helped Mira—steps forward. The mess hall hums with hushed voices. Forget the fact he's not an aeronaut; he's not even in Earth Force! He doesn't even have a bio! Whoever gets him as their pod leader is out of luck.

I cross the fingers on my other hand. *Don't call my name.* I glance at Cole. He scoots his chair back. What? If he's farther away, he won't get called?

Waters wears wrinkled tan chinos, a blue oxford button-down, and a corduroy blazer. Standing among the crisp, clean lines of the uniformed officers, he looks really out of place.

He clears his throat. "Good morning. The following cadets are in my pod." He looks down at the crumpled paper he holds in his hand. "Cole Thompson."

That stinks. Cole's face falls as he walks to the front of the mess hall.

"Lucy Dugan."

Bummer. I'd wanted Lucy in my pod. At least Lucy and Cole are together. I doubt he's too thrilled, but she's a familiar face.

"Marco Romero."

Marco slaps hands with the guys at his table before saun-tering to the front. He stands next to Cole, who inches closer to Lucy.

"Jasper Adams."

Whoa. I can't believe they actually placed me with my friends. I wish I had a different instructor, but I'm psyched about my pod mates. As I walk to the front, Lucy and Cole part, and I step between them. Marco leans over and shakes my hand.

"And finally . . ."

Lucy bounces on her toes beside me, and whispers, "No, no, no, no . . ."

"Mira Matheson."

Ahhh. So that's it. The girls at the table in front of us giggle.

"Okay, kids," Waters says. "Let's head out the back. We'll pick up Miss Matheson on our way." He crosses through the crowd at a brisk pace.

I turn to Cole, hoping to get his read, but his face is vacant. Marco and Lucy tail after Waters. I punch Cole on the shoulder to get him moving, and dash after them.

Mira's eyes are fixed on the porthole, even when our group surrounds her. Waters grips her shoulder with one hand and takes her slender fingers with the other. As he eases her away from the window, Mira turns. Her gaze darts around, landing on each of us for an instant, then traveling on. As her eyes light on Waters, she stands and allows him to direct her from the mess hall.

We trail after Waters down the corridor. No one speaks.

Waters still has Mira by the hand. He ushers us to the nearest chute cube.

"You kids learned how to use the chutes yesterday, right?" he says.

We nod.

He holds open the door and gestures for us to enter the cube. We exchange glances.

"What's the problem?" Waters asks.

"It's one at a time, sir," Cole says.

Waters laughs. "Do you think we have time for that? Come on. Let's go. And knock it off with the 'sir.' That's for officers only."

We crowd into the cube. There's just enough room for all of us to fit.

"Good," Waters says. "I was beginning to think you had a problem with directions."

Lucy makes a face behind Waters's back. I press my hand to my lips to stop from laughing.

"I'll punch in the override," Waters says. "Then you kids step up one after the next."

Cole shifts and watches the override over Waters's shoulder.

The chute sparks to life, and the sound of rushing air fills the cube.

"Let's go! Let's go!" Waters says.

Marco jumps onto the grate and—*whoosh!*—he's sucked in.

Waters presses a hand on Lucy's back, and she stumbles onto the pad. *Whoosh!*

I step on behind her. The suction yanks me up. Before I can blink, I'm flying through the chute. I pick up speed and soar around the corners.

I will never get bored of the chutes.

Thud. My head slams into something firm and rubbery. Was there a malfunction?

"Hey!" Lucy's voice calls out in the darkness. "Who is that?"

Lucy? I inch my arms upward, keeping them close to my body to fight through the drag. When they clear my head, I grab at the rubber. Sure enough, Lucy's shoes.

"Let go!" Lucy yells, and kicks with her foot.

"Cut it out!" I shout over the rushing air. "That hurt."

"Jasper?"

Before I can answer, something slams into my feet.

"Ouch!" Cole hollers.

I have an idea. "Cole, grab my ankles."

It takes Cole a second, but he manages to slide his fingers around my socks. I adjust my hands around Lucy's ankles. "Good. Now straighten out as long as you can."

I push down with my feet and up with my arms, and I sense the others doing the same. As our chain elongates, we pick up speed. We stretch out in a lean line and race through the chute.

"Wahoo!" I shout. Soon we're all hooting and hollering as we soar even faster.

I squeeze my eyes shut and drift in the thrill of the speed and the steady current of air against my skin.

We slide into an awkward pile in the chute trough. Cole on top of me on top of Lucy.

"Get off!" she shouts. Or at least, that's what it sounds like. Her voice is pretty muffled beneath Cole and me.

"What are you clowns doing?" Marco asks.

"Now, now, everybody off. Clear the chute. Quickly now. There are others in the queue." A squat man with messy hair pulls at my shirt with one hand and has Cole's collar in the other.

"Didn't I say quickly? Yes, quickly now. There, there. Don't be alarmed. You'll get the hang of the chutes with time. Just get out of the trough quickly."

I stumble out behind Cole. The strange man is wearing a long white lab coat and small wire-rimmed glasses. Glasses? Who wears glasses anymore? As the man leans down to help Lucy, I whisper in Cole's ear. "Who is that guy?"

Cole shakes his head. "I have no idea."

A gust of air from the chute announces the next arrival. Lucy had just lifted her foot from the trough when— *whoosh!*—Waters and Mira sail in.

"Good. We all made it." Waters climbs out of the trough

and helps Mira out after him. He nods at the strange man. "Kids, this is Gedney. He'll be helping us along." Waters swings the cube door open and twirls his arm around in a circle. "Let's go. Everybody out."

"Yes, yes," Gedney mumbles. "Everybody out. Not a second to waste. Not a single second. Very important we keep moving."

Lucy turns to me, her eyebrows raised. I shrug. No, I have no clue who he is. But I'm getting surer by the second we got bum luck with our pod assignment.

Waters takes off down the hall. All the officers at the space station stand straight and walk with confidence—it is Earth Force, after all—but Waters's walk is different. He has a bounce to his step that gives him an air of independence. It's like he knows a secret joke, and if you're lucky, he might share it with you.

We hurry to catch Waters. Gedney takes up the rear and herds us along. He keeps up his muttering—"Hurry, now! Keep moving! Quickly!"—and every time I turn around to look at him, he's glancing nervously over his shoulder. His posture is horrible. Worse than a Tunneler's. He hunches so far forward, I worry he'll lose his balance and fall on his face.

Waters stops at a door locked by a bio screen. "Here we are. The pod hall." He leans in so the sensor can scan his right eye, and the door buzzes open.

The hall overflows with Bounders. I recognize most of them from the ship or the dormitory. Some of the cadets say hello, but most keep to their pods. So this is how it's going to be. All pods for themselves. It's probably Earth Force's way of drumming up competition in the Academy. Florine even said there'd be a contest.

We pass several open pod rooms. Most of them are set up like small classrooms: two rows of student desks facing a teacher's table at the front, and a huge tech screen pulled down on the rear wall.

Lucy halts in front of one of the rooms. I glance inside. No surprise, it's Sheek's pod. Ryan knocks my shoulder as he brushes past me into the room.

"Sorry," he says.

"No worries," I say. "Is this your pod room?"

He stands too close, right in my personal space. "Sure is," he says. "I heard you're with our resident freak. Bummer."

That makes me mad. Who is he to call Mira a freak? I ball my hands into fists. Wait a minute. . . . Why am I jumping to defend Mira? Don't I think she's kind of a freak, too? Ryan stares at me with an odd, questioning look on his face. I just turn and stomp away. Better to be rude than start a fight, I guess.

I catch a glimpse of Han's pod room as we pass. One wall is lined with photographs he's taken in space. A pang of envy twists in my gut. When I see Regis and Han talking by the instructor's desk, it twists even more.

"Okay, here we are." Waters stops in front of the last door in the hall.

The very last pod room. Yet another sign we're the rejects.

Waters opens the door and stands aside for us to enter. The room doesn't look a thing like any of the other pod rooms we passed. Instead of desks, beanbag chairs are scattered around the room. A shag carpet the color of grass covers the floor. The walls are painted a sky-blue that gradually shades to a midnight ceiling twinkling with thousands of pinpricks of light.

Whoa. Weird.

"Dude," Marco says. "You really let loose with the decorating. Where'd you even find this stuff?"

Deep waist-high bookcases circle the room. On the top shelves are lots of unusual objects—lava lamps in shades of crimson and lime and aqua, squishy balls with rubber tendrils in different shapes and sizes, vases with prickly light sticks, and swaths of material of all sorts of textures.

Seriously. Where did he find this stuff?

Lucy creeps up beside me. "Is this a joke?"

I shrug. "You talked to Florine. Did she ever mention this guy?"

Lucy shakes her head. "Do you think they accept transfer requests?"

Waters closes the door and adjusts the lights. Or really, he just turns the lights off, so the room is entirely lit by the lava lamps and the night sky (or ceiling, whatever). He crosses to the middle of the room and plops down on a beanbag. Despite his being twice the size of a kid, he somehow has mastered the art of sitting on these things.

"What are you waiting for? We need to get started." He pats the beanbag. The little foam balls inside swish with each pat. "Sit."

I sink into a cobalt-blue beanbag. The beans mold around me, pulling me deeper into their foam. All sense of proper sitting or military form is lost to that bag.

The others claim bags, too—except Gedney. He buzzes around by the door, checking the readings on mounted screens. Marco and Lucy sprawl on their bags like me. Cole somehow manages to stay upright on his purple beanbag, but he can't last long. Mira lies on her belly on top of a lemon-yellow bag. She faces away from the group. Her fingers rhythmically stroke illuminated sticks in a cylindrical vase. The lights on the sticks dance in a pattern connected to her movements. Once I fix my gaze on the lights, I can't tear it away.

"Jasper," Waters says, "we'll start with you."

7

I SPACED OUT AGAIN. I HAVE NO IDEA what I'm supposed to be starting on.

"Sir?" I try to sound polite and enthusiastic. Maybe that will make up for not paying attention.

Waters smiles. It's one of those grown-up smiles that says both *You're a good kid* and *I've got something on you.* "I was just telling the group," Waters says, "I think we should get to know one another better, say a few words about ourselves. And no 'sirs,' remember?"

"Ummm . . . okay." I haven't really prepared for that kind of question, which I guess is pretty stupid, since of course the teachers will want to get to know us. "Well, I'm from East. District Eight. I have a younger sister, Addy. She's a Bounder, too. So she'll be coming to the Academy next spring when we're here for our third tour." I hoped that was enough, but they all still stare. "And I play the clarinet." Why did I say that? That is the last thing I want them to know about me.

As soon as the word *clarinet* slips out of my mouth, Mira flips forward on her beanbag. She pulls her knees into her chest and wraps her arms around them. Her liquid brown eyes lock on mine, and I swallow my gasp. Her eyes hold the most boundless amount of space I've ever seen. I could latch on to those eyes and stay. I shake my head and turn away.

The other cadets look from me to Mira and back again. I feel my cheeks flush. Waters nods approvingly before turning to Marco. "You're next, hotshot."

Marco jumps up and paces back and forth across the pod room. "Marco Romero. Amazonas. Older brother not a B-wad. Nothing else to say. Except I'm really curious why we're holed up in this love den while everyone else appears to be learning."

Waters laughs, a deep, hearty sound that rises up from his belly and pushes out into the pod room. "Love den?" he says. "I've never heard that one. And how come you called yourself that—B-wad? It's not exactly the most flattering term. I won't tolerate it in this pod room."

I wondered the same thing. On the passenger craft, Marco lectured the other cadets about using that word. Seems a little hypocritical to me.

"I didn't call myself a B-wad." Marco crosses his arms against his chest. "I called my brother a B-wad."

"You said your brother isn't a Bounder," Waters says.

"He's not. But if he were, he'd deserve to be called a B-wad."

Marco and Waters lock eyes in some sort of showdown. There's nothing the groovy lights or cushy seats can do to ease the tension. Waters lets several seconds pass before speaking. "Have a seat, Marco."

Marco doesn't budge, and he doesn't break his stare. What will Waters do if Marco refuses to sit? Waters isn't flustered. He stretches out on his tangerine beanbag and clasps his hands behind his head. His long legs, crossed at the ankles, cover half the width of the green shag rug.

Marco shrugs and returns to his seat. Waters nods at Lucy. "Miss Dugan."

"Okay. Hi, everyone. I'm Lucy Dugan. I'm super excited to be here. We've been waiting for this day for, like, our whole lives, right? Anyhow, I'm from West. Americana West. You probably knew that. I'm a web actress, just like Sheek. Or an aspiring actress, at least. I love to write. I've written thirteen full-length screenplays. So stereotypical, right? West, actress, screenplays? And all my friends . . ."

I try to listen to Lucy, but she just goes on and on. I tip my head back and close my eyes. How many times have I called someone a B-wad without really thinking about it? When have I actually understood what it means? That the *B* stands for *Bounder*? That the wad stands for—to be honest, I have no idea what the wad stands for—but it means freak, weirdo, loser. The word hurts. It's not a huge hurt like the way it feels when the kids at school tease me about my clumsiness or my clarinet. But each time I hear the word, or say the word, or even think about the word, a tiny dagger stabs me in the gut.

"And so what I'm really hoping to get from this is first, friends, lots of friends, and all of you are a great start. And knowledge—I know I'll learn a lot here, Mr. Waters. And of course, I'm really honored for this chance to serve my planet." Lucy talks for so long, it feels like something is missing when she finally shuts up.

"Thanks, Lucy. Cole, the baton passes to you."

"Thank you, Mr. Waters." Cole sits up so straight, it's like he has a rod stuck through his spine. How on earth does he do that? I sink a little farther into my beanbag.

"My name is Cole Thompson. I'm from Americana East. District Seventeen. Grade Six. I have no siblings. I've read all publicly available information on Earth Force and the EarthBound Academy."

Waters leans over his hunched knee and stands. "Thank you, Cole. I can tell you're very informed."

Understatement.

Waters walks over to the corner where Gedney is still fiddling with the screens. "Now let me introduce you to my main man. Kids, this is Gedney."

Wait a minute. What about Mira? How come she gets a free pass?

No one else seems to notice. They're all staring at Gedney. It's like Mira's not even here.

"Gedney is an important fellow," Waters continues. "Probably the most important person you'll meet at the EarthBound Academy."

You'd think Gedney would stand up straighter when all eyes were on him, but he actually hunches more. I really have no idea how he manages not to topple over.

"He's one of our key tech developers," Waters says. "Some folks call him Einstein, but I like to call him the Gadget Guru."

Gadget Guru Gedney. It has a certain ring to it.

Gedney inches away from Waters. "No, no, no. Don't make an asteroid out of a rock fragment. You kids are the important ones. No need to waste time on me."

"Always the pinnacle of modesty, Gedney," Waters says. "And cut it out with all the rush. They're here now. It *is* time."

Waters locks eyes with Gedney until Gedney nods.

I have no clue what they're talking about. Hurry. Don't hurry. I'm kind of with the Gadget Guru: let's just get on with it. Whatever *it* is.

"That's it for the meet and greet," Waters says. "We have daily pod sessions, and after we cover the basics, we'll start the bounding protocol in a week or so. And now I'll let the Gadget Guru distribute the tablets."

As Gedney digs through a crate in the corner of the pod room, my glance slips from one of my pod mates to the next. Marco with his fiery and impulsive personality. Lucy, friendly but never shuts up. Cole . . . What did Marco call him? Ahhh, yes. Wiki. The Fact Man. And then there's Mira. Mysterious Mira twirling on the tarmac to music only she can hear. What do they think of me? Me and my clarinet. At least I've managed to keep my klutzy ways out of the equation.

Gedney hands each of us a tablet. It doesn't look much different from the one I have back on Earth. The upside: it has a cool Earth Force insignia stamped on the back. The downside: I'm sure it has almost no connectivity. Media silence. No contact with parents, friends, anyone from the outside for six weeks. I bet the chance of our playing *Evolution* is zero.

"You're still with us, right, Jasper?" Waters asks. He stands by the door and waves his arm, shooing us out.

Heat floods my cheeks as I nod. I zoned out again? Geez, I have to work on the focus thing.

Everyone else is already on their feet. Well, everyone except Mira. When it's just the three of us left, Waters crosses to Mira's beanbag and takes her hand. He pulls her up and walks her to the door, his hand pressed firmly against her back.

When we reach the door, a silver button on Waters's lapel beeps. "That's my com pin reminding me of the very important briefing that was scheduled this morning and which I promptly forgot about." He removes Mira's delicate fingers from his own and places them in my palm. "Walk with Mira to the lecture hall. Okay, Jasper?"

"Yes, Mr. Waters." I don't think I have a choice, but it's weird. Holding hands? I don't even like holding Mom's hand. Mira's fingers are long and bony and cold.

We step into the hall packed with cadets from other pods. The bright glow of the florescent lights bears down on us, and the steady hum is like a bee buzzing in my brain. My nerves swim up from my belly and tickle the back of my throat, making it hard to breathe.

Mira's hand, which a second before lay limp in my grasp, deftly laces with mine and squeezes, jolting me with grounding pressure. My strength doubles, like somehow I'm tapping into her reserves.

I turn to her, but she stares off to the side, a foggy film across her eyes.

As we set off down the hall, I tighten my grip on her hand. *Hi, Mira. It's nice to meet you.*

· *EF* ·

The lecture hall buzzes with kids. A podium stands on an elevated platform at the front of the room. Rows of long, crescent-shaped tables stretch across the floor, which slopes down to the platform. Cadets gather in clusters, their Academy tablets spread on top of the tables claiming their spaces. As I scan the room for Cole, Mira slips off to a corner. I almost go after her, but Waters only asked me to escort her to the lecture hall. Check.

Two strong arms grab me from behind and pin me in a headlock.

"Get off of me!"

The arms release, and I spin around.

Marco steps back, hands up. "Whoa, Chief. Chill. Just having some fun."

I look down at my feet and think about Ryan and the stolen shoe on the passenger craft. "Yeah, well, it wasn't funny."

"Okay, whatever. Let's grab some seats. Unless you'd rather sit with your girlfriend." Marco tips his head in Mira's direction.

"Yeah, right." That's all I need. The whole Academy

thinking I'm paired up with Mira. I mean, I think she's okay, but that's it.

Marco starts down the aisle, and I follow. We join a group of the back bunkers and toss our tablets onto their table. I still can't spot Cole in the mass of kids.

"Hey, Marco," Lucy's voice calls from the row behind us. Marco and I both turn around.

The girl next to Lucy dives under the table. Lucy rolls her eyes and points at her. "Meggi wanted to meet you."

"And you're her spokesperson?" Marco asks.

Lucy grins. "Something like that." She pulls Meggi up by the shoulders. The girl's face is almost purple. *Hi,* she mouths, but no sound comes out.

"Don't mind her," the girl on the other side of Lucy says. She has clear blue eyes and strawberry-blond hair. "She's afraid of boys."

"Who are you?" Marco asks.

"Annette," she says. She twists her neck so her eyes lock with mine. "You're Jasper, right?" She has a funny way of talking. Toneless.

"Uh . . . hi," I say. I feel the color creeping into my cheeks, too, so I flip back around in my seat.

Behind me, the girls erupt in giggles. Great. I'm a complete loser.

Maximilian Sheek passes our row, heading for the podium.

MONICA TESLER

So that's why they laughed. I almost wish they'd been laughing at me. A few targeted girl giggles would be better than sitting through a whole lecture with Sheek.

"Thank you," Sheek says as the cadets clap. "Thank you. You're too nice. Thank you. Really now—quiet down." The claps fade as Sheek waves his hands in an oh-too-obvious attempt at modesty. "Thank you again. I'm thrilled to be teaching at the EarthBound Academy. After all, you Bounders are the future of quantum entanglement space travel. Admiral Eames asked me to join you this morning for your first lecture, to give you an overview of the history of the Earth space program. For most of you, this will be a refresher, but it's a good place to start."

Sheek talks and smooths his hair and talks some more. I try to pay attention, but I fade in and out. He's right: most of what he says I already know. The early space program—reaching the moon and Mars. Then the discovery of the Higgs boson that led to propulsion advancement to FTL, faster than light speed. Finally the discovery of the element occludium, the missing link for quantum entanglement space travel. In other words—drum roll please—bounding. That's when our exploration of the universe really took off. With the speed of bounding, humans have managed to chart and investigate hundreds of star systems. We've also explored dozens of planets, like the Tunneler planet, containing much-needed ore and other natural resources.

Marco passes me his tablet under the table. He'd typed a message: *Do you think he'll talk about you-know-who?*

The alien in the med room? I shrug. I hope he will, but my guess is the alien is under wraps, off limits, super security-clearance only.

I tune in when Sheek talks about first contact and the treaty with the Tunnelers. I think maybe he'll give us the real scoop on what happened during the diplomatic envoy—did it really go down without any blood or combat?—but he just sticks to the published history. And next on the agenda is the Incident at Bounding Base 51. He glosses over it. Just the basics: failed mission, quantum ship never materialized, aeronauts' atoms lost somewhere in the cosmos. I guess he doesn't want to make us too nervous, since the whole reason we're here is to learn to bound.

That's it. No mention of the alien in the med room.

As Sheek wraps up, Florine Statton waltzes down the row. The lights in the hall cast a glare off her white teeth.

"Wow! What an introduction to the EarthBound Academy!" she says once she reaches the podium, sounding suspiciously enthusiastic. She grabs Sheek's right bicep with both hands.

"Why, thank you, Miss Statton." Sheek smiles at Florine and winks at the class.

Marco passes me his tablet under the table again. Someone

sent him a Photoshopped GIF of Sheek and Florine in silver aeronaut suits, kissing on the bounding deck.

I cover my mouth to keep from laughing.

There's silence in the lecture hall. Florine stares at Sheek. Sheek stares at Florine. Then at us. Then at Florine again. Meanwhile, Florine seems totally love struck. Someone, say something please!

Sheek gestures at the podium.

"Oh yes, silly me," Florine says. She angles over the microphone without letting go of Sheek.

"I have details about the pod competition." Her voice is back to its normal boredom level. "Each week the pods will be ranked based on their combined scores. Scores will be based on three criteria: quizzes, relay races, and bounding percentages. The first rankings will be posted at the end of week two. Bounding will count double, but we won't begin the bounding protocol until the end of week three, when the first assessment is made. There will be a prize for the top-ranked pod. We'll announce more information soon."

Florine still clutches Sheek's arm. He tries to be discreet, but we all see him struggling to get free from her grip while she talks. It's so funny, I can hardly hear Florine over all the muffled giggles. When she finally stops talking, she drags Sheek up the aisle and out of the lecture hall.

We wait for someone to come and dismiss us. Eventually,

when no one shows, we grab our tablets and head for the aisle.

I finally spot Cole. Front row—I should have known. He chats excitedly with Ryan and a couple of cadets I recognize from the dorm. He probably knows what the prize is for the first-place pod. Yet another reason to stick with Cole. He catches my eye as he walks out of the lecture hall. He doesn't look too happy about my seating choice.

As the cadets start out the doors, I search the room for Mira. The area where she'd been sitting is empty.

· EF ·

Dinner is worse than breakfast. I thought I was digging into a huge plate of buttered noodles. Nope. Tofu strings. And no butter, either. The tofu strings are just slimy. Six weeks of this stuff? Yuck. I'll go home a lot skinnier than when I left.

Ryan and Cole don't seem to mind.

"How can you eat that?" I ask.

Ryan shrugs. "It's good." I get a great view of the half-chewed strings in his mouth.

"Me?" Cole says. "I knew what to expect. I'd read all about the space station food, so I didn't have high hopes. It might improve. We'll learn about the garden initiatives in Subsistence class with Captain Suarez."

I push my tray toward Ryan, who gladly off-loads my tofu strings, then I shove away from the table. "I'm going to see if they have any more carob-coated fruit balls."

When I turn the corner for the cafeteria line, I nearly collide with Regis. He has a huge bucket in his hand. Two guys from his pod, Randall and Hakim, are with him. They each carry a bucket. And Marco is there, too, empty-handed.

"What are you guys doing?" I glance into the buckets. They're filled with the slimy tofu strings.

"Having a little fun," Regis says. "You in?"

I have a bad feeling in my gut, but I fall in behind Marco as Regis leads us out of the mess hall.

Regis sends Randall ahead to scout as we make our way to the nearest chute cube.

"Okay," Regis says. "What's the time?"

"Almost eighteen hundred hours," Hakim says. "She'll be here in two minutes."

"Good," Regis says. "Perfect timing. Load it up."

Regis, Randall, and Hakim dump their buckets of tofu strings into the chute's arrival trough.

"Whoa," I say. "What are you doing?"

"Setting up a little welcome party for Meggi," Regis says.

Meggi? Lucy's friend? The one who dove under the desk?

Randall laughs. "We used Marco here as bait. Told her he wanted to meet her at the chute cube at eighteen hundred sharp."

For real? I look at Marco. He grins.

Oh, that's mean. Really mean. Really slimy and mean.

But I must admit, it's really funny.

The red light flashes in the chute cube. Incoming.

"Quick!" Regis yells. "Everybody out! We'll hide around the corner."

We dash away from the cube and down the hall. We peer around the corner at the arrival trough. *Bam!* Someone slams into the chute and is instantly drowning in tofu strings.

We burst out laughing. I hold my stomach with one hand and bite down on the other to keep from making too much racket. More noise wouldn't have mattered much, though. The shrieks coming from the chute cube would have drowned out almost anything.

The girl in the arrival trough is struggling to climb out, tofu strings clinging to her hair, covering her clothes. Wait a minute. . . .

She isn't wearing the indigo uniform.

Are those . . . ? Sunglasses . . . ?

"Oh no," Hakim says.

"That's . . . ," Randall says.

"Florine Statton!" Marco says.

"Run, run! Go! Go! Go!" Regis yells.

We tail after him down the hall as fast as we can. Of course, it's really not that fast, because we're practically choking with laughter.

When we finally reach the boys' dorm, Regis climbs up on

the table and entertains the room with the story of our prank. I laugh along and throw in a choice nugget about how the tofu strings in Florine's hair looked just like slithering snakes. A modern Medusa.

Instant legend.

THE FIRST FEW DAYS FLY BY. THE FOOD hasn't gotten any better, but I'm getting used to life at the space station. We spend mornings in pod session, and afternoons in lecture. Even Waters, Gedney, and the tricked-out pod room are growing on me.

Of course, all that could change drastically. We're scheduled to start specialist classes this afternoon. I'm not worried about Subsistence and Technology, but Mobility makes my stomach twist. As far as I can tell, it sounds like glorified gym class. And let's just say gym isn't my thing. Plus, it's taught by Bad Breath.

"Jasper." Waters looks down at me in the cobalt beanbag. "This is important information. Please stay with us."

Pay attention. Right. I have to work on that.

"As I was saying," Waters continues as he walks a labyrinth around the beanbags, "you all know the basics of quantum entanglement space travel—bounding, that is—and if you don't, I'm sure they'll cover it in agonizing detail in your lectures." Gedney laughs and Waters smiles. Some private joke, I guess. I stretch out on my beanbag and watch the stars twinkle on the ceiling.

"Let's quickly review," Waters says. "We're able to move within space almost instantaneously by bounding. We have a base here at the space station, and we have a base at the destination. The atoms here—we'll call it home base—have a corresponding set of atoms waiting in the quantum field at the destination base—everything from the quantum ship to the equipment to the aeronauts themselves. Once the bound is initiated, the destination base atoms receive all the information from the home base atoms, and the home base atoms are left in stasis . . . empty, if you will . . . in the quantum field. That's the wavy space you see at the launch site. Does anyone know how the quantum fields are created?"

Cole's arm shoots into the air. "An inventory of every required atom is taken, starting with the ship. The quantum field is filled with the receiving atoms. Without being too technical, the bounding atoms are mapped into their receiving atoms via the space station's computers, and then the destination base is ready to receive the bound."

"Good," Waters says. "You've done your homework, Cole. Impressive. What could go wrong? Jasper this time."

Bounding Base 51. The Incident. That's where Waters is going. "If the mapping is messed up," I say, "the bound fails."

"And what exactly does that mean?" Waters asks. I guess he isn't going to gloss over it like Sheek did during lecture.

I've watched web runs of the Incident at Bounding Base 51 hundreds of times. Everyone has. It's part of Earth's collective memory. The reason the Force reintroduced the Bounder genes as insurance it would "never happen again."

I clear my throat before answering. "The quantum ship wouldn't materialize at the destination base. The ship, the aeronauts, everything would be lost." My voice fades at the end. The sheer gravity of it hits too close. A failed bound. That could be my fate. The EarthBound Academy isn't all fun and games. The stakes are real. And they're high.

"Everything would be lost," Waters repeats. He settles onto his beanbag and rests his hands on his knees. "I know that's scary. This is difficult, risky work. You knew that coming in, but I know it's hard when you're staring right at it."

"What exactly happens to the atoms when they're not received?" Lucy asks. "Where do they go?"

Waters leans forward, tightening our circle of beanbags.

"Lucy, that is one of the great mysteries. No one really knows."

"You mean they're just lost in space?" she asks.

Waters nods. He looks at Gedney before continuing. "Maybe this is a childlike notion, but I hope someday we'll solve that riddle and bring those aeronauts home."

A heavy silence fills the pod room. We talked about the Incident a lot growing up. Mom and Dad wanted to demystify all the lore around it, since Addy and I are Bounders. My parents were on their honeymoon when the Incident at Bounding Base 51 occurred. They watched the bounding mission on the webs. Everyone did. The quantum technology was still so new and awe-inspiring. One second the ship was there, the smiling aeronauts waving good-bye, the next second it was gone. Just that. Gone.

A lot of things happened the year after the Incident. All of Earth's space programs and militaries merged to create Earth Force. Admiral Eames stepped to the helm. A few months later Earth Force announced the Bounder Baby Breeding Program. All male-female couples were tested for the Bounder genes. A positive test meant physician-assisted procreation to guarantee a Bounder baby. The government always said it was optional, but from what I've overheard from my parents, that wasn't really true.

As I sink deeper into my beanbag, I can hear Mom's voice swell:

Mom: I don't get it. What on earth are a bunch of kids going to do?

Dad: We've been through this. Their minds are better suited to perform the bounding calculations.

Mom: Better than computers? Come on. None of it makes sense. You know there's something they're not telling us.

Dad always dismisses her fears, but she never let it go.

When I drift back from the memories, Waters's bounding talk is over. He pages through a few screens on his classified tablet. "Listen up. Here's the schedule. You're headed to the main hall for full Academy lecture, then to Mobility. I won't spoil the surprise, but let me just say that the Gadget Guru will be joining you for your Mobility class today."

· *Ef* ·

The hangar doors are shut, closing it off from the wild open space beyond, and there's no sign of the gunmen from the first night. Still, the place is scary. The walls are four stories high and twice as wide. Plus, the junior officers are there, the mean ones from daily wake-up call. They'll be assisting in Mobility class. As soon as I walk in, I spot Bad Breath. No way do I want his rank odor washing over me. I head to the opposite side of the hangar.

The junior officers place us in formation facing a large crate at the front of the hangar. Marco slips in next to me as they're forming my row. As soon as the officers step away, our formation falls apart. Our lines are crooked, our spacing bunched, and at least half of the cadets (including me) are so fidgety, we look like we're practicing dance moves. We Bounders aren't exactly living up to formal military standards.

"Well, look who it is," Marco says. Gedney's stooped form emerges from the hangar's side door, inching forward at a snail's pace. Geez, for someone who wants everyone to rush, he doesn't exactly operate at Mach speed.

Two plebes enter the hangar behind Gedney. They push shoulder-high carts piled high with gray backpacks. They position the carts alongside the crate and help Gedney climb up. That makes me nervous. Gedney on top of a crate? I can't imagine that will end well.

Gedney's mouth moves, so he must be talking, but I doubt anyone's listening. Gedney, with his civilian clothes and hunched posture, doesn't have the cred to hush a hangar full of twelve-year-olds.

"Shut up, you little freaks!" someone bellows. Bad Breath. What a surprise. He marches to the front. "You're not here to talk; you're here to be taught!" he yells. "So shut up!" He stares into our ranks, daring any of us to speak.

Marco leans over. "He's the one who roughed you up, right?"

I nod and whisper to Marco what Cole told me about Bad Breath's rank.

"You got something to say, plebe?" Bad Breath stares at me.

"No." I will my voice not to shake, but it doesn't work.

Bad Breath's face lights up with a satisfied smile. "No, what?"

Sir. I have to say it. I have to cower to the bully in front of everyone.

"Wasn't his answer clear?" Marco yells. "He said no."

I turn to Marco. I'm happy for the support but—geez—does he have a death wish?

Rage boils beneath Bad Breath's eyes. "Was I talking to you, plebe?"

"My guess is, you were talking to everyone," Marco replies. "Your job is to get things quiet for Gedney. And we're quiet. So I have no clue why you need to call out my friend. Especially since it was me talking."

"Is that how you see it, plebe?"

"Yes," Marco says.

"Yes, what?"

Great. Here we go again. Back where we started.

Marco smiles. And now it's his turn to look wickedly satisfied. "Yes, Auxiliary Officer Johnson."

I can't believe it. Marco called him out in front of the entire Academy, highlighting his pass-over for aeronaut in front of all the little bounding prodigies. Marco, you rock.

Red rushes into Bad Breath's face, and his cheeks puff up

like he's going to explode. I bite my lip to stop from laughing.

"Back. Of. The. Line." Bad Breath deflates as he speaks, each word slipping out in a puff of air.

"So I'm at the back of the line? Big deal," Marco whispers. "Chin up, Jasper. He can't touch us." Marco slaps me on the shoulder and heads for the back.

"Okay, now, very good." Gedney jumps right in, pulling the attention away from Marco and Bad Breath. "I'm distributing special devices today. Very special, indeed. Form two lines. Let's go. Quickly."

We break off into lines, one in front of each bin. Gedney nods to the plebes, who each hold up a backpack. They look like standard packs to me. The only difference is the indigo-and-orange Earth Force seal embroidered on the front pocket.

"One at a time," Gedney says. "Come through the line and get your pack. Quickly."

We rotate through the lines. When I reach the front, the plebe tosses me a backpack. It looks like my school bag at home. What a grand fuss over nothing.

I head over to Cole and Ryan, who already have their bags. Cole looks like he's just been given an awesome birthday present.

"What are you so pumped about?" I ask.

"You'll see," Cole says.

"What? The backpack? You're kidding, right?"

Cole doesn't respond, but he bounces on his toes.

The bag is made of a rugged material and has reinforced zippers. Okay, so it's obviously a high-quality backpack, but seriously, what gives?

One of the plebes up front whistles, and all eyes turn to Gedney.

"You now, you over there." Gedney waves at Regis.

Regis looks around, probably making sure Gedney is actually talking to him. His buddies laugh. Randall pushes him between the shoulder blades, sending him stumbling forward.

"Fine, fine," Gedney mumbles. "What's your name?"

Again he looks at his friends. "Regis," he says.

"Say it loud now, son. I doubt they heard you in the back."

Regis blushes, but he shouts his name. I glance at Cole and Ryan. They both have huge grins. They're probably thrilled to see big man Regis quake a little. I admit it's pretty awesome.

"Regis, my boy," Gedney says, "you get to be the guinea pig. Suit up. Quickly now."

One of the plebes helps Regis into his backpack, carefully adjusting the shoulder and chest straps.

What is this? A fashion show? Did Gedney call us down here to watch Regis try on a backpack? For someone so concerned with getting things done fast, it sure seems like a waste of time.

Regis must have been thinking the same thing. He spreads his arms out to the sides as if to say, *Okay, dude, is this it?* A condescending smile spreads across his face as he glances back at his buddies. I guess Regis is feeling a little more sure of himself, not that I'm surprised. All of this is just further proof I'm stuck in the loser pod with Waters and his sidekick, Gedney.

But Cole's still all lit up like a streetlight. Maybe I'm missing something.

"Good, good," Gedney says. "Now, tell me, Regis, are you afraid of heights?"

"Me?" Regis laughs. "Uh, no."

"That's good." Gedney nods to the plebe. "Walk him to the practice area and hand him the controls."

Controls? The plebe escorts Regis to the other side of the hangar. He unzips small pockets on either side of the back-pack and pulls out two straps, each with a throttlelike grip at the end. He places the grips in Regis's hands.

Regis doesn't look so comfortable anymore.

"Turn around, son. Face me," Gedney says. Regis squares his body toward Gedney. "Good. Now, Regis, do you see the red button on the top of the grip?"

Regis nods.

"Okay, hands together now," Gedney says. "Gently push the buttons with your thumbs."

Regis does as he's told. As soon as he touches those red buttons, the backpack goes rigid, whistles like a fierce gale, and shoots Regis straight into the air.

"Whoa," I say, but I doubt anyone hears me above the other gasps and hollers. Regis is heading for the roof of the hangar. If he doesn't stop soon, he'll crash.

I tear my eyes from Regis and turn to Gedney. He's waving his arms, signaling for us to quiet down. "Hello, Regis? Can you hear me?" he yells up to the rafters.

"Yes." Regis's voice shakes as he answers. I bet he wishes he said he was afraid of heights.

"Good. Keep your thumbs on the red buttons, and push the second buttons with your pointers."

Regis stops rising. He hovers in the air. The backpack puffs out behind him like an inflated balloon. His legs dangle and sway. One of his shoes falls to the floor and bounces.

"Good, good. That's it, my boy. Now carefully press down with your third fingers."

Regis jerks around in the air. It looks like the backpack has a mind of its own.

Gedney tries to coach him. "Gently. Yes. No. The third fingers, boy!"

The backpack pulls Regis right, then left. He drops several meters until he hangs in the air about three meters from the ground. "What do I do?" yells Regis. He sounds

MONICA TESLER

so panicked, he makes my blood pressure rise a few notches.

"Your first three fingers, son!" Gedney shouts. "Only make sure you don't—"

Regis plummets to the ground, backpack first.

"Take your thumbs off the red buttons," Gedney continues, too late.

Regis strikes the ground and then bounces back up. I didn't notice it before, but the entire far side of the hanger has a swath of black netting stretched a few inches above the ground.

"A trampoline," Cole whispers next to me. Ahhh, so that's why his shoe bounced. It doesn't look like any trampoline I've ever seen, but Regis's body rebounding back up in the air confirms it.

Gedney hobbles over to the practice zone and pulls Regis off the net with the help of one of the plebes. He hurries Regis back to the center of the hangar. "Fine. Very good. Nice first flight. Thank you for volunteering." Gedney might not remember he picked Regis out of the crowd, but I'm sure Regis knows he didn't volunteer.

"These packs are very important," Gedney continues. "You must master them. Most places you'll travel as Bounders have gravity pulls very different from what you're used to. You'll need your packs to get around."

Despite Regis's precarious flight, all of us inch closer to

the two backpack bins. Sure, I'm nervous, but I can't wait to buckle into my backpack and press those red buttons.

"Okay, then," Gedney says. "Regis, you stand up here with me for a demonstration. Hold up those controls so everyone can get a look. Top buttons—the red ones—those are for your thumbs. They control upward propulsion. First finger button is hover. First and second together is forward. First three fingers depressed takes you in reverse. Grab all buttons at once to go down. Gradually, that is. As Regis so aptly demonstrated, if you simply let go of the controls your descent will be greatly aided by gravity."

That last comment draws a few chuckles, and Regis's face turns red.

"Come on, now," Gedney says. "No time to waste. Come grab your blast pack."

I elbow my way to the middle of the blast pack line. After each group suits up, one of the plebes takes the cadets to the practice zone for a tutorial. Most cadets get the hang of it after a few tries.

Cole's group heads over to the practice zone before I do. Cole is small. The plebe has to pull the straps super tight to secure him in the pack. Cole keeps bobbing his head and hopping on his toes as he stares at the controls, listening to the last words of advice from the plebe.

When the plebe steps back from the net, he gives the go

MONICA TESLER

signal. Four of the kids shoot straight into the air. Cole doesn't move. He keeps his eyes glued to the controls. He's frozen. I cringe. How embarrassing.

Then Cole raises his head, nods, and lifts off. He comes to a perfect stop midway to the rafters and then banks left. He travels halfway across the tarp, stops, ascends fifteen meters, then banks right. He zooms to the exact same spot on the other side, lowers, then flies left again. I'm stunned. Cole executed a near perfect square in the air. Compared to the other kids soaring haphazardly across the hangar, nearly colliding with one another midair, Cole achieved some bizarre mastery on his first flight.

I'm not the only one who notices. When Cole lands on the tarp, whispers run through the line.

"Wow."

"Did you see that?"

"Was that really his first flight?"

Lucy punches me on the shoulder. The line kept moving, and I let a huge gap open in front of me. I glare at her but quickly catch up. My group suits up next. Lucy and I will be flying together.

As the plebe fastens me into my pack, my blood pulses with excitement. I can't wait to push those red buttons. I mean, how hard can it be? Cole made it look like a piece of cake. And if he can do it, I'm sure I won't have any trouble.

I step onto the tarp while the plebe reviews the instructions. I mostly tune him out. I listened to Gedney the first time.

Lucy pokes me in the ribs. "Pay attention, Jasper."

"And most important," the plebe says, "don't release the red buttons. Go!"

I jam my thumbs down on the red buttons and shoot into the air. I sail toward the rafters, leaving Lucy and the other cadets meters below. That's right. Eat my airstream.

The blast pack pulls me up while my body weighs me down. It's the strangest mix of odd and awesome. No cadet has anywhere close to my altitude. Jasper Adams, Blast Pack Master. So what about Cole and his fancy moves? I'll fly higher than anyone.

"Slow down, Jasper!" Lucy calls. Seriously? Like I'd let you catch me?

"Jasper! Loosen up!" the plebe shouts from the hangar floor.

Sure. In a sec. I'll need to change course soon. The rafters are a few meters ahead.

That's it, just a litter farther. Wait. Now what? First and second together. Good. I bank right. Too far right. First three fingers. Left. Too far left. Oh no. I majorly overcorrected. Right again. What's hover?

Shouts rise up from below, but they reach me in a jumbled

mess. And, okay, I panic. I squeeze and release the controls in a random pattern that sends me zigzagging across the hangar. The pack jerks my body like a rag doll.

All I remember are the red buttons. I grind my thumbs against them and release my other fingers. My pack accelerates straight for the roof.

I hear the screams and Lucy's high-pitched squeal. "Jasper, stop!"

When my head hits the roof, I must release the red buttons, because gravity steps in and pulls me straight to the ground.

"HE'S WAKING UP!" LUCY'S HIGH VOICE
jabs at my brain like a dull cafeteria knife. Please, not now.
It hurts.

I flutter my eyelids, but I can't keep them open for more
than a second. Moving them at all exhausts every muscle
in my face. Someone squeezes my hand. Lucy. No one else
would do that.

"Jasper? It's Lucy." *Yep.* "You've been in an accident."

No joke. Plunging four stories to the hangar floor definitely qualifies as an accident, trampoline or not.

"Can you hear me, Jasper?"

My eyes flutter again. Opening them is getting a little easier, but everything is out of focus. Lucy is here. Her wide eyes gaze down at me, and her eyebrows are pinched. There's someone else. Cole. It must be Cole.

"Cole?"

The fuzzy figure approaches. "I'm here."

"How on earth did you do that?"

"What?"

"The box. In the air." I lift my head, and the room whirls.

"Quiet, Jasper," Lucy says. "You need to rest."

Shoes tap across the floor. "He's awake?" Waters. Great. I'm sure my fall will do wonders for my placement in the pod.

"Jasper, are you awake?" Waters asks.

I focus hard and manage to nod.

"Good. You'll be fine. You're mighty bruised, but no significant injuries. I had them sedate you so you could rest—that's your biggest issue right now—but you'll come out of it in the next few hours."

I force my chin into a nod again. I'm not thrilled about being sedated, but all I want is to slip back into oblivion.

"We have work to do, Jasper," Waters says. "I expect you there with the pod tomorrow morning. And no more stunts. The whole operation's a bust if you're not in one piece."

Stunts? I wish. That would mean I had control over what

happened in the hangar. Yeah, right. I guess I didn't leave my klutzy ways back on Earth like I planned.

Lucy squeezes my hand, then a chorus of footsteps moves toward the door. I assume they all left, but I don't have the energy to check. Maybe I'm wrong. I could swear someone is watching me.

· *Ƒ* ·

The next time I open my eyes, something dark and hairy hovers in the air above my face. I squeeze my eyes shut. Geez. Whatever meds the docs pumped into me have me seeing things.

Arrr. Kit. Kit. Rarrrgh. Kleek. Guttural grunts and clicks rumble through the room.

What on earth? My eyes fly back open. I'm not seeing things. A Tunneler dressed in a white medical coat stands next to my bed.

"How are you feeling?" the translator box says.

It takes a second for me to catch my breath. "Ummm . . . I guess okay."

The Tunneler's hairy hand clutches a thermometer. He zaps it in my ear. *Kleek. Arrr. Arghhh. Kit. Kleek.* "Normal. That's a good sign. Open your eyes wide."

He shines a light in my face and taps a note into a tablet that rests beside my bed. This is so surreal. I haven't been this close to a Tunneler since that day on the air rail, the day

MONICA TESLER

before I left for the Academy. My mind spins. There are so many things I should ask him.

"Are you from the Paleo Planet?" I ask.

He grunts and clicks in a fast frenzy. The translation box says: "Ha! Ha! Ha!"

When he settles down from his fit of laughter he says, "You Earthlings. All you ever ask about is the Paleo Planet. No. I'm not from there. None of us are from there, although a lot of my people work there now. I've never been to the Paleo Planet. I don't even live in the same galaxy."

Whoa. Okay. Sorry I asked. He's just as touchy as the Tunneler on the air rail. Is it him? Nah, I don't think so.

The Tunneler crosses to a medical cart on the other side of the room. He walks all hunched, like Gedney.

"I've heard it's nice, the Paleo Planet," the Tunneler says as he walks back with pills in his hand. "That's where you cadets are headed for your end-of-tour field trip, right?" He hands me the pills and a glass of water.

"Yep," I say. "So where *do* you live?"

He grabs my wrist and takes my pulse. "Gulaga."

What? "Where?"

"P37, to you," he says, "Gulaga to us. It's not like you call Earth P1."

Earth. P1. As in Planet 1. I laugh, which makes my chest hurt.

"Get some rest, Jasper. You'll be feeling much better soon. Close your eyes and think about your field trip in a few weeks."

"Thanks," I say as my eyelids sag. "See ya."

I don't hear his good-bye. I'm already dreaming of the saber cats and the wildeboars and all the amazing things I'll see on the Paleo Planet.

· E_F ·

"Red Baron, you awake?"

I wasn't, Marco. But I am now.

"Hey, can you hear me? Did you check this place out?"

Is he blind? I'm lying, sedated, on a medical bed. I'm certainly not checking much of anything out. Still, I feel better. I open my eyes without much effort. Marco is in front of me, pulling open the drawers of a medical cart.

"What are you doing?" I ask.

"What does it look like? I'm snooping around. Seeing what I can find out about this place."

I press down with my hands and manage to push myself up on the pillow. My head throbs as I take in my surroundings. A medical room. Oh, I get it. *The* medical room. As in the medical room with the green alien on the bed. As in the bed I'm currently lying on. A wave of nausea hits me in the gut.

"This is where they had the alien?" I ask.

"Bingo," Marco says as he moves on to the next medical cart.

I sit up and look around. Sure enough, it's the same room.

I glance behind me at the windows. "You were right. I can't see anything through that glass."

"Ahhh, but she can see you," Marco says. He faces the windows and blows a gigantic kiss at the blacked-out glass.

"Why'd you do that?" I ask.

Marco turns back to the medical cart, pulling out vials and reading their labels. "Jealous? I was blowing a kiss to your girlfriend."

"What on earth are you talking about?"

"Oh, come on. You know, the woman of few words. Dancing Queen."

"Mira?" I can't make anything out through the windows. "She's up there?"

"Well, she was," Marco says. "Who knows if she stuck around after I popped in and interrupted her silent vigil?"

"She was watching me?"

"Like I told you, Romeo, she's into you. I saw the way she looked at you when you mentioned your clarinet."

Ugh. I knew that would come back to bite me.

Marco keeps talking. "What's with that, anyway? Who plays the clarinet? You're the kind of kid who puts the *B* in B-wad."

"What's that supposed to mean? For someone who doesn't approve of the word, you sure use it a lot."

"Yeah, yeah, yeah," Marco says. "What gives? Are you going to help me here or what?"

"Haven't you noticed I'm injured?"

"What do you take me for? The pity police? Get your butt off that bed. You'll have to be up for Waters in the morning anyhow."

He's right. I might as well get up. After all, Waters said none of my injuries were serious. I have to face the hangar humiliation head on. I might as well make myself feel better by helping Marco find some dirt.

I flip the blanket off and slide from the bed. When I transfer my weight to my feet, a tingling pain shoots from my hip up my back and down my leg on my left side.

"Ouch. Geez, that hurts." I fall back onto the mattress.

From the other side of the room, Marco lets out a long laugh. Nice. Real nice.

"The least you could do is have a little sympathy, B-wad."

"I'll try," Marco spits out between giggles, "but it will be hard after that stellar snapshot of your bruised butt."

Great. All I'm wearing is a hospital gown. Marco got a full whopping view of my rear side.

"Shut up and help me find my clothes," I say, and toss one of my pillows at Marco.

I ease off the bed again and hobble over to the mirror on the opposite wall. I turn my back to the reflection and peer over my shoulder.

"Keep snooping around," I shout at Marco, "and keep your

eyes off my butt!" I let my gown fall open in back. A huge bruise the size of a grapefruit blossoms across my left hip. The center is a deep purple; the edges are pink. That must be where I hit the ground. I jab a finger into the bull's-eye of the bruise. Yep. That hurts.

"Catch," Marco hollers. My balled-up clothes slam into my head.

"Gee, thanks." I bend to pick up my uniform, and a whole new wave of pain ripples through me. "And I appreciate your not looking, like I asked."

"Shut up and get dressed," Marco says. "I could use another pair of eyes."

I pull my uniform on and walk over to Marco. He's rummaging through a glass cabinet against one of the walls.

"Find anything?" I ask.

"Nothing out of the ordinary. Unless you consider these out of the ordinary." He pulls open one of the drawers. It's filled with leather straps, metal cuffs, and chains.

"Are those the restraints they used on the alien?" I ask.

"Sure looks like it."

"Do they need those for their other patients?"

"I doubt it. I mean, metal cuffs and chains? Seems a little extreme."

"Maybe if someone is in pain . . . ?" I ask.

"Or maybe if someone is trying to escape," Marco says.

He raises his eyebrows. I'm sure he's thinking the same thing I'm thinking, because at that moment my mind is filled with the image of the alien on the table. And the armed guards at the door.

Marco and I bolt for the door. He beats me there. Bolt is probably a stretch when it comes to my ability to move right about now.

The door is open—Marco, Waters, and the other kids were able to come and go without a problem—but it's clear the door is equipped with sophisticated security.

"Look," I say, "this is one of those bioscanners like they have in the pod hall." I tip my eyes toward the device.

"That's weird." Marco stands next to me and examines the scanner. "Why would they have a scanner on the inside of the room?"

I shrug. I have no idea. "Don't eye scanners make sure only certain people can get in?"

"Or make sure only certain people can get out," Cole says from behind.

Marco and I both jump. How long has Cole been standing there? And more important, how are we getting out of this one?

"Geez, Mr. Fun Facts," Marco says, "didn't your mother ever teach you not to sneak up on people?"

Cole ignores Marco. "I guess you're feeling better, Jasper."

His eyes dart up at me. It's only for a second, but I think it's the first time he's looked me square in the eyes. Everything about him—his eyes, his voice, even the way he stands—is an accusation.

I'm annoyed. I mean, come on. Aren't I allowed to have more than one friend? Every muscle in my body aches. I'm still woozy from the drugs. I'm the laughing stock of the Academy. And I have to add angry Cole to my list of problems. Then, of course, there's the issue of the secret alien.

Marco places a hand on each of our backs and presses us toward the bed. "Sit, Wiki. You, too, Ace." Cole and I both sink down onto the mattress. "Here's the skinny." Marco looks at Cole as he speaks. "Fly Guy and I snooped around the first night and discovered a captured alien holed up in this very med room."

"A captured alien?" Cole says. "You mean a Tunneler?"

"No, no, no," Marco says, "a new kind of alien. He was this nasty green color and had a huge pulsing head."

Cole looks at me again. "Is he serious?"

I nod. "I know it sounds unbelievable, but it's true. They were working on him. He was injured or something. There was tons of security—at least five armed guards. Even so, the alien threw one of the doctors across the room."

"How come you're just telling me about this now, Jasper?"

There's really no way out. Cole is mad. I don't have an

excuse, and I'm too battered down to make one up. I shrug. "Sorry."

Cole looks away. "Whatever."

"Listen, Fact Man," Marco says, "you can be mad all you want later. Who knows how much longer we have in here before Waters or someone on the medical staff comes back? Do you want to help us snoop around or not?"

Cole balls his hands into fists. What? Is he going to hit me? I'm in bad shape, but I could still take Cole in a fight. I shake off the thought. Geez, Jasper, don't be ridiculous. Tense seconds pass before Cole bounces back onto his feet and briskly strides to the door.

"This looks like a standard bioscanner," Cole says. He punches a series of buttons on the keypad beneath the scanner, and a menu pops up.

"What are you doing?" I ask.

"I'm helping you," Cole says. "Isn't that what you want?"

"Yeah," I say. "Thanks."

Marco and I lean over Cole's shoulders as he pages through the menu. "Whoa," he says.

"What?" Marco and I ask together.

"That's weird," Cole says. "This door is equipped with an occludium shield."

"Occludium shield?" I say. "Doesn't that seem a little extreme? I mean, if they've got the guy all strapped down with those cuffs and chains, where can he really go? Plus, I thought occludium was only used for quantum movement."

Cole enters numbers on the keyboard. As each page loads, he enters more numbers.

"Dude, what are you doing?" Marco asks.

Cole keeps on pressing keys. "I'm accessing the security system."

"You mean hacking in?" Marco says.

Cole doesn't respond. He just keeps punching numbers on the keyboard.

"Are you sure that's such a great idea?" I ask. I stick my head out the door to make sure no one's in the hall.

"As long as we don't get caught, I'd say it's a great idea," Marco says.

"Yeah, but what are you looking for?" I ask.

A map appears on the security screen. Cole zooms in. "While you B-wads snoop around in here," he says, "I'm snooping around where it actually matters."

"What do you mean?" I ask.

"You said there was an unknown alien on board, right?" Marco and I both nod. "Well, then, what I want to know is, where is that alien now?"

He can figure that out? I lean over Cole's shoulder and stare at the map of the space station.

Cole raises his finger to the map. "There." He points to a

wing branching off from one of the space station structures. It's surrounded on three sides by open space.

"What?" Marco asks.

"That's a cellblock," Cole says. "And that cell right there is secured by an occludium shield."

YOU'D THINK GETTING DISCHARGED FROM the med room would be a good thing. Nope. Cole basically hates me. He hasn't spoken to me since he hacked the computer. Everyone else won't shut up. From the second I step into the dorm, I get ripped for my fall in the hangar. Regis is the worst. I can't get that kid off my back. As I remember it, Regis wasn't exactly a superstar with the blast pack.

Morning lecture is mind-numbingly boring. Edgar Han talks to us about the science behind quantum entanglement, the building blocks of bounding. I should listen. I know the basics of QE, but Han is going way beyond the basics.

"So, in other words," Han says, "the two particles are related, intertwined, if you will, no matter how far apart in space they are. Thus, when one particle departs point A, it simultaneously arrives at point B. It bounds. This is what makes intergalactic travel not just possible, but practical."

At the end of class we're quizzed. I probably do okay. I mean, I already knew most of what Han talked about, but there's no way I got everything right. The quiz counts toward our pod rankings. I really need to start paying attention.

We have lunch right after lecture. I find Lucy and drag her to a table in the back of the mess hall. I'm sure the guys will tease me about it, but I just can't take any more. As soon as we set our trays down, Meggi and Annette come through the line and join us.

"How are you feeling?" Lucy asks when we sit down. Tofu dogs are the lunch entrée. And yes, they're definitely the source of the stale hot dog smell that never leaves the space station. My appetite evaporates.

I shrug. "Okay, considering I'm pretty banged up from the fall. No one will shut up about it. The whole thing stinks, you know?"

Lucy smiles and pats my hand. "Listen, Jasper. They'll get over it. As soon as they have something—or someone—else to latch on to, you'll be old news. Trust me."

"Maybe you're right," I say, "but it's not doing me much good today."

"Have you noticed none of the girls are teasing you?" Annette asks.

I laugh. "I thought that was because you're just nicer."

"Please," Lucy says. "Girls are meaner than boys times ten. No, the reason they're leaving you alone is because they have someone else to target."

"Who?"

"Who do you think?" Annette asks.

"Mira?"

The girls nod. "She snuck out again last night," Lucy says. "Sent the whole dorm ringing with sirens and whistles and flashing lights."

"No one got any sleep," Meggi says.

"Where was she going?" Was she watching me again?

"Beats me," Lucy says. "But I'm glad you dragged me over here this morning. All the girls keep bombarding me with questions. They think since I'm in the same pod as her, I have some grand insight into her psyche."

"You mean, you don't?" Annette says in a flat tone.

Lucy rolls her eyes. "Shut up. You, too, Meggi. Don't even start."

I scan the mess hall. Mira sits in the back near the porthole again. She presses her hand against the glass, her fingers splayed like a fan. Part of me wants to go over and sit with her, try to connect, but there's no way I'm going to set myself up for more ribbing.

The girls jabber away about Mira and her midnight escapades. Somehow that leads to nail polish and Maximilian Sheek's line of hair styling products. I stare at Mira's long braid and her thin arms. What's going on inside your mind, Mira? How do I reach you?

"So I'll show you around. We're scheduled to go back this afternoon. It's like our post-class leisure time."

"Go where?" I ask.

"The sensory gym," Lucy says.

"The what? Wait. Where are Meggi and Annette?"

"You zoned out, didn't you?" Lucy asks. "You're worse than Meggi, and she can't pay attention for more than two minutes at a time. How did you two make the cut? Never mind. I'll tell you again. The sensory gym's in the same structure as the pods, the next hall down. And Meggi and Annette left to sit with their pod more than a minute ago."

Lucy describes the sensory gym, with its trampolines and tents and climbing ladders and rope swings and ball pits. It sounds like Waters's tricked out pod room. Next, Lucy fills me in on all the gossip from the girls' dorm. Then she tells me every detail about her morning conversation with Florine. By the time she takes a break from talking, lunch is almost over.

I love that about Lucy; she can easily fill your time. And when I tune in, she usually has something mildly interesting to say.

My gaze wanders back to Mira. She rises from the table and floats from the mess hall. I want to follow her, but I don't.

"And here she is," Lucy says. She looks at me, probably waiting for some sort of reaction.

"Who?" I ask.

"Oh, Jasper." Lucy shakes her head. "Florine, of course." She nods to the front of the mess hall, where Florine stands with a handful of officers.

"May I have your attention, puh-*leeeze*," Florine says from behind her sunglasses. "Today we start the pod competition. This week's rankings will be based on quiz scores and Mobility relay race placements. Next week's scores will include the bounding assessments, which will be double weighted. We'll post the rankings here in the mess hall after dinner. Best wishes to all the pods."

A relay race with our blast packs? My stomach flips, and I haven't touched my tofu dog. I'm not looking forward to strapping back into my blast pack after my fall. Knowing I'll have to race makes me cringe.

Lucy slams her hand on the table. "Jasper! I'm talking to you! You better stop acting like such a space cadet and focus, if we're going to have any chance of winning."

I grin. "But I am a space cadet. . . ."

She slaps my arm. "You know what I mean. We all need to pitch in if we want a shot at top pod, especially since we'll have to carry her weight." Lucy turns toward the porthole, obviously expecting to spot Mira. "Where'd she run off to now? She better show up at pod session. Or better yet, maybe she won't, and we can convince Waters to ax her from our pod."

There's no way Waters will do that, so I don't bother responding. Lucy doesn't notice. She's already talking about a drama club show she starred in last year.

We leave the mess hall and meet up with Cole and Marco at the suction chute. When Cole sees us coming, he stuffs his hands into his pockets and starts to stomp away from the chute cube. He's ignoring me? What is this? Third grade?

Marco grabs Cole by the shoulder. "Where do you think you're going, Wiki? I missed out on the fun and games with the chute the other day. Show me how you made that human chain."

"No, thanks," Cole says. "I'm riding solo."

"Oh, come on," Marco says, "leave your beef with Jasper out of this."

Cole doesn't respond, but blood rushes to his face and colors his cheeks.

Lucy marches up to the door and pushes it open. "Come on, boys. There's no room for these little spats. You heard Florine. It's all about the pod now."

"That's all good, Sunshine," Marco says, "but we're down one, if you haven't noticed."

Lucy's face darkens. "Good. As far as I'm concerned, Mira's a liability, something we'll have to work around if we want to win this thing."

As quickly as the shadow on Lucy's face arrived, it fades. She steps onto the chute platform and flashes us a smile. "So, who's with me?"

I follow Cole and Marco into the chute cube. Cole's still mad, but I'm optimistic. After all, Lucy's right: we'll have to work as a pod. And that means we all have to get along.

"Well?" Marco says. He's staring at me. In fact, all of them are staring at me. Even Cole.

"What?" I ask.

"How do we do this? You know, the mega fast human chain."

Why are they asking me? Any of them could figure it out. Lucy and Cole did it with me the first time. They stand there, waiting for my answer, like I'm the missing glue that can make it all stick.

"Okay, well, ummm . . ." I stink at breaking things down into steps. I just know how to do something or I don't. Like, for example, I clearly don't know how to fly the blast pack.

They still stare. I have to come up with something. I close my eyes and picture us in the chute. First I hit Lucy's shoes with my head. Then I reached up and grabbed her ankles and yelled at Cole to do the same. When we connected, I urged them to stretch out as far as they could.

"So, how 'bout this," I say. "Lucy, you go first. Marco, you stand ready. As soon as Lucy lifts off, you step onto the platform and try to grab her ankles before she's completely sucked in. Cole, you go next. I'll take the rear."

"You're grabbing my ankles?" Cole asks me.

"Do you have a problem with that?"

Cole pauses. Lucy and Marco bounce on their toes, antsy to get going. Cole tips his eyes to mine for a second and then turns his body toward the chute. "No problem."

"Good," I say. "If for any reason you miss, just get into the chute as fast as you can and make the grab inside. And remember to stretch out. It gives you speed."

Lucy rubs her hands on her pants and steps up to the chute. "Here goes," she says, and presses the button.

A loud whooshing fills the chute cube, and Lucy is sucked up. Marco is quick. He's on the platform and sailing up after Lucy in a flash, his hands locked on to her ankles.

Cole hesitates and misses the grab by a solid second. He looks back at me, a question on his face.

"Just go!" I yell. "Make the grab in the chute." I push Cole, and he stumbles onto the platform. As soon as he's sucked up, I take his place. There's no way I'm going to screw this up. Not when I'm the one who gave the directions. Not when Cole is the kid in front of me.

My hands clamp onto Cole's ankles, and my body is yanked into the chute.

"Where are you guys?" Marco shouts.

"We're coming!" I yell. The wind plasters my hair against my face, covering my eyes. I stretch my arms and legs out as far as I can. We accelerate, closing in on Marco and Lucy.

"I think I'm close!" Cole shouts.

"Make the grab!"

Bump. We caught up. Cole and Marco connect, and we zip forward: a four-person chain barreling through the suction chute.

"Woo-hoo!" Marco yells.

We rush through a straightaway, accelerating every second. Tears stream from my eyes, and my stomach drops as we fly through the dark tunnel.

Without warning, we bank right. As the last in the chain, I whip around the corner. My left leg bangs against the side of the chute, sending currents of pain up my bruised hip. Still. It's awesome.

The chute echoes with our screams. I hope no one's behind us. They'll think we're badly hurt (which isn't too far from the truth, in my case).

I slam into the arrival trough on top of Cole, who's on top

of Marco. Somehow Lucy managed to jump out of the way. I guess she learned her lesson the last ride.

Cole pushes me. "Get off."

Geez. Settle down. I climb out of the trough and extend a hand to Cole. He ignores me and climbs out the other side.

Marco takes my hand and hops off. He pats me on the shoulder. "Nice work, Captain," he says. "That was incredible."

"Yeah, Jasper," Lucy says. "Thanks."

You're welcome? What did I do?

Cole's already headed for the pod room. We race to catch up.

"Okay, crew, let's get settled," Waters says when we arrive. He grips my shoulder and squeezes. "Welcome back, Jasper. I'm glad you're on your feet."

We sink into the beanbags and stare at Waters.

"So you gonna explain how to bound today, Teach?" Marco asks. "Give us the goods we need to ace this competition?"

Waters studies us with a grim face. "No. I'm not."

We look around at one another. Why not?

"I'm not," Waters continues, "because the whole pod's not assembled."

The other cadets look at me. I shrug. No, I have no idea where Mira is. Come on, people. Didn't we just ride here together in the chute? Why would I know any better than you where Mira is?

"I don't get it," Lucy says. "Why do we have to wait for her? It's not like she's going to help us. She's the reason we're going to lose. Seriously, Mr. Waters, why is she even here? How did she make the cut?"

Waters's face grows rigid, and his eyes drill into Lucy. She shifts in her seat and glances at me. I'm sure she's looking for my support, but I turn away.

"Mira is a member of this pod," Waters says, "just like you. She's critical to the success of this pod. In fact, I may go so far as to say Mira is the most critical factor to the success of this pod. You'll do well to remember that, Miss Dugan."

"Yes, Mr. Waters." Lucy dips her chin and stares at the green carpet.

"Jasper," Waters says, "please bring Mira to the pod room. I expect you'll find her in the sensory gym."

It takes a second for his words to register. Does he really want me to search for Mira? Why me? Why is it always me? I guess I don't have much choice. I haul myself out of the beanbag, leave the room, and wander out of the pod hall.

Lucy said the sensory gym is in this structure. I head away from the chutes toward the part of the building I haven't explored yet. An obnoxious horn blows as a mini Spider Crawler zips around a corner, heading straight for me. I jump out of the way just in time to avoid being run over. The robot abruptly stops in front of the chute cube, stretches up on its spindly legs to unlock the door and activate the chute, then crawls onto the platform. *Whoosh!* It's sucked into the tube.

Those things are creepy.

I turn down the hallway where the robot came from. It looks the same as every other hallway—bright lights, green-gray walls, lots of chrome metal. Most of the doors are secured with a bioscanner. If Mira is in one of those rooms, I'm locked out.

The door at the end of the hall is open, so I head that way. As I enter the room, I'm enveloped in soft warm light. All the harsh florescent bulbs have been replaced with natural glow orbs. I almost feel like I'm outside. Back on Earth.

Rings and rope swings hang from the ceiling. Ladders and climbing walls rise to elevated platforms. Slides and fireman poles lead back to the ground. My shoes sink with each step. I bend down and press my fingers into the floor. A deep mat cradles my feet.

I don't get this place. It's completely anti–Earth Force, like Waters's love den.

A tent is in the corner. I peer inside. Piles of pillows and blankets are stacked against the edge. I could definitely lose some time in there. Unfortunately, I have a job to do. I drop the door flap.

A row of trampolines is against the far wall. They're lined up one after the next all the way to the edge of a large pit. A knotted rope hangs from the ceiling above the pit. What on earth is in there? I cross over and peer in. The pit is filled with tiny silver beads.

Awesome.

Mira will have to wait a minute.

I glance over my shoulder, making sure I'm still alone. Then I walk back to the door and look down the hallway. No one. I skip to the far end of the trampoline wall and slip off my shoes. I hoist myself up and bounce a few times before taking off.

Hop.

Hop.

Hop.

Grab the rope.

Swing and drop.

I sink into the bead pit. The little silver spheres part just enough to let my body through, then rush to mold around me. The metal is cool against my skin. I lay my head back, close my eyes.

For the first time since arriving at the space station, I relax. I forget all about Bad Breath and the blast pack. I don't care about Cole. I slip deeper into the bead pit and let myself drift.

The soft tinkling of piano keys tickles my ears. What is that? The music grows louder, more intense. I've heard the song before, but I can't place the memory. Where's that music coming from?

I drag myself out of the bead pit and follow the sound. A hallway I didn't notice before opens from an inside corner of the sensory gym. At the end of the hall is a small room with a black grand piano.

The door is open. The notes tear out of the room and run down the hall, pulling me toward them. By a magnetic force, I'm drawn to the music, to the piano, to Mira. And there she is. Her long thin arms are spread wide above the keys, jabbing and pounding and commanding the instrument. Her body sways and jerks in time with the beats and measures. I move, too. I can't help it.

Mira's eyes are closed. She tips her head back so her chin lifts from her neck in a straight line. The long braid holds most of her hair, but golden wisps escape and float above her head like a halo. She looks as small and delicate as a bird but as strong and masterful as a thousand kings.

Then the tone changes, and her chin drops. Her head rolls forward to her chest and pivots loosely between her shoulders. Her whole body caves in as a hollow sadness drones from the piano. The room is filled with melancholy.

I am filled with melancholy.

And I'm sitting up in bed, Addy at the foot, playing her violin, my clarinet gripped strong in my hands.

The music fades to a whisper as Mira's slender fingers brush the keys in a final chord. I sigh. I'm as relaxed as I'd been in the bead pit.

She hears me. My sigh. But she doesn't look at first. She opens her eyes and stares at her fingers. Her body shifts then. Slowly. Like she needs a separate second to take control of each muscle. To bring them back.

Then she looks at me with her bottomless eyes.

My heart falls to the ground, and I'm not sure I can speak. Then I shake my head, cough once, and say, "I've come to take you to the pod room."

"MIRA, JASPER, GLAD YOU COULD JOIN
us," Waters says when we enter the pod room. "I was telling
the others something important while you were out, so I'm
going to say it again. There is only one way you'll succeed
here at the EarthBound Academy. And only one way you'll
succeed as Bounders, and that is by working as a team. . . ."

Waters's mouth moves, but I can't hear his words. All I can
hear is the melancholy music streaming from the piano, filling the hall, filling my mind. I can't look at Mira. If I did, I'm
sure I would melt. I'm sure everyone in the room would know
what happened. Not that anything *did* happen. She played

the piano. Okay, she played the piano better than anyone I'd ever heard. And she knows I play the clarinet. So we have a musical connection. Big deal.

"Jasper," Waters says, "this is critical. You need to be engaged. I'll wait until you're ready to join us."

Everyone stares. Cole glares. Great, just great. Another space out. I press my hands into fists to stay focused. "Sorry."

"Let's get started," Waters says. "You'll be taught the basic bounding mechanics for the ships during your classes. In pod sessions, we'll be focusing on new technology." He and Gedney exchange a suspicious glance.

Cole perks up. "New technology?"

Waters nods. "That's right. Okay, here goes—" Waters opens his mouth, but no words come out. He rises from his beanbag and drags his fingers through his hair. "I feel like there should be a musical accompaniment to this announcement." He looks at Mira, but she doesn't react.

Why is he acting so weird? I turn to Cole, who turns to Lucy, who shrugs. There is definitely something going on.

"Boss, come on, don't leave us hanging here," Marco says. He hops up and crosses to the bin of spiky balls in the corner. Marco never sits still for long.

Waters's slow gaze circles the room. "Gedney, the gloves."

Gedney hobbles over to Waters with a pair of shiny gloves in hand.

I look at Cole again. His eyes blaze with excitement, but I can tell he doesn't know what to expect.

"Gloves?" Marco asks. He plops down on his beanbag and tosses a bumpy purple ball from hand to hand.

"I'll let Gedney do the honors," Waters says. "How 'bout a demo, old man?"

"Well, yes, no time to waste." Gedney steps to the center of our circle, and Waters dims the lights. Gedney shakes out the gloves and slides them onto his hands. He's careful, meticulous, making sure each finger is perfectly in place—a slow process for someone always urging us to hurry. He smooths the end seams of the gloves midway up his forearms.

Gedney's hunched body straightens as he raises his arms out and up. Moments before, he seemed small, forgettable, but as he lifts his arms, he morphs into something commanding.

Then he jerks his hands in the air.

Currents of light race through the gloves to the tips of his fingers and then out into the pod room. First ten then twenty then a thousand rays of light shoot out of the gloves, dancing and darting and weaving together like an army of spiders spinning their webs into the greatest net ever known. And then he's pulling and gathering the lines of light into a great ball. A great ball of yarn made of strings of light, knotted together in a perfect orb. Gedney has it there between his fingers, molding it, massaging it, gathering it together until it acquires a certain quality or symmetry that seems right, certain. Like it's the only design it can possibly be.

And then Gedney disappears. Or maybe he doesn't. Maybe I just blinked. Because he's there, and the ball of light is gone. The air behind him shimmers for a second and then is still.

"Ummm, what just happened?" Lucy asks.

Gedney's shoulders roll forward, and his knees shake. When I'm sure he's about to collapse, Waters eases him onto a beanbag. Gedney pulls the gloves off finger by finger and lays them lengthwise across his lap.

"Seriously," Marco says, "what on earth was that?"

I don't have the faintest clue. It was the coolest thing I've ever seen, but I have no idea what it was.

Cole jerks up in his seat. He taps his fingers. He mumbles to himself. Then his face lights up like a lantern. "You bounded," he says.

What?

Gedney nods. "Indeed, I did."

"But how?" Cole says.

"Wait a minute, Geds," Marco says. "Just slow down. What does he mean, you bounded?"

Waters places a hand on Gedney's shoulder. "Just that, Marco. You all just witnessed Gedney bounding through space. A very small space, yes, but he bounded."

"How is that possible?" I ask. Bounding requires all kinds of sophisticated computers and calculations and precautions. You can't just free-bound. That's the stuff of sci-fi stories.

"Gedney's gloves make it possible," Waters says. "Gedney is the mastermind behind this incredible new biotechnology. A biotechnology you were born to master."

· *EF* ·

"But free-bounding?" I ask. "Bounding through space without a ship? How could that not have been leaked to the media?"

Lucy, Cole, Marco, and I huddle around a rear table in the mess hall. I thought we should debrief from the pod session, and I want to keep my mind off the afternoon's Mobility class.

"You heard him," Marco says. "It's top secret. Highest-level clearance."

"Yeah, I heard him about the clearance," I say, "but that doesn't make it clear. Why would we need to keep it secret? What's compromised if it's disclosed? You'd think they'd want people to know about the greatest scientific advancement in modern time."

"Unless," Marco says, "there's a threat no one knows about."

Marco's eyes drill into me. If this were a mystery movie, the camera would be zooming in for a close-up, and suspenseful music would be playing.

"You mean . . . ? You couldn't possibly . . . ?" I say.

Marco nods. I cover my face with my hands. I don't want to believe the gloves have anything to do with the alien prisoner, but I can't ignore the uncomfortable feeling in my gut.

"What are you talking about?" Cole asks.

Marco gives Cole a crooked stare. Even I know it means *shut up.*

It flies right over Cole's head. "What?" he says, indignant.

"The med room," I whisper.

Cole's eyes widen. "Whoa . . . I guess it's possible."

"Oh, come on," Lucy says. "You boys stink at secrets. Just clue me in, will you? It'll be easier on all of us."

Cole shrugs, and Marco gestures to me, giving me the honors. Well, I guess there isn't a lot of downside in telling Lucy.

"There's an alien being held captive on the ship," I say.

We lean forward, awaiting Lucy's reaction.

"So?" Lucy asks.

"So, it's not a normal alien—not that there's anything too normal about an alien—but this one's not a Tunneler. Marco and I saw him on the first night. They had him in the med room. The same one I was treated in. And let's just say he wasn't friendly."

Lucy rolls her eyes. Her hair is tied in ribbons again, even though Bad Breath made her take them all out in our last Mobility class. "So they've made contact with a new alien species. So what? I'm sure the public's not always the first to know. They're a lot more careful with disclosure since the Incident at Bounding Base 51. And just because one alien is a bad dude who needs to be locked up, it doesn't mean we have to condemn his entire species."

"Fair point," Cole says, "but this isn't just a normal disclosure delay."

"What do you mean?" Lucy asks.

"Waters said the Bounders were born to master the glove technology," Cole says. "That means Earth Force has had the technology, at least in the infant stages, since before we were born, before they started *breeding* us . . ."

I hadn't thought of that. Earth Force started breeding Bounders almost thirteen years ago. They've known about the glove technology for over a dozen years and never a whisper reached the media. Mom was right. There's a lot Earth Force isn't telling us.

"And if the alien has something to do with the gloves," Cole continues, "then maybe they've known about him for that long, too."

"Oh, please," Lucy says. "What would an alien today have anything to do with a technology developed before we were born?"

"I'm not sure," I say, "but I have a gut feeling it's all connected."

"And don't forget," Marco says, "Techie here discovered

the alien prisoner is secured by an occludium shield." Marco swings his arm around Cole, who flinches and scoots his chair over. When he realizes he's now closer to me, he flinches and shoves back.

"Occludium?" Lucy says. "I thought occludium was only used to stabilize atoms involved in quantum space travel."

"Yeah, well, it must be used for security, too," Marco says, "because they sure called in the heavy guard for the alien."

"So let me get this straight," Lucy says. "They're holding an unfriendly alien prisoner at the space station, and it's all hush-hush, right?"

Marco shoots me a glance. "*Unfriendly* is not quite a strong enough word, but yeah."

"And they've been waiting for more than a decade for us Bounders to wave our hands around in their fancy gloves, right?" Lucy flips her wrists in a dramatic flourish.

"Is that really a question?" Cole asks. "We've been through this."

"So, why all the secrets?" she says.

Marco laughs. "Well, that's the million-dollar question, sweetheart, now, isn't it?"

"Don't call me sweetheart."

Marco and Lucy argue, but I tune them out. Images swirl in my head—the heavily secured hangar, the armed guards in the med room, the alien on the table, the occludium shield.

"That's it!" I say. "The occludium shield!"

"What about it?" Cole asks.

"The occludium shield doesn't just stabilize atoms for quantum travel; it can prevent quantum travel. As in it can block bounding!"

"And?" Lucy says.

"And so the only reason we need that kind of shield is if bounding is used offensively—you know, to attack."

"I'm not following you, Ace," Marco says.

"What if the gloves aren't just a new technology?" I say. "What if they're a weapon? And what if the aliens have the technology, too?"

"A weapon?" Lucy says. "Come on."

"No, really, think about it," I say. "Wouldn't it be awfully convenient to pop up on your enemy unannounced?"

"Use the gloves to bound to your enemy's exact location?" Cole asks.

"Exactly," I say.

"Genius," Marco says.

"And that's why they need the occludium shield," Cole says, "to block the alien from bounding."

"Ex-*cuuuse* me."

I jump at the sound of the voice. Florine Statton is the last person I want eavesdropping as we talk about the alien. She strolls around our table until she stands behind Lucy.

"Someone hasn't been following directions." She pulls one of the ribbons out of Lucy's hair and curls it around her pink-polished fingernail. "No ribbons, Lucy dear. Now, all of you need to pay attention. There's a schedule to follow. The bell sounded for transition to Mobility more than five minutes ago. Do not forget you serve at the pleasure of the admiral and you've taken an oath to follow orders."

Five minutes ago? I guess we missed it. We were all too focused on the mystery of the gloves and the alien. Florine flushes us up from the table and shoos us out of the mess hall.

When we reach the chute cube, Marco jumps onto the platform. "Ready, Bounders? Same order as last time?"

He doesn't wait for an answer. He pushes the button and shoots into the tube. Lucy grabs his ankles before he disappears.

Cole hesitates. Geez, that kid has horrible timing. As I'm about to shove him onto the platform, he turns around.

"I think you're right," Cole says.

"About what?" I ask.

"The gloves. They're a weapon."

Cole's talking to me again? "What makes you so sure?"

"Before I came to the Academy, I read everything I could find on the Bounder Baby Breeding Program, going back for years. Once I came across a military document. It probably wasn't supposed to be released, but I doubt many people could find it. It was archived and encrypted on a secure site, but the encryption software wasn't current, which is why I was able to decode it. I wouldn't say I'm a hacker, but I have a certain way with computers. . . ."

"Yeah, no kidding. I saw you in the med room, remember?"

Cole nods. "Anyhow, the military document set forth the protocol for the genetic testing—what our parents had to undergo to see if they carried the Bounder genes."

"Okay," I say, "so the military was involved. We knew that. The military took over the space program after the Incident at Bounding Base 51. They formed Earth Force."

"Right," Cole says, "but do you know what the original name of the Bounder Baby Breeding Program was?"

"What?"

"Operation *Ultio*."

"Okay . . . ," I say.

"Don't you know what *ultio* means?"

"Ummm . . . 'ultimate,' maybe?"

"No. It's Latin."

"Look, Cole, I don't speak Latin. No one does. Other than you, apparently."

"It's Latin for 'revenge.'"

Whoa. *Ultio.* Revenge. No way. That could only mean one thing. The Bounder Baby Breeding Program is Earth Force's long-term offensive to stick it to the aliens. Gedney said the

Bounders were born to master the gloves. That has to mean the gloves are weapons. So what does that make the Bounders?

What does that make us?

We catch up to Marco and Lucy in the hall leading to the hangar.

"What happened to you clowns?" Marco asks.

"Cole couldn't make the grab," I say, sneaking a nervous glance at Cole.

Cole stares at his shoes. "Yeah, what he said."

Hmmm. So Cole and I are tight again? Sharing secrets? I'm not really sure when we turned the corner, but I'm not complaining. Plus, Cole gave me a lot to think about.

· E_F ·

So I was distracted. It's not like every day you learn about a new biotechnology you were born to master. Biotechnology that might actually be a secret weapon. That's why Mobility was a bust. Or, at least, that's what I'm telling myself as I lie here in my bunk, hiding out, trying to avoid more teasing, at least until dinner. Either that, or I'll have to admit I'm just as inept as everyone's saying.

Honestly, though, we were a genuine air rail wreck. Mira wouldn't even fly. She sat in the corner, folded in upon herself, staring into space. I'm sure the other pods just chalked it up to her being a freak, or whatever they're calling her.

But then there was me.

I suited up in my pack and listened closely to instructions. I had to save face after the first blast pack lesson landed me in the med room. Bad Breath set up an obstacle course. We had to fly over and under and around barrels and raised launch platforms and beams suspended from the ceiling. It was a relay race, pod against pod, one pod member after the next. Bad Breath agreed to let Cole go twice since Mira wouldn't join. It was that or be disqualified before we even started. Looking back, I bet he agreed for the joy of watching me humiliate myself.

The race started out great. Cole has a real knack for the pack. He pulled out to an easy lead. Marco and Lucy fell back a little, but we were still in the game. I stood at the starting line, gripping the controls, reviewing the route in my mind. I was ready.

When Lucy tapped my hand, I lifted off. I could have flown a little straighter, that's for sure, but all in all, I had a good start. I made it around the first group of barrels and under the platform (barely, my feet touched the ground, but I don't think anyone saw). A couple of cadets passed me, so I raced to catch up. I soared up to the rafters, pushing my pack as fast as I could.

Then things got ugly. I tried to take a sharp dive over the beam to make up some time, but I cut it too close. The strap of my pack got tangled around a metal post sticking out the

MONICA TESLER

top of the beam. I was jerked back in the middle of the air and left hanging from my straps thirty meters up.

I tried to shake loose, but it was no use. If I let go of the grips, I'd fall. And there was no way I was gonna let that happen again. I hung there, kicking my feet, but all I managed to do was kick my shoe off. As it plummeted to the ground, I stopped flailing. I had to accept that things didn't work out quite as planned.

After the last cadet from the other pods crossed the finish line, Bad Breath sent Cole up to rescue me.

When we made it to the ground, something hard slammed into the back of my head.

Behind me, Regis, Randall, and Hakim were slapping high fives and laughing hysterically. My shoe lay on the ground next to me.

"Oops," Regis said. "I forgot to say catch. Great flying, Jasper. Hang in there. Get it—*hang* in there?" His buddies thought that one was hysterical, too.

I stuffed my foot into my shoe and ran out of the hangar, straight to my bunk. If rankings weren't posting tonight, I'd probably skip dinner. I'm sure Regis has dreamed up some choice rips to throw my way in the mess hall, especially if the rankings turn out the awful way I'm predicting they will.

· *EF* ·

Shockingly, tonight's dinner doesn't stink, but that's the only glimmer of good news.

Ridders marches into the mess hall. He holds a huge piece of paper in his hands that ripples out behind him like a cape. He grabs some tacks from his pocket and whips the paper, scrawled with pen, up against the wall.

Lucy is out of her seat as soon as Ridders enters. By the time he pegs the paper up, at least half of the cadets crowd around him.

Me, I stay put. The only one left at the table with me is Marco. I shove a huge bite of lettuce and radishes from the hydroponic garden into my mouth and chase it with a thick bite of the grilled cheese sandwich the kitchen coughed up from somewhere.

"Paper? Pens? What is this? The twentieth century?" Marco says.

I swallow the grilled cheese. "If they posted the rankings on tablets, someone might try to hack in or slap it up on EFAN or something."

"Why aren't you over there?" Marco asks.

"Come on. You saw how I flew today. We're gonna tank." Marco shrugs.

"What about you?" I ask. "You're not over there either." I take another bite of my sandwich. When I close my eyes and ignore the lingering smell of tofu dogs, it almost tastes like Mom's cheesy garlic bread.

"What's the rush?" Marco kicks his feet up onto Lucy's empty chair. "You think I won't find out unless I push through a crowd? Sometimes it's better to let it come to you."

"I'll remember that." Yeah, the next time I'm looking for some free therapy.

Cole slumps back to the table, dragging his feet, staring at the ground.

"Go ahead," I say through another mouthful of grilled cheese. "What's the damage?"

He doesn't look up. "Last place."

Well, it's not like I didn't see it coming. "At least tell me Han's pod isn't winning."

Cole doesn't respond. Great. Regis is leading, first of all twenty-six pods.

Yep, dinner is the only thing that doesn't stink. I cram the rest of my sandwich into my mouth, shoot up from the table, and shove in my chair. As I stomp out of the mess hall, my chair clangs to the ground behind me.

AS WE MARCH TOWARD NEXT WEEK'S
rankings, my flying barely improves. Fortunately, we have
Mobility just twice a week, so there's only so much damage I can
do. I focus extra hard at lectures and in Technology and manage
to ace two quizzes. At least I'm not total dead weight for the pod.

Plus, I'm not going to let anything get me down this morning. It's finally our turn to suit up for a mission aboard a
quantum ship. That's right—we get to bound. We've heard
pod after pod tell stories of their missions—what the inside
of the ships look like, how cool the other bases are. Now we'll
be the ones making the quantum leap.

We're excited. Super excited, even. But no one could miss the nerves that cling to us like determined flies in a storm. Marco's color is off. His face has a green cast beneath his olive skin. Lucy talks more than normal, which I didn't know was possible. Cole doesn't look at anyone. Not even for a second. The only one who seems unaffected is Mira. She's within her normal range of odd.

I shove my breakfast aside—which is a bummer because it's waffles and contains no tofu whatsoever—but I don't want the waffles showing up during the bound. Puke might really mess up the replication mapping.

After breakfast we meet up with Waters, who escorts us through the station and across the chutes to the bounding deck. I've seen the quantum ships on EFAN hundreds of times, and we saw the fleet out the window when we arrived at the station, but I'm still not prepared to see them up close.

The quantum ships aren't huge, not compared to the passenger craft that brought us to the space station, but they're ridiculously intimidating. Perfect spheres. Eight meters in diameter. Giant drops of liquid metal. The surface glistens and ripples in the light of the floods. The ships rest on raised pedestals and are held in place by retractable scaffolding manned by the Spider Crawlers. Just then, the Crawlers— huge remote-controlled robots with eight legs, four for walking and four for working—surround the third ship in the fleet, attach their limbs to its malleable surface, and peel off the top.

That must be our ship.

Waters herds us onto the bounding deck. As we approach the ships, Edgar Han emerges from behind the scaffolding.

He grips Waters's hand. "Good morning, Jon."

Waters shakes his hand, then turns to us. "You all have met Captain Han. You're in good hands. Enjoy the ride."

"You're not coming with us?" Lucy asks.

Waters laughs. "No. I've had my share of bounds. I can't say I have much of a stomach for them."

Great. That does wonders to calm my nerves. I'm glad I passed on the waffles.

Han ushers us into the locker room adjacent to the bounding deck. He hands out bounding suits and shows us where to get changed.

"Remember," Han says, "nothing on your body other than the suit." He gives one of Lucy's ribbons a tug. "Nothing."

Lucy nods and bites her lip. Lucy, quiet? That sure doesn't make me feel any better.

We meet back on the bounding deck ten minutes later. We're all zipped up in the skintight silver suits with the orange insignia. Circles of transparent breathable membrane frame our faces and allow us to see out. We look hysterical, like five scuba divers without any water. As soon as we see one

MONICA TESLER

another, we crack up. For a minute I forget my nerves about the bound.

Han's head pops out of the ship, encased in the same slick suit as the rest of us. "Great, you're here. Let's load. The ladder's around back."

As we parade around to the rear of the ship, the Spider Crawlers click their long legs and shuffle to the side, letting us pass. Their sensors follow us with beams of ultraviolet light. Creepy. How come no one's ever made a horror flick about these things? *Attack of the Killer Crawlers? Giant Robot Spiders Take Over the Earth?* I swing wide to avoid brushing up against their metal limbs.

I've seen the inside of quantum ships on EFAN specials, but I'm still surprised. The ship is basically empty. Screens and terminals hang from the ceiling in the center of the ship, and the periphery is lined with passenger carrels. But that's it. I mean, it makes sense. Everything inside the ship needs to be replicated, so they keep it as bare-bones as possible. Still. It's creepy.

One by one we hop off the loading platform into the belly of the ship. We circle the interior wall, lining up one after the next, each of us filling one of the man-size indentations that look way too much like half coffins, and buckle in with the thick black straps.

My breath is all caught up in the back of my throat, and my pulse throbs in my ears. I pull at the suit that has melded against my body. The material constricts my neck and threatens to suffocate me. I promised myself before we stepped onto the bounding deck I wouldn't think about the Incident at Bounding Base 51. I broke that promise as soon as I saw the quantum ships. What if we don't materialize? What would it feel like to be lost in space?

Han must realize I'm basically hyperventilating, because he grips my shoulder hard and lowers his head level with mine. "Jasper, relax. All of you, take some deep breaths. Nothing will go wrong. I've piloted this mission a thousand times. Literally, a thousand. At least. Imagine you're back home at one of those summer fairs. You've all been to one, right?"

I nod. My parents take Addy and me every July.

"Good. You know those rides where everyone stands on the inside edge of a circle and then the ride spins faster and faster but everyone stays glued to the wall because of the centrifugal force?"

Yep. I rode on one last year. Dad puked after.

"Okay," Han continues, "this is just like that ride. Except for one important thing. Once we bound, this ride will be over in a nanosecond."

I press my eyes shut, calling up the image of Addy and me and Dad on that ride. The Blender, I think it was called. The sun was bright that day. Addy grinned at me just as the ride started. Sweat beads glistened on her freckled nose.

The *tick tick tick* of the Spider Crawlers sound near the hatch, and a squishy noise like stepping in rain-filled shoes but ten times louder echoes through the ship. Then most of our light is gone. The Crawlers have sealed the hatch.

Han pushes a button above his head and a control system drops down in front of him. He pages through screens on a large see-through monitor. "I'm running the bioscan now. Next I'll perform the final mechanics check. Then we're out."

As Han conducts the scans, I look at my friends. It's funny. Usually, I think we're big stuff—you know, the future of Earth Force and all—but we all look pretty small in the quantum ship. Cole and Lucy hardly take up any space in their compartments. Their straps are cinched all the way, and still they aren't tight. Mira's a waif with her long blond braid tucked inside her suit. Marco is tall, but he's thin as a reed next to Han.

"All set," Han says. "I'm commencing the bound sequence."

The screen shows a camera shot from outside the ship. The Spider Crawlers have removed the scaffolding. All that's visible is the edge of the bounding deck and the infinity of stars. And right in the middle is the pocket of wavy space, the quantum field through which we'll bound.

"Five, four, three, two, one . . ."

Bam!

Smashed.

Crushed.

Wrung.

Flung.

Puffed.

Stuffed.

Done.

I open my eyes. Blink hard. Lift my hand in front of my face and unfurl my fingers. I suck a huge vat of air into my lungs that a second before were as flat as pancakes.

"Did we make it?" Cole asks.

Han laughs. "I hope so. Either that or we're all lost together in some alternative dimension." When no one laughs, Han adds, "Joking."

The loud squishy noise sounds again, and then a weird light fills the ship. A stranger's voice shouts over the intercom. "Welcome to Bounding Base 32, kids!"

A Crawler inserts a ladder into the ship, and we climb out one by one onto the loading platform. As I drop down onto the bounding deck, I look around. Bounding Base 32 isn't all that different from the space station—just a lot smaller. A couple of structures connected by chutes, a narrow bounding deck, a hangar for standard crafts. And a dozen armed gunships surrounding the base.

Hmmm. Security's awfully tight here, too.

"So, how was it?" Malaina Suarez asks when we walk into Subsistence class after our bounding mission. She's pulled forward a dozen overhead garden racks hung with tomato vines. Five pots of romaine lettuce rest on the table.

"Awesome," I say.

"Yeah," Marco says as he grabs his pair of gardening gloves. "It rocked."

"When do we get to do it again?" Lucy asks.

Cole smiles. And, believe it or not, so does Mira.

"I'm glad you had fun," Suarez says.

Regis, Randall, and Hakim walk in. We're paired with their pod for Subsistence. Hakim has a black eye. That's the second one this tour. Those guys can't stay out of a fight for more than five minutes. I wonder if Regis gave Hakim the shiner, or if they picked a fight with another pod. Maybe I'm not their sole target.

"The first bound is really special," Suarez continues. "I'm happy you could do it together. You're officially quantum aeronauts now." Suarez goes into the back for fertilizer.

"Yeah," Regis says, "you're aeronauts. Hope you liked it. It's the last chance you'll get to bound this tour." The three of them laugh. They really crack themselves up.

"What are you talking about?" Marco says.

"Haven't you heard?" Randall says. "The top pod gets to

take the first free-bound with the gloves in front of the entire Academy on the last day of the tour of duty. That's the prize in the competition."

"So you better get ready to watch me," Regis says, raising his palms for Randall and Hakim to high-five.

The first free-bound? I didn't even think we'd start free-bounding until our second tour, at the earliest. I'd give anything to be the first to bound. I'd also give anything to make sure Regis is *not*.

"What makes you so sure you're gonna win?" Lucy says.

"Oh, we'll win." Regis steps in front of Lucy and glowers down at her. "And I'll tell you something else. With Jasper's stellar blast pack moves, you've locked up last place."

"Shut up, Regis," I say.

Regis spreads his arms wide. "Okay, Jasper. Let's wait and see. Second rankings post tonight after dinner. We'll let the scores do the talking."

Suarez walks back in carrying a huge tub of squiggly things. "Worms," she says. "Nature's fertilizer. Come on, now. Grab a handful, and let's get to gardening."

· *Ef* ·

After lunch, Cole, Marco, Lucy, and I head to the sensory gym. We need a chance to decompress. My muscles are tied in knots. I'm drained from the bound and angry at Regis. It's a bad combo. I need a break. We all do.

As we skip down the hall, laughter spills from the sensory gym. I'm excited. I can almost feel myself launching off the trampoline and sinking into the silver bead pit.

As soon as I step into the gym, I can tell something is off. A strange energy swirls in circles, and the laughter is too high-pitched. Plus, once I look around, I'm sure something isn't right. No one is on the trampolines or in the ball pit or on the monkey bars. They're all crowded in a circle in the middle of the room. Closed in. Focused on something in the center.

Marco pushes his way into the circle, and the rest of us follow. Two people are in the center: Regis and Mira. Mira is on the ground, curled tight in a ball. Her eyes are squeezed shut, and her entire body shudders. Regis walks around her, circles her, stalks her. Every few seconds he reaches down and pokes her with his finger or pulls a strand of her hair loose. And each time he does, the circle laughs, like Regis is the epicenter of a sick, rolling wave.

"I said talk, freak," Regis says. "What? Are you deaf, too? Deaf and dumb? Or just crazy?"

A chorus of echoes blasts out.

"Freak."

"Dumb."

"Crazy."

The chorus stokes Regis. His eyes are ablaze. "Why did you come here, freak? Don't you know we hate you? Don't you know you're the reason we take so much flak back at home? Because everyone thinks we'll end up like you?"

He reaches down and grabs Mira's braid, ripping her chin back. "Look at me, freak! Answer me!"

At first Mira's eyes are vacant, like she can't really see. Like she's staring at the one-way glass in the med room. Then something kicks in. Her eyes dart across the faces, frantic, searching. Until they come to rest on me.

Help me. I hear her in my brain and in my bones and in my blood. And in the lingering memory of her music. *Help me.*

I lunge into the center of the circle. "Stop."

Regis spins around. When he sees me, his eyes glisten with amusement. "What did you say?"

"Stop." I wish I screamed it. Stepped right in his face and hollered. But all I can manage is to keep my voice level, my gaze certain.

"Is this a joke?" Regis walks the edge of the circle, drawing in supporters. "What? Is she your girlfriend? Perfect. She's the queen freak and you're the freak who can't fly."

"Shut up," I say.

Regis laughs, and most of the others laugh with him. "And who's gonna make me?"

I suck in air. My exhale comes out in a stuttered rhythm that marches in time with my racing heart.

"Me," a voice calls from behind. Marco steps to my side.

Anger rolls off him like storm clouds in a fast-moving front. His hands are balled into fists, and his jaw is clenched. He walks right into Regis's space until they're practically touching. Then he lowers his voice to a strong whisper, low enough to sound menacing, but loud enough for everyone in the circle to hear. "If you ever lay a hand on anyone in my pod again, I will beat you so bad, you'll be shipped in the first shuttle to Earth and you'll never come back. Are we clear?"

Regis doesn't give ground immediately. He keeps his eyes locked with Marco, but I can tell he's crumbling. His shoulders slump, and he seems to shrink.

"Whatever, man," Regis says. "Be a B-wad."

Regis stomps out of the circle. The cadets disperse. Meggi and Annette pause, waiting for Lucy to join them. She doesn't.

"I am," Marco calls after him.

The other cadets turn around. They seem curious. What does Marco mean?

Marco laughs. "I am a B-wad. We're all B-wads. Don't you know that?" Marco keeps laughing long after Regis leaves the sensory gym. His laugh is dark and wild and knowing. I want to shutter up my brain to keep it out.

My hands shake. The rest of me is frozen, rooted to the spot where I stepped from the circle into Regis's space. How did I do that? Long strands of leftover fear and live anger weave together and tighten around my neck. I'm suffocating, just like on the quantum ship.

Mira cowers on the ground. She still needs my help.

I force myself to move. I try to get Mira up by myself, but she won't budge. She curls back into a ball and tucks her head to her chest. I plead with her to get up. My voice is strained. A grapefruit-size something sits in my throat, making it hard to talk and almost as hard to breathe. The lump grows, and I bat at my eyes. Why do I have to cry? I'm not sad. I'm not anything anymore except angry.

Lucy is mad, too. She stomps around the sensory gym, fuming. "Oh, for goodness sake," she says. "Why'd you have to make us choose sides?"

"What on earth are you talking about?" I growl.

The other cadets have left for pod session. It's just us, the loser pod, left.

"It's not like I care about that jerk Regis," Lucy says, "but I have friends in the other pods, okay? Why does it have to be us against them?"

"I don't see it that way, Lucy." I'm not really interested in her social woes. "Give me a hand here."

She kneels on the other side of Mira, and together we manage to haul her up into a sitting position. I stroke Mira's hair out of her face and squeeze her hand. *You're safe now, Mira.*

"What choice do you think we had?" Cole asks Lucy.

"Anyhow, it's for the best. It's all about the pods now."

I lie back on the mat and drape my arm across my face. "Yeah, well, now I guess our pod's a huge target."

"Don't be so sure," Marco says. He lifts the flap to the corner tent he stormed into after the blow-up with Regis. "We're a bunch of freaks, remember? No one thinks we're a threat."

"Speak for yourself," Lucy says. "I'm no freak."

Maybe I *am* a freak. I always felt like a freak back home. Trying to act normal. Trying to hide the fact that I'm a Bounder. Maybe we're all freaks. Who cares anyway? It doesn't matter what I am as long as I can make sure Regis and all the bullies like him can't touch me. Or Mira. Or anyone in my pod. We need to stick it to Regis and his band of Bad Breath wannabes.

I channel my boiling emotions into a single word: *Ultio.*

"We'll just have to prove them wrong," I say. "One way or another, we have to win this thing."

We slowly make our way to the pod room. Thankfully, the hall is clear. All the other cadets are already in pod session. If Waters is surprised the five of us show up together—Mira wedged between Cole and me—he doesn't say anything. As soon as we drag Mira in, settle her on the tangerine beanbag, and slump down onto our own bags, Waters claps his hands.

"Okay, team. Let's go. Gedney's expecting us."

Gee, thanks for waiting until after we got settled.

"Where are we going?" Marco asks.

Waters doesn't answer. He opens the pod room door and impatiently waves with his hand for us to get out.

"Do we get to try the gloves?" Lucy asks as she leaps from her beanbag. "Do we each get our own pair? Who goes first? When are they posting the rankings?"

Waters studies Lucy's face. "Yes," he says.

"Yes what?" she asks.

"Yes to the first question. If you think I can keep all those other questions straight at the same time, you greatly overestimate me."

Mom is like that. She cannons out the questions, one after the next. A picture of her forms in my mind. The lump in my throat comes back, and I bite my lip. I'd give anything for an hour at home with Mom and Dad and Addy. I'd trade every last meal at the space station for one taste of Mom's chocolate chip cookies.

The whole mess with Mira drained me. I let the others shuffle out before us. Of course they expect me to get her. I don't exactly mind, but I sure don't understand. From the first pod session, I've been responsible for Mira. I have to admit, it seems right, but it's also totally hilarious. I mean, since when am I the caretaking type? Addy has to take care of *me*, and she's a full year younger. I never thought I was up to the job.

I crawl across the green grass carpet to Mira's beanbag. Her hair sticks out in a million places. Man, do I hate Regis.

As I'm about to reach for Mira's hands, she lifts them. She laces her long fingers through mine, weaving our hands together. When she looks at me, a wave of calm soothes my homesickness, and I know it's her way of saying thanks.

I close my eyes and savor the moment.

Waters is waiting. I lead Mira out of the pod room.

"Good, we're all accounted for," Waters says. "Let's not keep Gedney waiting. You know how he is about getting to things quickly."

I fall in line behind Marco.

"Nice of you to join us, J-Bird," he says.

We follow Waters through the exit at the end of the pod hallway and into another corridor. "J-Bird?" I ask Marco.

"Yeah, you know, *J* for *Jasper* and *Bird* because of your sick fly skills." Marco thinks he's hysterical. I'm pretty sure Cole chuckles, too. Is it ever gonna end?

"Give it a rest, Marco," I say.

"What? You want me to stick with Ace?"

"Just shut up. Really." J-Bird? I guess it's kind of funny. Why is Marco okay with his teasing, but Regis is such a monster? I guess it's because Marco has my back, and Regis wants to break me.

"All right," Waters says. "Here we are." He stops in front of a door armed with all kinds of security. "Where are the girls?"

I spin around. I swear Lucy and Mira were right behind me. My pulse quickens. Has something happened to them? Did they run into Regis and his pack?

A few seconds later the girls emerge at the end of the hall.

"Lucy, Mira, you need to stay with me when we're going to the training room," Waters says. "This area is highly restricted."

"Sorry, Mr. Waters," Lucy says. "We had to take care of some girl stuff."

I look at Marco, and he shrugs. I don't even bother looking at Cole. Then I realize what's different. Mira's hair is swept back in an intricate braid and tied with an emerald ribbon.

"You fixed her hair," I whisper to Lucy.

"I couldn't just let her go around looking like that, now, could I?" Lucy spouts. But she can't fool me. Lucy's finally coming around. She considers Mira part of our team.

"Okay, now step up one after the next," Waters says. "The computer's been preprogrammed with your lens signatures, and everyone entering this room needs to be approved."

After Marco and Lucy are scanned, I step up to the door and lean in with my right eye open wide. It creeps me out knowing the computer is accessing all my data based on an eye scan. I sigh in relief when the scanner buzzes. I passed its test.

After we're all scanned, Waters holds the door open so we can enter.

As soon as I set foot in the room, I lose my bearings. The room is black—black floors, black walls, black ceiling—but it isn't completely dark. I can't figure out where the light is coming from. I can see, but all I can see is blackness. Once Waters closes the door behind us, I can't tell if I'm standing on the floor or on the ceiling. I try to walk and nearly trip, sure I'll go tumbling through space.

"Good, good, not a second to waste." Gedney emerges from somewhere. Another door? A screen? Suddenly he's just there. Air prickles my skin. Something is blowing, brushing against my clothes, raising the hair on my arms. I can't tell its source.

"Welcome to the Entanglement Zone, or Ezone," Waters says. "You're lucky. You're the first pod to come here, the first to post results for the rankings." And then under his breath he adds, "Although luck had very little to do with it."

"LET ME TURN IT OVER TO YOUR GUIDE,
Gedney," Waters says.

Gedney hobbles to the center of the Ezone. His arms swing
heavily by his side. Sure enough, he wears the gloves.

When he reaches the center, he turns to face us. "Yes, we
should get going. No reason to delay."

He raises his hands into the air. Pulsing currents of light
race to his fingertips. In the blackness, the brilliant light
blinds me. And just as the room is black, devoid of color, so
is the light. It has no color—just brightness.

The pulsing continues. I fixate on the light until my heart

aligns with the pulsing of the gloves, and my blood pumps to the same rhythm. I float, fall, reel in space. What on earth is this place? I'm afraid but filled with awe.

"Ezone Bounding Training Protocol, initiate," Gedney says.

As soon as Gedney utters the command, a billion pinpricks of light, each as bright as the pulsing light on Gedney's hands, fill the room. And they're everywhere. Above, below, behind. The light fills me, too. I glow from the inside.

It's just too much. Every ounce of awareness I have sparks to life. I gasp for breath, and my right leg buckles. I throw my hands out in front to brace my fall, and tangle with someone already on the ground.

"Jasper?" Lucy whispers. "Is that you?"

"Yeah, it's me." As I stare at a shimmering outline of Lucy, I'm sure it's her only from her voice.

"What is this?" she asks.

"I have no idea."

She gropes in the darkness until she finds my hand. She clutches me like she'll be lost in space if she lets go.

"Okay, that's a start," Gedney says. "Don't fret; you'll adjust."

That's *it*? Don't *fret*?

"Look, Einstein," Marco calls out, "you've got to tell us what's going on here."

Yeah, no kidding.

"Very well, Marco. Can you make it to me? You'll be first."

A glowing blob that must be Marco creeps toward Gedney. He waves his hands in front, trying to swat a path through the light.

"Walk right through, son. Nothing's going to hurt you," Gedney says.

Gedney pulls a second pair of gloves from somewhere and helps Marco ease them onto his hands.

"Good, a perfect fit," Gedney says.

Lines of light race from Marco's fingers.

"Whoa!" Marco yells. "Oh man. I don't know about this, Geds." Marco's voice vibrates with fear and exhilaration. His body jerks around like a giant bug has landed on him and he's trying to shake it off.

"Now, now, give it a second," Gedney says. "The gloves are just binding with you. It's a strange experience the first time."

Lucy leans over and whispers in my ear. "I can't do this."

I'm thinking the same thing. I squeeze her hand, hoping she'll think I'm trying to boost her confidence rather than hang on for dear life.

Marco's body finally quiets. He holds his hands in front of him and examines his palms. "What the heck happened?"

"The gloves have established a direct cerebral link via your neural system," Gedney says.

"English, please, Geds," Marco says.

"The gloves are synced with your brain."

"Oh, of course," Marco says, laughing nervously.

"Try this," Gedney says. He reaches forward and gathers all the light in front of him. He packs it together like a snowball. Where the light just was, there is blackness.

"How?" Marco asks.

"Just try," Gedney says.

Marco reaches out. He drags his hands through the air, but nothing happens.

"Think about what you want to do, Marco. Focus on the outcome. Find the connection between the gloves and the brain."

Marco pulls his gloves through the light more slowly this time. At first nothing happens. Then a small pocket of blackness appears. He corralled some of the light with his left hand.

Marco laughs again. "Oh wow. I can't believe it. This is unreal." His ball of brightness grows bigger, and the pocket of blackness surrounding him expands. "You guys gotta try this."

"And they will," Gedney says. "Step over here, kids. I'll get you set up with the gloves. We'll run through a few exercises and then bound right in. Ha! I love that pun."

My sight is starting to adjust. I can tell who's who, and I have a general sense of direction. Marco seems okay, and there's no real way to avoid it anyhow.

I push to a squat and lean toward Lucy. "We've got this. Let me help you up." I pull her to her feet, and we make our way to Gedney.

"Lucy, right, here you go," Gedney says, handing her a pair of gloves. "And these are yours, Jasper."

The gloves are surprisingly thin. I expected to find wires or sensors to account for the light, but the material is gauzy. I push my hand into one glove and remember me and Addy playing with Mom's stockings when we were little. The material stretches against my fingers and molds into place like a second skin.

With both gloves on, I wait. At first I feel nothing. I ball my fingers into a fist then flex them out in a fan, waiting for them to ignite. I'm completely focused on my hands, so when my brain jolts, I jump.

"What is that?" I shout. Another jolt, like Dad is turning the ignition key on the hovercraft we rented for our family vacation in the scorch zone. Something almost catches but doesn't.

Then the third time—jolt and *jolt*. A live wire races out of my brain, around the curve of my neck, through my shoulders, and down my arms, all the way to the gloves. When the current crosses the glove line, my hands glow even brighter, and the current runs right out my fingertips.

"This is awesome!" I yell.

I turn in a circle, arms outstretched, watching my hands stream through the glow-pricked blackness. I've never felt more alive.

"Good, good. Gather around. No time to delay," Gedney says.

We line up in front of Gedney. Even Mira. She looks different. Taller, maybe, although I have no idea why.

Cole waves a lighted hand in my face. "Isn't this technology amazing?"

"Yep, it's super cool," I say.

"That's an understatement," Marco says.

"Okay, listen," Gedney starts. "This first game I'll call Catch. Grab a partner and stand two meters apart. Gather the light together like I showed Marco and then toss it to your partner. Every time you make a pair of catches, take a step back."

Cole and I head to a corner, or at least what I think is a corner. The Ezone is still ridiculously disorienting.

"Do you know what you're doing?" Cole asks.

"I haven't tried yet." Gedney said to focus on the outcome. I close my eyes and visualize the connection between my hands and my brain. Yep, the current is definitely still there. I picture my body as a pinball machine, and my brain as the release bar. I envision what I want to do and—*bam!*— shoot the message into the current. It races down my arms and into my hands, which feel like magnets or machines or something totally unlike the mere appendages they were a few minutes ago.

I focus on the light field in front of me and nudge a few of the glowing orbs. Sure enough, as long as I cling to the connection with my brain, they move at my will. I cluster together a couple hundred sparklers and wad them into a ball.

"Ready?" I call to Cole. He has a similar sphere of light he's kneading with his hands, but mine is definitely bigger.

"Almost," he replies.

"Think fast!" I yell, and hurl my ball of light at him.

"Hey!" Cole ducks as my light-ball whizzes by his head. "Not fair!" The ball sails beyond Cole and then breaks apart. The light scatters outward from the core in a hundred different directions.

I crack up. "What did you think it was going to do to you? They're just a bunch of silly lights, remember?"

"Yeah?" Cole says. "Well, then, catch this!" He chucks his ball at me. And, okay, I'll admit it's a little unnerving to have a huge ball of light barreling at me, but I'm not about to lose face. I brace for impact and hold up my gloves, focusing on catching. When the ball is about a foot in front of me, I somehow stop it. The glowing mass hovers in the air between my gloves.

"Nice catch," Cole says. His voice sparks with excitement.

My smile reaches from cheek to cheek. Hands down, playing with the gloves is the coolest thing I've ever done.

Focusing on the ball, I bend my arms into my chest and push. "Catch!"

By the time Gedney stops us, Cole and I are on opposite sides of the Ezone. Our ball is the size of a small boulder, but it weighs nothing. I toss it into the air and bop it to Cole, just like the giant beach balls the crowd keeps aloft at the futbol games Dad takes me to each spring.

"This next exercise doesn't require a partner," Gedney says. "It's basic practice for the assessments and rankings. Please gather around in a circle."

As I make my way to Gedney, I gather up a handful of light. I sneak up behind Lucy and dangle my fingers above her, letting the twinkles rain down onto her head.

Lucy jumps and spins around. "Jasper! Cut it out! You scared me."

"That was the goal."

Lucy grabs at the light around her and hurls it at me.

Just as I'm about to get Lucy back, I'm doused from behind by a downpour of light as big as the boulder Cole and I built.

What on earth? I whirl around. The only one behind me is Mira. Mira did that? My face must gloss over in shock, because that's definitely how I feel.

Mira doesn't say anything—she certainly doesn't own up

to it—but I could swear her mouth turns up on one side. A smile? A smirk? An involuntary lip twitch? I'm not sure.

"Okay, kids," Gedney says. "Focus here. Fun is fun, but we've no time to waste. Spread out. You need at least three meters on either side of you. Good. Now, close your eyes. Relax. Picture yourself as made of light. Connect with the light. Try to tap into your composition."

I close my eyes, but I have no idea what I'm doing. Picture myself as the light? What is this? Some weird spirituality? Can't we go back to tossing light-balls?

"Excuse me, Gedney," Lucy says. "I don't get it. What do you mean 'connect with the light'? What does that have to do with the gloves?"

"It has everything to do with the gloves," Gedney says. "Sense your own light. Tap into the source."

Lucy looks at me. I shrug. That seems to happen a lot when Gedney's talking. I close my eyes again and think about the light. The connection between the gloves and my brain is intense; it courses through me. Is that what he means by tapping into my source? I really don't have a clue.

Cole exhales sharply. "Can you at least give us the objective?"

Waters walks into the circle. He must have been hanging back along the edge of the Ezone. "Gedney, if you don't mind, maybe I can step in here."

Gedney moves aside, muttering. He's too quiet to hear, but I bet it's something like *No time to waste* or *Don't delay*. I hold back a laugh. That guy cracks me up. He moves like a snail while he urges us to rush. Whatever. Somehow speed and learning how to tap our inner sources don't really match up.

Waters reaches into his pocket and withdraws a pair of gloves. He fits them onto his hands, pressing firmly on his fingers to align the fit. He lets his arms hang loosely by his sides, and jogs in place. Then his body jerks like he's been struck—the neural connection—and he holds his hands out as the current blasts toward his palms.

"I will never get tired of that," Waters says with an enormous grin. "Anyhow, Gedney is the mastermind, but I'm perhaps a little less murky. Let me get to the meat of this. The light is a manifestation of matter, but not all matter. It's a manifestation of the matter available to construct all of you. That's why you needed to provide a bio signature to enter. The Ezone is preprogrammed to recognize your matter composition. When Gedney activated the program, all the matter that is you and can be used to construct a replica of you appeared in this room. Your building blocks, if you will."

"I don't get it," Lucy says. "We're not made of light."

"No, you're not," Waters says. "But the bright light against the blackness makes an excellent training room. And if you remember Gedney's demonstration in the pod room, when you use the gloves to manipulate matter in order to bound, the gloves enable the matter to glow."

"Building blocks?" Cole says. "That's not possible. The building blocks of organic matter are far too small to see. There are lots of lights in here, I'll give you that, but nowhere near equal to the number of atoms needed to rebuild us. If that's what you're suggesting."

"You're right on both counts, Cole. That is what I'm suggesting. And atoms are certainly too small to see with the naked eye. But, as it turns out, atoms are smart. And they're even smarter in the presence of those gloves. The atoms in this room sense you. They've given you a head start by assembling in larger masses."

"Smarter in the presence of the gloves?" Cole asks. "I don't understand. How is that possible? I've never read anything about that kind of technology."

"Well, Cole, some of this you'll have to take on faith—partly because I don't know the answers, and partly because the answers aren't mine to impart."

Hmmm. What exactly does that mean? The answers aren't his to impart? As in *secrets*? I never knew before I came to the EarthBound Academy, but Earth Force is full of secrets. The alien prisoner pops into my brain. I can't see a connection, except for the secrecy, but I'll have to give it some thought later. I have enough to focus on now.

"So, your job is to gather together your building blocks. Assemble the atoms needed to replicate yourself."

"Great," Marco says. "No problem. Except how the heck are we supposed to do that?"

"It's hard to explain, but you just know. Your brain knows on some innate level, and you can tap into that level through the gloves. I'm not good at it. Gedney's the best. Well, I should say, Gedney's the best for now. We suspect—in fact, we've bet our careers and, dare I say, the future of humankind—on the assumption every one of you will be better at this than anyone has ever been before you."

"Why?" I ask.

"Your brains are better attuned to this. You have an advanced ability to open your minds and absorb limitless stimuli without triggering your filtering systems. And you have the ability to process all that information. Simply put, no one other than you Bounders is capable of that because we bred it out of our genes. Ha! I'm still pained to think about it. Genetic engineering was hailed as one of the biggest advancements of the twenty-first century. Humanity's own technology is its greatest folly."

There is so much packed into Waters's words, I can't begin to digest it all. Filtering systems? Genetic engineering? I guess it boils down to a simple fact: Bounders can work the gloves. That's why we were born.

"Okay, so grab a spot," Waters says. "Spread out. Focus.

Think about what I said, and hopefully it will help you tap in. Try to gather the materials necessary to replicate yourself, the first step of bounding. You'll have half an hour to prepare, and then we'll test."

"Oh no, no, no. Wait a second . . . ," Lucy says. "You're going to rank us? Already? We're not nearly prepared. We need more help, more guidance. I mean, how can you expect us to master this in half an hour?"

"Your concerns are noted, Lucy. No one expects perfection. You'll be given a score based on the percentage of correct material you gather. In four weeks we hope all of you will be at one hundred percent. We'll start free-bounding Academy-wide in your second tour of duty this fall. And, as you may have heard, the top-ranked pod will be the first to free-bound on the last day of this tour."

I stare at the blackness behind my eyelids. Tap in to my source? Ummm, sure. Fear creeps up my throat and presses against my windpipe. I'm not afraid of the gloves or the light or even the idea of free-bounding. Not anymore. What I'm afraid of is much worse. I'm afraid I'll fail. I'm afraid I won't be able to do it. I'm afraid I'll be as much of a disaster with the gloves as I am with the blast pack.

I force a gulp of air down my constricted throat and focus. The current between my brain and the gloves sparks. I sense the power, but I'm not sure how to access it.

Let go. The words appear in my brain. Mira? No way. I thought I'd heard her cry for help in the sensory gym, too. But how could that be possible? Still, for a split second I was sure she was there. There, as in, *inside my brain.*

Well, it's worth a shot. I relax my muscles, starting at the tip of my toes and moving upward. By the time I reach my neck, my body feels like jelly, and I'm not sure how much longer I can stand. My eyes roll inward until I see a faint orange-yellow glow that must be coming from inside my brain. Without warning, my brain grows—larger and larger—its energy pushing outward so I'm not sure it will be contained by the four walls of the Ezone.

And then I'm there. I'm part of the light. Everything slows, and even the smallest spark sharpens with exquisite detail. Just like Waters said, I know. I know what is a part of me, and what isn't. There is a natural attraction between the lights that can bond together to form a replica of me. There is no other possible solution. It's just right, in the purest way I've ever known.

My heart whips around inside my chest, but I'm no longer afraid. I'm overwhelmed with a joy unlike anything I've ever felt. I am comforted, because I know with certainty everything in the universe is right and ordered and made of equal parts logic and intuition.

I pull together my light. Reaching, grabbing, reigning it

in. When I've harnessed all the light within reach, I flash my gloves to the corners of the Ezone, where the other lights float. I reach out with my mind and draw them to me.

The brightness in the room grows more concentrated, and the patches of blackness expand. The other cadets are harnessing their light, too. Cole has a small sphere in front of him. He still gathers light within reach. Marco's and Lucy's spheres are bigger. Mira, though . . . at first I think I must be seeing things. Her sphere of light is enormous, at least twice as big as mine. She stands still, her hands by her sides, serenely gazing at her light.

Waters claps his hands. "Good. Nice work. All of you. We're off to an excellent start. Gedney, kill the program."

Without warning, the room darkens. As the light extinguishes, something is yanked from my chest. I sink to the ground and bury my head in my knees. Exhausted. Empty. Lonely.

"We'll start the testing now," Waters says. "You'll each be tested individually. You'll have sixty seconds to gather your light. Your score will be based on the percentage you've gathered. The pod's score will be posted to the Academy rankings. Bear in mind, your scores will be posted as a cumulative number: one pod, one score. No one outside our pod will know the internal score breakdown. And I expect to keep it that way. Understood?"

We grunt our agreement, but we're all so tired, we don't have much more in us than that.

"Remember," Waters says, "the pod that places first in the rankings will free-bound in front of the entire Academy on the last day of this tour of duty."

Marco catches my eye and nods. Yep. We have to win this.

"Lucy, we'll start with you," Waters says.

"Really?" she says. "Can't someone else go first? Or, if I have to go first, do they really all have to watch? I mean, it's not that I don't love spectators. I'm an actress, you know. But I haven't mastered this. Like, at all. And I really want a chance to practice before—"

"Lucy, get ready." Waters waves around a mechanical device. "Gedney cooked up this clever measuring tool— a quantum caliper—to gauge your percentages. The clock starts in ten seconds."

Lucy hops up and dashes to the center of the Ezone. A few seconds later the lights appear. At first she does nothing.

Come on, Lucy! Do it for the pod.

She raises her arms and reaches for the light. I'm impressed; she's fast. She carves a huge circle of black around her. When Waters calls time, she has a good-size sphere of light.

"Nice work, Lucy," he says. "You clocked in at twenty-three percent. Cole, come on up."

Cole walks to the center of the Ezone. "Before I start, can we talk through strategy? I'm not sure how to begin."

"You'll get the hang of it," Waters says. "This is all about practice."

Cole shifts his weight from foot to foot. When Waters starts the clock, he throws his arms out by his sides. He waves his hands, brushing the light around him, but his sphere grows at an agonizingly slow pace.

"Okay, Cole, you got the first one under your belt," Waters says. He checks the quantum caliper. "Four percent. Next time try not to think so much."

Cole looks crestfallen. It's one thing to disappoint yourself—another thing to disappoint your pod. I know all about that, thanks to the blast pack. When Cole slumps down next to me, I pat him on the back. "You'll do better next time, for sure."

"Jasper, you're up," Waters says.

Watching Cole brought on even more nerves. Lucy hit 23 percent. I have to beat that. I close my eyes and shake out my arms, waiting for Waters to start the clock.

As soon as he says go, I open my eyes and take stock. The light comes into focus, and I tap in, sensing what I'll need. Then I'm off. I scoop the light as fast as I can. When I've gathered everything within arm's reach, I pull light from across the room.

"Time," Waters says. "Very nice, Jasper. Fifty-seven percent."

Fifty-seven percent? Yeah. That rocks. I'm not klutzy at all with the gloves. In fact, somehow the gloves make me feel like I'm in total control.

"Dude, that was incredible," Marco says. "How'd you do that superhero magnet move?"

I shrug. "Just tapped in, you know. To my inner source."

Marco laughs. "Yeah, right, so easy."

"Marco. It's you," Waters says.

Marco pushes up and crosses to the center. "Let's get to it, then. Let me tap that inner source."

As Marco grabs and pulls at the light, he scrunches his face up like he's in pain. He definitely has an edge on Cole, but I can see his weakness. He's trying too hard, like he has to force everything rather than finding the natural flow.

"Stop," Waters says. "Excellent first try. Thirty-one percent."

That's good. And Marco shows promise. He'll do better next time. That leaves only Mira.

Mira strides to the center of the Ezone. Again, she seems taller, or, I don't know, maybe more elegant? Like I even know what that means. The word just popped into my brain when I looked at her.

Waters starts the clock, and Mira lifts her arms. Light races toward her. She isn't grabbing the lights; she's commanding them, beckoning them to her. Effortlessly. Her arms glide in wide scoops and falling arcs. Amid the sparkles, she dances.

And then she is still. Like before, she stands motionless in front of a large sphere of light.

Waters hasn't called time.

Lucy looks at me with her eyebrows raised. I shake my head. What is Mira doing? Doesn't she know her score affects the whole pod? Come on, Mira. Not this, too.

The seconds tick on.

"Time," Waters says with a strange tone in his voice. It's hard to describe—too quiet and a tad questioning.

The light before Mira vanishes, and her shoulders slump like something has been ripped from her. She walks past us toward the door of the Ezone and leans her forehead against the wall.

"Well?" Lucy asks.

"What?" Waters says in that strange tone.

"Duh. Her score," Marco says.

Waters doesn't respond. He simply stares at Mira.

Gedney shuffles out to meet Waters. When he reaches him, he grips Waters's shoulder to steady himself.

"As I suspected." Gedney says, reading the quantum caliper. "One hundred percent."

"ONE HUNDRED PERCENT? I MEAN REALLY, one hundred percent?" Marco whispers. "How the heck did she do that?"

Cole, Marco, and I huddle in a corner of the boys' dorm before breakfast.

"Don't talk about it anymore," Cole says. "My score is just too humiliating."

"Come on," I say. "You'll nail it next time. Plus, no one can hack like you. No one."

"Don't call it that," Cole says. "I'm just good with technology, okay?"

"What do you mean, don't call it that?" Marco asks. "You're the best hacker around, and you should be proud of it. Speaking of which, I'm not too bad of a thief." He opens up his blast pack and pulls out a classified tech tablet, the kind Waters and all the officers carry.

"Where'd you get that?" I ask.

"A good thief never gives up his secrets," Marco says. "Plus, the important thing now is we have it. So tonight Hack Man here can break into the system, and we can figure out more about you-know-who."

"You mean the alien?" Cole asks.

Marco glances over his shoulder. "There's a reason I didn't say the word, Genius. Do you want everyone to know?"

"Are you sure that's a good idea?" Cole asks. "What if we get caught?"

"We won't." Marco looks around again and then shoves the tablet back into his pack. "We'll do it later today after Ezone, right before they post the rankings. No one will notice we're gone. Everyone will be too focused on their ranks."

I eye Cole. He nods.

"Okay," I say. "It's settled. After Ezone. Just us. Now let's get going, or we'll be late for breakfast, and I heard they're serving waffles." I've been thinking about those waffles ever since the quantum ship ride, and there's no way I'm going to miss them again. A whole stack of waffles with my name on them is waiting in the mess hall. With tons and tons of hot, gooey maple syrup.

· E_F ·

Our showing the second day at Ezone is better than the first. Gedney explains (and Waters translates) how to use the gloves to sense the quantum field, push the replication atoms through the field, and bound to the destination. Then we practice everything but the very last step, the actual bounding.

When it's time for testing, everyone improves except Mira, who has no room for improvement. She holds strong at one hundred percent. Even Cole manages to muster a double-digit score. If we can sort things out with the blast pack—boost my skills and get Mira to fly her leg of the relay—our pod will be a real force in the competition.

Our percentages improved so much, Waters lets us out early as a reward. We walk as a pod down to the sensory gym to kick around before dinner. Mira floats into the music room. Lucy and Cole jump on the trampolines. Marco hauls himself on top of the crossbars and stands.

"Hey, Jasper!" Marco calls. "Come on up. Let's have a chicken fight."

"No, thanks." I wouldn't stand a chance against Marco. Plus, it's a good ten-foot drop. I take off my shoes and join Lucy and Cole on the tramps.

Lucy touches her toes in the air. "I used to take gymnastics, you know. I had the best pike in the class. I wanted to keep it up, but my mother made me choose—drama or gymnastics. And my true calling is the screen." She bounces even higher, splitting her legs out to the sides and waving her hands in a flourish.

She nods at Cole. "You try."

"Uh, no," Cole says as he jumps to her downbeat.

"Oh, please? Pretty please? It's fun." Lucy flashes Cole a dazzling smile. He turns eight shades of red. Cole has no idea how to handle Lucy. Not that I do. She keeps pressuring him until he shakes his head in exasperation.

"Fine," he says. He scrunches up his face and takes half a dozen giant jumps. Then he hikes his legs high in the air . . . and crashes down on his butt.

I crack up. "Nice, dude. Great form."

Lucy stifles her giggle. "You'll do better next time."

"There won't be a next time," Cole grumbles.

I take off down the row of trampolines, bouncing in long strides, and then launch for the ball pit. My body disappears into the beads.

Cole sits on the trampoline, and Lucy joins Marco on the crossbars. As we decompress from the day, Mira's music dances into the gym. Her song is spirited and bright, like a music box.

"She can really play," Marco says.

"Yeah," Lucy says, "no kidding."

"Hey, Maestro!" Marco shouts at me. "Why don't you grab your clarinet? Join her for a duet?"

"I'll pass," I say. Why did I ever tell them about my clarinet?

We're quiet, adrift in Mira's music. I close my eyes and sink deeper into the pit. Maybe I doze. I don't notice when the music stops. My eyes jerk open when the beads shift against my skin.

Mira's long body slides into the pit. She submerges to her chin. Her golden hair fans out behind her, shimmering against the silver of the beads. She stretches, and our legs touch far beneath the surface. Her eyes are closed, but a lazy smile spreads across her lips.

I tense. Heat floods my face like a spotlight is trained on me. On us.

But I don't move my leg. We stay in the pit—legs touching— for a long time.

"Okay, team, time to eat," Lucy finally says. "And then time to find out how far we've risen in the rankings."

I don't want to move, but we don't have much time to get rid of the girls and hack the classified tablet Marco stole. I ease out of the pit and hoist myself up onto the edge. My leg is warm where it touched Mira's. I'm careful not to look at her. I join Cole and Marco by the crossbars.

"You and Mira, go ahead," I say to Lucy. "We'll meet you there. We have a guy thing to do."

Lucy narrows her eyes to slits. "A guy thing?"

"Like my man says"—Marco swings his arm across my shoulder—"a guy thing."

Cole shifts nervously behind us. If we don't get the girls out soon, he'll blow our cover.

"Trust me," I say. "You don't want to know."

Lucy raises her eyebrows. Oops. That sounded way too intriguing.

"No, really," I say. "It's gross."

Lucy crinkles her nose. "Gross, as in, bodily function gross?"

"Yeah," Marco says, "something like that."

"Come on, Mira, we're outta here." Lucy grabs Mira's hand and starts for the door. "They're posting the rankings at dinner. Don't be late!"

Once the girls disappear down the hall, Marco slaps me five. "Bodily function? Good one."

"What did she think you meant?" Cole asks.

"Who knows," I say. "Sweat, farts, poop, something worse. Who cares as long as it scared them off?"

I lead Cole and Marco into the music room. Cole and I sit on the piano bench, and Marco plops down on a wobbly chair in the corner. He pulls the classified tablet from his pack and hands it to Cole.

Cole slides his fingers across the screen. "Most of this stuff is highly restricted. It's not like I'm going to be able to bypass the security in the ten-minute window before we have to get back to the mess hall."

"Just focus on the alien prisoner," I say. "Find out how we can break into the cellblock."

"Why?" Cole asks.

"So we can take a little field trip, Wiki, okay? Just do it," Marco says.

"No way. I'm not breaking into the cellblock," Cole says.

"Oh, come on," Marco says. "No one's told us jack about the alien. If we don't find out for ourselves, we'll never know."

Cole looks at me.

"He's right," I say. "Plus, Earth Force has been waiting on us for twelve years—you know, to work the gloves we were born to master and stuff. What would they really do to us if we got caught?"

That logic seems to work on Cole. His brows point down in a V as he stares at the tablet. He taps in numbers and pages through screens at Mach speed. Every few seconds he mumbles to himself, "Hmmm. Okay. I see."

Marco can't take it anymore. "You see what? Clue us in here, Hack."

Cole flashes his palm in Marco's face. "Hold on a minute."

Swipe, tap, scan, swipe, tap, scan. I peer over Cole's shoulder, trying to make sense of the numbers on the screen. Time keeps ticking. We have to head out soon.

Cole flips the tablet over in his lap and sits up straight. "Okay. He's held in Structure Eighteen, Cell Seven. I have an idea how we can pass through security. Now all we need is a plan to distract the duty guard long enough for us to get through the door."

"Lucy," Marco and I say at the same time.

"That's what I was thinking, too," Cole says. "Lucy can talk to anyone. But the more people who know our plan, the more likely we'll get caught."

"Yeah," I say, "but I'm not sure we have a plan without Lucy. We have a few more minutes. See what you can find about the Incident at Bounding Base 51."

"Oh, come on," Marco says, "that theory is bogus. What could the alien prisoner possibly have to do with the Incident? Let's use our time for something other than a shot in the dark."

"Trust me," I say. "I have a hunch."

Cole runs his fingers across the tablet. He pages through screens, shaking his head. "There's nothing. I told you, it's restricted."

Marco stands. We need to head out.

"Wait, wait, here's a medical note," Cole says. "It was written the day we arrived. The day you and Marco saw the alien in the med room." Cole glances up at me with an annoyed face.

Dude, get over it. "Go on," I say.

"It's still in draft form, so it hasn't been restricted yet." Cole scans the note. His face is creased in concentration.

I lean forward, trying to read the medical note on the screen.

"These are lab results," Cole says. "For blood type, there's some weird code I've never seen before. But underneath, there's a handwritten note."

"Seriously, Fun Facts," Marco says, "just spill it. What does the note say?"

The color drains from Cole's face as he speaks. "Blood type matches samples recovered from the Incident at Bounding Base 51."

A strange quiet eclipses the room. At first we don't dare look at one another. We don't want to admit just how huge the implications are. But when none of us can come up with a plausible, less horrible, less explosive explanation, we have to look at one another. It isn't news you can bear alone.

"You mean," Marco says, "the alien was there? At Bounding Base 51?"

I nod. "The Incident at Bounding Base 51 was no accident. That alien—or at least his buddies—caused the Incident."

We stare at one another but say nothing. The connection

between the alien and the Incident at Bounding Base 51 weighs us down. I mean, what is there to say, really? Nothing. Everything.

"The time . . . ," Marco says.

We're going to be late for dinner. Lucy is going to be furious. We race out of the sensory gym for the chute cube.

Screams come from up ahead. When we round the corner, the cube is lit up with flashing lights. Annette is inside the cube, pushing buttons. Meggi is standing in front, screaming.

"Help! Help! Oh, thank goodness," Meggi says when she sees us.

"What's going on?" Marco asks.

Meggi looks at me when she answers. She's still too embarrassed to look at Marco. Someone must have told her that the tofu strings were meant for her, not Florine.

"It's Ryan," she says. "He's stuck in the chute."

"What do you mean?" I ask.

Meggi tries to answer, but all she chokes out is a sob.

I rush inside the cube. "What's going on?" I demand of Annette.

She seems oddly calm as she points at the blueprint of the space station. "There," she says. "See the chute? Meggi and I made it through fine. But Ryan didn't make it. As soon as I stepped out of the trough, all these alarms started sounding, and the trough sealed shut."

A thick metal barrier has slid down where the trough opening used to be. I look at the blueprint of the space station. Where the incoming chute is supposed to connect to the structure, there's a red blinking square indicating a malfunction.

"Cole!" I yell.

He appears beside me in the cube.

"See what you can find out in the systems."

Cole pages through the screens. "Chute's sealed, too. Good. At least we know he wasn't launched into space. Okay, I'm pulling up a camera visual."

A live view of the exterior flashes up on the screen. The chute has disconnected from the space station. It swings through space like a windsock, flopping this way and that, knocking against the space station structures.

"He's in there?" I ask in horror.

Annette nods. Meggi stands beside her, sobbing.

Whoa. If the seal doesn't hold, he'll be sucked out of the tube and killed instantly.

My mind spins a mile a minute. "Marco, quick, find another route to that structure. Get help! Cole, check the systems, see if there's a way to reverse the suction and pull him out. Do it!"

Marco dashes out of the cube at a full sprint. Cole hacks at the screen. Time stretches, and I feel useless. Meggi still sobs. I grab her hand.

"Okay, here," Cole says. "There's an override, but it's manual. It has to be done in the other cube. The cube where the chute is still connected."

"What has to be done?" I ask.

"A switch." He points to one of several switches mounted next to the control panel. "It reverses the suction of the departing chute. It's a fail-safe for just this situation. But it has to be activated at the other cube."

"Why isn't anyone doing it?" Meggi yells. "Why isn't anyone getting him out?"

Cole points to the blueprint. "I don't know why, but the alarm isn't sounding there. Probably no one knows there's a malfunction."

My mind empties of everything except what I have to do. I step onto the grate for the departure chute. According to the blueprint and camera visual, it's still intact.

"What are you doing?" Annette asks. "This whole chute cube could be malfunctioning."

"Cole, see if you can sound the alarm on that end," I say. "I'll flip the switch when I get there."

Cole's eyes widen. His face goes white. "You're not . . . ?"

"We don't have a choice," I say.

Cole's face hardens, and he nods. I push the activation button, and the familiar swirl of wind fills the cube.

I'm sucked into the chute.

I try to keep my mind blank. I can't think about the fact that I'm soaring through a malfunctioning chute. I focus on my breath, keeping it slow and even, as I pick up speed.

A loud noise fills the chute, and I'm slammed against the side. *Bam!* I'm flung against the other side. *Bam!* The chute's come loose, just like the one Ryan is in.

The suction holds. It pulls me through the chute as I whip back and forth.

Finally a light appears ahead. The chute spits me out into the arrival trough. I jump up and search for the switch on the control panel. Alarms sound. Cole must have found the override.

I flip the switch, and the cube hisses with suction. Shouts ring out from the hallway. Marco and a contingent of officers dash for the cube. I stare at the chute vent at the top of the cube.

Ryan emerges headfirst. Somehow I manage to dive beneath him and break his fall. Good thing he's small, or he would have crushed me. He's unconscious, but I can tell from his ragged breathing he's alive.

Ridders lifts Ryan from my arms.

"Are you okay, Jasper?" he asks.

I nod and follow Ridders out of the cube. He takes off with Ryan for the med room while the other officers work to fix the chutes.

Marco shakes his head as I slump toward him.

"Dude," he says, "you are one messed-up Bounder. You know that, right?"

Meggi, Annette, and Cole race down the hall.

"Are you all right? Is Ryan safe?" Meggi asks.

"I'm fine," I say, "and I think Ryan will be, too."

"What about you, girls?" Marco asks, staring straight at Meggi. "How are you?"

Meggi moves her mouth, but no words come out.

"Let's go," I say. "They're waiting for us in the mess hall."

Lucy meets us at the door. Her glare freezes us in our tracks. "Where have you been?" When she sees Meggi and Annette, she fumes. "I thought you said it was a guy thing."

Mira hovers behind her, twirling her hair around her finger and bouncing on her toes.

That's weird. Usually Mira is on her own in the mess hall.

"What's going on?" I ask.

Lucy places her hands on her hips. "I'll tell you what's going on. They posted the rankings."

"OKAY," I SAY, "THEY POSTED THE RANK-
ings and . . . ?"

Regis and his pod head our way. We're blocking the exit. Regis doesn't change course. He walks directly toward me, stopping inches from my face. "Hope you enjoyed the med room, Jasper, because you'll be seeing it again soon."

Marco takes a step closer. He has my back.

"Is that a threat, Regis?" I say. "Because I'm scared. Real scared."

"You should be," Regis says. He brushes my shoulder as he leads his pod out of the mess hall.

As soon as he disappears from view, I spin back to Lucy. "What is going on?"

"That's what I was trying to tell you before you went and picked a fight with Mr. Friendly over there. . . ."

"I didn't— Oh, never mind. Just tell us what's up."

Lucy points to the rear of the mess hall. "The rankings are what's up. As in, literally. They're up. They've been posted."

I glance at the back of the room where the big white poster is plastered on the wall. "And?"

"And we're in first place," she says.

Marco, Cole, and I dash to the back wall of the mess hall. My jaw drops when I see the rankings. First place. Regis's pod slid to third.

"Now I get why Regis is mad," I say.

"Why everyone's mad," Lucy says.

"Who can blame them?" Marco asks. "They got their butts kicked."

"Not like I helped," Cole says.

"Oh, stop the pity party," Lucy hisses at Cole. "It's not like any of us did much. It was all her." Lucy turns, likely expecting Mira to be right behind her, but she isn't. She must have slipped away while we were looking at the scores. "Well, great. She's gone again. I'm thrilled she shot us up in the rankings, but it doesn't change the fact that she's . . ." Lucy lets her words drop off.

"A freak," I say, "I know you were going to say it. Geez, Lucy, you're no better than Regis."

"I didn't say it, Jasper, thank you very much. And don't you dare compare me to that vat of used ship grease. Plus, what word would you use?"

"A girl, okay? A girl, like you. And a Bounder, like all of us."

Some cadets still shuffle out of the mess hall. A couple mutter weak congratulations. Others avert their eyes. A few glare. When they've cleared out, I spy Mira at her familiar perch by the porthole.

"J-man, Lucy has a point." Marco throws his arm over my shoulder. "We've pulled ahead, but the other pods will catch us. The only way to keep the lead is to show up as a pod. That means Mira needs to show up. Play by the rules. She's our ace in the pocket for the bounds, no doubt, but we've got to get through to her. If they're ever gonna take us seriously as a pod, we can't have all the focus be on your flight high jinks and Mira's flip-outs."

"Fine." I don't have the energy to fight about it. If they expect me to say something, I'll just go do it. I turn and head for Mira's table. "Come on," I call over my shoulder. "We're a pod, remember?"

I pull out the chair next to Mira. The others take seats, too. They look at me. All of them. Well, all of them except Mira, who is the only person whose attention I need. She presses her fingers against the porthole, and the others press me with their glares. Who made me the spokesperson?

This is going to be awkward. I close my eyes and try to remember the tact Addy uses when she explains things to me she thinks are painfully obvious.

"Listen, Mira," I say. "We're top in the rankings, thanks to you. I don't know how you do that magic with the gloves, but I think it's awesome"—remember the pod—"*we all* think it's awesome." I look back at the others, hoping someone will jump in.

"He's right. We do," Lucy says, and nods at me to go on.

Gee, Lucy, thanks for the help. Never could have done it without you.

"Anyhow," I continue, "what I'm trying to say is, you need to pull it together a little more. You know, during Mobility and in the dorm. Even here in the mess hall. We really need you to act more like a team player. For the pod."

Mira doesn't move. Her right hand is splayed against the window; her left dangles loosely by her side. She gives no sign she's even heard me.

My mind flips back through all our encounters. I remember guiding Mira into the hall after our first pod meeting. How I took her hand and somehow she made me feel strong and safe.

The last thing I want to do in front of everyone is hold Mira's hand, but I'm not coming up with any other strokes of genius. I wipe my palms against my uniform pants and reach with my right hand for Mira's left. I gather up her fingers and awkwardly thread them with my own. I keep our hands beneath the table. If the others see, at least they're nice enough not to say anything.

"Mira, you're part of our pod. We're glad you're part of our pod. But you need to start acting like it. Do you understand?"

I stare at her, and the weight of everyone else's stares cuts a hole in the back of my skull. Mira's hand lies limp in mine. Then, ever so slowly, her fingers curl and press against the back of my knuckles. Her right hand drops from the porthole, and she turns to face us. Her murky eyes slip across the table until they lock with mine and come into focus.

Mira dips her chin. A nod, maybe?

Good enough.

· *EF* ·

The good news: I managed to get through to Mira. It helped that Lucy convinced Waters we needed the security alarms turned off in the cadet dormitories so Mira could go to the music room without waking everyone up. There was never a big formal announcement about the alarms, but we knew he worked it out. Marco checked the boys' dorm to see if the alarms had been deactivated there, too. He slid out into the hall and back in one night. I braced for the alarm, but nothing happened. The next week Mira flew during blast pack practice, rode the chutes with us to pod session, and even sat with us in the mess hall. We held the lead in the rankings for the next post.

The bad news: my flight skills barely improved. We always placed in the bottom half in the relay. Some of the other cadets struggled, too, but I was the worst.

Even though we've been first-place pod in the rankings for two weeks in a row, the other pods have to be creeping up. Everyone's percentages are improving. Mira's perfect score is not as much of an outlier anymore. Marco and I both cleared 75 percent. Unless I get my act together with the blast pack, we'll be passed for sure.

No matter what I try, I can't get the hang of the pack's control straps. My brain knows where it wants to go, but something gets messed up in translation.

And Regis won't let me forget. Not even for a millisecond.

I'm thinking it all through as I lie on the hangar floor, staring up at the crossbeams, watching the other cadets zoom by in their packs. I just took out half a dozen empty barrels in my last practice pass at the relay course.

Regis flies low and hovers right above where I'm sprawled on the ground, trying to heave one of the barrels off my leg. "No words," he says. "I have no words for how awesome it is to watch you fly."

I manage to heft the barrel off me. Regis kicks over another that lands on my stomach.

"I'm finally starting to understand it." Regis has a sinister smile on his face. Whatever he finally understands is going to be a real treat.

"What?" I should keep my mouth shut, but I stink at that.

"I couldn't figure out how a klutz like you could be in the first-ranked pod," Regis says. "But now it's all coming together. See, I was right. There's no way you and Dancing Queen are in the best bounding pod. It just doesn't make sense. The pod leaders rigged the last two rankings. They've fluffed up your scores to make the rest of us try to chase you."

"Yeah, right," I say.

Regis lands on the hangar floor and stands over me. "My only question is, are you in on it? Or are you stupid enough to think you're winning for real?"

"Shut up, Regis," I say. "You don't know what you're talking about."

Regis laughs. "Oh, I think I do." He soars off for the finish line.

· E͞F ·

I try my best not to let Regis get to me. It's easiest when we're practicing in the Ezone or hanging in the pod room. I wish all Academy classes were taught in pods. It's the one place I can relax and be myself.

Marco and I wait for Cole after pod session. He stayed late to talk to Gedney. When he steps out of the room, he has a ginormous smile on his face.

"What's with you, Wiki?" Marco asks.

"Gedney helped me figure something out."

"What?" I ask. "You're all lit up like a firecracker."

"It's a surprise," Cole says. "I'll show you when we get back to the dorm."

We have half an hour to kill before mess hall. I planned to use the time studying for the Technology quiz, but with Cole all fired up, it doesn't look like I'll be getting much studying in.

As soon as we make it to the dorm, Cole grabs a seat at the center table. The dorm is maybe half full; about twenty-five cadets mill around. Cole flips his tablet face up and activates projection mode.

Instantly a military formation shows in the air space above the tablet.

No way. *Evolution?* I say.

Marco leans against the table. "Hack Man, you've outdone yourself!"

Cole grins as he manipulates his men in the projection. "No hacking. The Gadget Guru helped me out with this."

"But how is that possible?" I ask. "I thought all external communications were disabled and banned. You can't play *Evolution* without access to the webs."

"True," Cole says, "unless it's in beta mode." Cole explains that Gedney downloaded the beta version of *Evolution of Combat* onto his tablet for free play. Since Cole's tablet is the host, anyone can join the game via their tablets automatically.

"Genius!" Marco says. "Dude, what level is this?"

"World War Two," Cole says. He reaches into his pocket and pulls out his WWII figure. He places it on the table with his scimitar-wielding Crusades figure.

"Of course the Hack Man is a game master," Marco says. "That's incredible!"

Cole checks his health points and stockpile. He rearranges the force formation and subs in some new majors. I study his strategy. It's impressive. He's playing a long game, but it looks like he'll take the battle, too. He really is an *Evolution* genius.

I pull my tablet from my pack and link with Cole's game. He assigns me two captains and explains the offensive. Marco straddles the chair on the other side of Cole and joins as a captain of an amphibious unit.

Before long all the cadets in the dorm sit at the table with their tablets. Cole directs the advance, and we storm the beach at Normandy. Our offensive line stretches the entire length of the dormitory table. Our soldiers dash for the beaches. I can almost feel the spritz of water from the raging waves and the give of sand against my feet.

For the first time in weeks I don't feel the pod divisions. I don't remember how much I suck at the blast pack. I don't think about the alien behind the occludium shield.

We're just a bunch of guys playing *Evolution*. And we kick butt.

· Ef ·

"Do you know what they're saying?" Lucy asks when we drop our trays down at dinner.

Oh no. I have a sinking feeling I know exactly what they're saying.

"I'll tell you," she says.

Of course you will, Lucy.

"They're saying it's rigged. They're saying we're really in last place. They say some of us have the lowest Ezone percentages in the whole Academy. Can you believe that? We've got to do something."

"Wait," Cole says. "Who's saying that?"

Marco looks up from his tablet. Even Mira shifts her weight in Lucy's direction.

"Everybody," Lucy says. "I heard it from at least five different girls in the dorm. Even Meggi and Annette are starting to believe it."

Marco shrugs and looks down at his tablet. "Who cares? It's not true."

"I care," Lucy says. "I thought we were going to do something about this. You know, start acting like a real pod so they'd take us seriously."

"What if they're right?" Cole says. "My percentages might be the lowest."

"Oh, please," Lucy says. "You hear only the part of a sentence that pertains to you, Cole. Or, in this case, doesn't pertain to you but you think does because you're half delusional and completely self-centered. Your percentages are climbing. You're not the worst. You're just the worst in our pod."

"Gee, that's comforting," Cole says. "Thanks."

As they bicker, a great weight forms in my chest, like someone enclosed my lungs in an iron cage. This is my fault. We've been so focused on Mira, we haven't bothered to admit the obvious. My complete failure at flying combined with Regis's grudge against me has doomed the pod. They'd be better off without me.

They're still fighting, but I tune them out. When Lucy's midsentence, I stand.

"Look," I say in a too-loud voice, "I'm sorry, okay? I've tried to work on my flying, but I just suck. Live with it."

Lucy calls out to me as I rush to the dishwasher to drop off my tray, but I don't look back. I've got to get out of here. Unfortunately, that's not really an option on a space station. The lights hum, and the walls close in around me as I follow the sensor stripe to the dormitory and the small comfort of my bunk.

The bunks hum with snores. Thank goodness. This day couldn't have ended fast enough. They posted the rankings right after dinner. Cole and Marco filled me in when they returned to the dorm. We've slipped to fourth place. Regis and his minions hounded me right up until curfew. I camped out in my bunk, my nose in my tablet, betting they'd eventually get tired of teasing a nonresponsive bump on the bed. When I wouldn't take their bait, they harassed Cole, who was so down about his Ezone percentages, he was probably having nightmares that everything Regis said was true. At least they left Marco alone. And, hopefully, the girls fared okay. Mira's oddities are old news, and Lucy can hold her own.

I count the minutes after lights-out until almost an hour has passed. That's long enough. Everyone should be asleep. I slip the case from my bunk frame. The leather gives against the press of my thumb, and the metal clasp is cool. I flip open the top and peek inside. The sheen of my clarinet reflects the dim light of the night runners. As I slide my fingers across the dark wood, I shiver. It's the same feeling I have when Mom makes chocolate chip cookies. The high starts before the first taste.

I know the alarm is off, but no one else does—well, no one other than Marco and Cole—so I have to be quiet. I dangle my legs down from the top bunk and drop the remaining distance to the floor. I'm grateful Cole campaigned for the front bunks. I only have five meters to cross to the exit.

Luck is with me. Finally. I'm due some luck. I make it out of the dorm and all the way to the sensory gym without encountering a single person. The halls are empty. Almost too empty.

The sensory gym is dark. I trace the wall with my fingers to keep my bearings. When I reach the corner, I turn toward the music room. I don't reach for the light switch. Something about playing music in the dark feels powerful. And the last time I played—alone with Addy on my final night at home— was in the dark. I want to connect the nights. Anchor them in time and space with a huge sweeping arc, so I know there's always a place for me. A place where I feel safe and loved. A place where no one judges me.

The piano dominates the room. I slip along its side, finding my space in its sleek curvature, resting my case on its wood. I lift my clarinet from its velvet cradle and fit its pieces into place. As I raise the reed to my lips, I erase the humiliation of the blast pack—my failed launches and wacky turns and crippling crashes—at least for a moment. I am in control.

The first note is dead on, and I push until the tone rattles the legs of the wobbly chair in the corner. I close my eyes and let the music guide me. Let it go. Let all of it go.

When the first notes from the piano rise up to meet me,

I'm not surprised. On some level, I expected them. I must have known Mira would come. Maybe that's why I'm here—to be with Mira—although I can't fully admit it.

Mira's music swells and weaves with mine. Our song holds echoes of the melancholy tune from before, but our crescendo peaks with joy and promise. The notes carry so much power, they can't be contained by the music room. They run into the sensory gym, prance along the trampolines, dash through the halls, fly through the chutes, and dance into the infinity of space.

When it's over, I take apart my clarinet and close the case. I glide my hand along the edge of the piano until I reach the keys. Mira stands, her faint outline visible in the darkened room. She takes both of my hands in hers. I'd let most of my emotion out in our music, but I let what's left flow into Mira. Homesickness, Regis, the nagging feeling something terrible is about to happen. I let go of the fear that I'm not good enough, that I'm holding back the pod. I release my utter bafflement about why my pod keeps looking to me to lead, and the big ball of awkwardness I know has something to do with Mira.

Her hands curl around mine. Her silent words sound in my mind.

I am here for you.

Hand in hand, Mira and I leave the sensory gym and walk

down the hallway that is as empty as when I first left the dorm. And then, all of a sudden it isn't. The sound of voices swells from an intersecting hallway and grows louder. A large group of people is approaching. Fast. And we're out of our beds after curfew.

"Quick, we need to hide," I say. A chute cube is a few meters ahead. I rush Mira inside. "Climb into the trough. Get far enough in so they won't see you."

Mira climbs into the chute, and I scoot in after her. There's only half a meter of flat space between where the chute takes a sharp turn down and where the arrival trough is visible from the hallway. In other words, Mira and I are crammed practically on top of each other.

I don't know what to do with my hands. Anywhere I set them, they seem to be touching Mira. Finally I just shove them under my butt. Her hair is in my face. I can't swipe it away because I'm sitting on my hands, so I try to blow it. That kind of works, but not really.

The whole thing is so awkward, I stop paying attention to the voices. Ah yes, the voices, the whole reason Mira and I are stuck in the chute in the first place. The voices are still coming. I inch forward with my head until I can see the floor in front of the chute cube. Dozens of pairs of feet shuffle by.

Where are they going? Or, the better question turns out to be: Where are they coming from?

A loud female voice stands out above the rest: "Thank you for the briefing tonight. We are prepared. There shouldn't be a problem as long as we follow protocol. Still, raising the alert to orange is the prudent course."

Admiral Eames?

"Admiral, I agree raising the alert level is imperative. Frankly, I'd feel better if it were raised to red," a second voice responds. I know that voice. Waters.

"Noted, Jon. Do not doubt we take your warnings very seriously. But in this instance, I don't want to create false panic. Canceling the field trip to the Paleo Planet would cause alarm and could derail the tourism initiative. Not to mention, I certainly don't wish to get us off the training timetable."

"Yes, it's best to hurry." Gedney's there, too?

"We're all aware of the time sensitivity," Admiral Eames says. "I understand there's a standout in the group."

"A few, actually," Waters says. "We knew of their aptitude going in, so we've grouped them in the same pod."

"That's wise," Admiral Eames says. "With these recent developments, we'll need them sooner than we expected."

Wind rustles Mira's hair and blows it back in my face. As I strain to hear Waters's response, a low hum drowns out his words. And the walls of the chute start to vibrate.

Oh no. Someone's in the chute.

MIRA'S ARMS WRAP AROUND ME AS SOME-
thing slams against us. We fly out of the chute into the arrival
trough. My head bangs roughly against the stopper.

I know it's bad. But it's actually worse.

Three other cadets fly into the chute cube, piling on top of
me and Mira. They bounce off surprisingly fast. And who can
blame them? They've found an unexpected treasure.

"Well, what have we here?" Regis grins down at us, flanked
by Hakim and Randall.

You have got to be kidding me. I guess my luck has turned.

Regis laughs. "The King of the Blast Pack and the Dancing

Queen having a little alone time in the chutes? Priceless."

My brain flips. There's no getting out of this mess. We're doubly busted. The admiral and Regis. I don't know which is worse. And I have no way to spin it. Mira is so freaked, she clutches my hand for dear life. The only silver lining is Regis and his minions will be busted, too. In fact, I don't think Regis realizes the admiral is standing just outside the chute cube.

"Is this what you two lovebirds do?" Regis says. "Sneak out at night and ride the chutes? No wonder Queenie set off so many alarms. She had to go meet her boyfriend."

"Shut up, Regis!" I say.

"Shut up, Regis," he mocks.

The door to the chute cube opens. "Yes," commands Admiral Eames. "You'd be wise to shut up."

Regis, Hakim, and Randall spin around to face the admiral. Their hands shake as they try to hold their salutes. I climb out of the trough and help Mira out after me before snapping to attention.

"What is the meaning of this?" the admiral asks. "Joyriding the chutes after curfew is against the rules."

Wow. Admiral Eames thinks we were riding with Regis. Well, no reason to correct her.

"I'm sorry, Admiral," I say. "It was poor judgment on our part. It won't happen again."

"You're right it won't, cadet," she says. "Or you'll be on the first ship back to Earth. Am I clear?"

"Yes, Admiral," I say in chorus with Regis and his two side-kicks.

I don't know if the admiral notices Mira's silence, but Waters jumps in right away. He inserts himself between me and Mira and places a hand on each of our shoulders.

"These two are mine, Admiral," Waters says. "I'll make sure they're disciplined. I believe the others are in Captain Han's pod."

"Very well," Admiral Eames says, and then addresses Regis and the other cadets. "You three return to the dormitory immediately. I'll inform your pod leader and make sure you're disciplined appropriately."

"Yes, Admiral," they say, and immediately depart in the chute.

"Good night," Admiral Eames says, nodding at Waters. "Keep your pod in check, Jon. We're counting on you." On her way out, she turns to Gedney. "Good work."

Gedney mumbles something incomprehensible and blushes.

I don't want to look up at Waters, but I know I have to. His arms are crossed in front of his chest, and he has a stern stonelike gaze.

"I don't know what you two were doing," Waters says.

"And I'm not going to ask. Let's just say, I expect it never to happen again. Got it?"

I look back down at my shoes. "Got it."

Mira doesn't respond, though I doubt he expected her to.

"Good," Waters says. "And one more thing. You two surprise me. I never expected you to be associating with the likes of that Regis character. I've been watching him. He's bad news. Who you spend time with in your free moments is your own business, but I'd think twice about him."

I open my mouth to respond—I don't want Waters to think I'm buddies with Regis—but he has already turned and pushed open the door to the chute cube.

Gedney winks. Oh well. At least *he* gets it.

· *EF* ·

The next week is brutal. No, really. *Brutal.* During lecture, someone runs a worm through the class server, and a huge heart pops up on everyone's tablets with the words *Jasper and Mira* written in the middle. Most of the class bursts out laughing. Even Marco laughs. And Ryan! Doesn't the guy remember I saved his life in the chute catastrophe?

Mira is checked out as usual, so I'm the prime teasing target.

I run for the door as soon as lecture ends and hide in the back of the mess hall during lunch. I nearly choke as I shovel food into my mouth as fast as possible so I can escape from here, too. Lucy corners me and demands to know what's going on. I shrug, shove a protein bar into my pocket, and sneak out the back door.

I kill time, stalking the halls and riding the chutes. If I keep moving, maybe I can outrun all the jokers who think their life missions are to remind me how much I suck. After all, the joke's on me. I waited my whole life to go to the EarthBound Academy. Surrounded by other Bounders, I'd finally find a place I fit, where I didn't suck at everything. Well, here I am. And I still suck.

At least this tour of duty is almost over. Yeah, so I can go back home and get teased for being a B-wad until my next tour, when I can come back and get teased for being a B-wad who can't fly.

I can't wait until pod session so I can stop running. But by the time I make it to the Ezone, I'm so exhausted, I don't know if I'll be able to function. Waters runs us through drills like he took pointers from Bad Breath. He's still punishing me for embarrassing him in front of Admiral Eames. Great. The harsh pod sessions are my fault, too.

After a particularly grueling glove exercise, Waters's com pin beeps, and he steps out of the Ezone. I lie on the floor and drape both of my arms over my head. Every time a thought pops into my brain, I shoo it away. I want a blank mind. The blanker, the better.

"Okay, kids," Waters says when he comes back in. "You're

lucky. No more drills today. I have to leave early. Gedney will finish up."

Leave early? I push myself up on my elbows. By the door, Waters talks with Gedney. I can't hear what they're saying, but Waters is angry about something. And he's in an awful hurry to leave. Good. Maybe Gedney will let us go, too. I wouldn't mind some free time in the sensory gym.

Gedney shuffles to the center of the Ezone and claps his hands. "Now, now, I'm glad Waters is gone. We can explore the extra features of these gloves." He withdraws his pair from his pocket and eases them onto his fingers. No such luck on getting out early, I guess.

"Extra features?" Cole asks.

Gedney nods. "Yes. Amazing technology, these gloves. Unlimited, what they can do. I've hardly scratched the surface of their capabilities. I expect you'll be teaching me a few tricks before long."

That's weird. I thought he invented the gloves.

Gedney drags an orange cafeteria chair to the center of the Ezone. "You all know the gloves can manipulate the necessary replicating atoms in order to bound, but here's something you might not know. These gloves can manipulate any atoms—for instance, the atoms that comprise this chair."

Gedney points his hands at the chair. Light shoots from his fingers. The chair rattles on its legs.

Wow. Cool.

"Can I try?" Marco jumps to his feet and stands next to Gedney. He waves his arms like a magician and then aims his fingers at the chair. The chair levitates a few centimeters above the ground.

I try next and slide the chair about two meters across the Ezone.

I'm feeling pretty good about myself. Better than I've felt in a while. When it comes to the gloves, I'm good.

"Come on, Jasper," Marco says. "Lift it."

I focus on the chair and shoot beams of light through my fingertips. The chair wobbles on its legs, just like it did for Gedney, then rises off the ground.

Yes! I'm doing it. I hold the chair aloft—five, ten, pushing twenty centimeters. It's awesome. I'm awesome. I've never felt more powerful.

My neural connection is suddenly severed. The chair launches high in the air and flies across the room, crashing into the wall. The shock knocks me off balance, and I fall to my knees.

What on earth was that? I might be good, but I'm not that good. I didn't throw that chair.

As I push myself up, a sick feeling stirs in my belly. *Mira.* She's the only one who is that powerful with the gloves. I turn slowly, knowing who I'll find, hoping I'm wrong.

Mira stands behind me, that serene look on her face.

Rage boils up from somewhere deep inside. Who does she think she is, staying disconnected from everyone all the time until the moment she can show me up? How dare she?

I charge at her, stopping right before her face. "Why'd you do that? What are you trying to prove? That you're better than I am? I already know that, okay? You don't have to go reminding me all the time. You win!"

Even as the words spew from my mouth, I know they're not fair. It's not Mira's fault I suck at flying, that I feel like I'm disappointing everyone all the time. But I'm angry, and Mira is an easy target. I'm sick of being teased, of always being on the outside. She's part of the reason. And it's kind of her fault everyone at the Academy thinks I'm her boyfriend. But I'm not. I'm not her boyfriend.

"I'm not your boyfriend!" I scream.

Mira buckles at the waist as if I'd struck her.

"Jasper!" Lucy yells. "What's the matter with you?" She places her hand on Mira's back and guides her to a corner of the Ezone.

I lean over, resting my weight on my knees, and struggle to catch my breath. In the corner, Mira sinks to the ground and pulls her legs to her chest. When Lucy sits down next to her, she flinches.

I am such a B-wad.

"Dude," Marco says. "Stellar. Way to take out our pod star."

Where's Gedney? Isn't this the kind of thing a teacher should be jumping all over?

Gedney reemerges seconds later. He carries a large metal bin. "I think we have a few more minutes," Gedney says. "Let's give these a try."

That's it? He isn't even going to lecture me? Somehow that makes me feel even more guilty.

"Grab your blast packs," Gedney says.

Is he serious? This day could not get worse.

"Jasper, come on up," Gedney says. "You'll be our guinea pig today."

For a long moment I don't move. I even think about refusing, but I'm such a sucker for that whole respecting authority thing. I push myself up slowly. If I can't swing a flat-out refusal, at least I can make them wait for me.

I drag my feet to the door, where we dropped our packs, and fish mine out of the pile. What is he going to make me do? Practice in front of the entire pod? Hammer home just how awful I am? I guess I have it coming. Humiliation is small payback for what I did to Mira.

The pack feels heavy on my back. Twice as heavy as usual. I inch to the center, staring at the floor, hoping Gedney might take pity on me and change his mind.

"Good, good," Gedney says. "Thought you'd never make it. But now we're ready. No cause to delay."

Yeah, yeah. Hurry, hurry, hurry. We get it, Geds.

"Do you remember what I said when Waters left?" Gedney asks.

I don't respond at first. What is this? A quiz? "You said it was unlimited what the gloves can do."

"Right you are. Unlimited." Gedney sets the box on the floor. "Jasper, reach up on the control straps of the blast pack until you feel where they connect. Remove them. You'll have to compress the latch with both fingers and pull."

I do as he says—find where the control snaps connect, and detach them.

"Good. Now put those old straps in the pack pocket." Gedney bends down and pulls a pair of silver straps out of the box. "And put these on."

Now this is getting interesting. Once I've put the old straps in the pack, I connect the silver ones. Can this really be what I'm thinking? Can the gloves control the pack?

"Give 'em a whirl," Gedney says.

I hold the new straps out in front of me. No buttons. I place one in my right palm and one in my left. And squeeze.

Immediately my brain is aware of the pack. No, not aware. Linked. The pack is part of me. The connection courses through my veins.

I frame my intentions and shoot a message from my brain to the gloves exactly like we've been trained. Instantaneously I launch.

I soar to the rafters and bank right. The connection between my brain and body sizzles. I'm in complete command of the pack.

"This is awesome!" I yell. I fly low over my pod mates, tapping Marco's head with my toe, and then pull up hard for the ceiling. I'm in control. I am incredible.

Down below, Marco and Cole are suiting up with the new grips. Marco lifts off. We chase one another through the Ezone.

When I finally slow to a hover, Marco zooms over. "You perked up."

"Yeah." I shake the grips. "These are the best."

Marco shrugs. "They'll take some getting used to."

"What?" I say. "Don't you think they're better than the standard control grips?"

"Sure, eventually they will be. But I'm used to the controls. What can I say? You're better than I am with the gloves, and I'm a heck of a lot better than you are with the old-fashioned control straps. Keep flying, Ace."

Marco takes off into a figure eight. I'm about to follow when someone's foot makes contact with my butt. Hard. I drop a few meters before regaining control. "Hey!" I spin around to face the kicker.

"Sorry," Lucy says, although her tone doesn't sound too apologetic. "I would have tapped you on the shoulder, but I have my hands full." She lifts her fists, which hold the grip controls. "I'm done picking up after you, Jasper. Get down there and straighten out your own mess." She tips her head to the corner of the Ezone where Mira sits.

Yeah, I've been ignoring that issue. I figured if I flew fast enough, I could outrun the truth about how mean I'd been.

Mira hugs her knees and rocks. Every few seconds she shudders. She isn't in much better shape than the day we found her with Regis in the sensory gym. Guilt grips me. I never meant to do that. Lucy is right. I need to clean up my mess.

I lower myself to the ground next to Mira. I have no idea what to say. I was a jerk—how do I come back from that? I take off my pack and sit down.

"I'm sorry, Mira," I say. "I know that sounds lame. This place is just getting to me, you know? And I took it out on you. I'm sorry."

Mira doesn't respond. She bows her head to her knees and keeps rocking. It's going to be rough. I'm not very good at the whole girls and emotions thing. Addy would say that's an understatement.

"It's just . . . I'm jealous of you, okay? The way you are with the gloves. Like they're part of you. I feel that way sometimes, but for you it looks as natural as breathing. And it's not just that. . . ." My mind flips in circles. My feelings for Mira are all over the place; the last thing I want to do is match them up with words. "I'm mad at you, too. I'm mad at you because I need you so much."

There. I said it. And once I've said it, I know it's true.

Mira peeks above her crossed arms and stops rocking.

I keep talking. "I have no idea how you do it. I mean, you don't even speak, but you seem to understand me better than anyone else here. And sometimes—I know this is going to sound crazy—but I hear you inside my brain. Yeah, I know, I must be losing it. How can I know someone's voice when I've never even heard her talk?"

Mira unfolds her long limbs and stretches her gloved hands out in front. The chair she lifted lies on the ground a few meters from where we sit. One of the legs is askew from the force with which it hit the wall. Mira's gaze latches on to the chair, and she points at it with her right hand.

"The chair. I know, I was a B-Wa— A jerk," I say. "I'm sorry."

Mira doesn't react to my words. She keeps her finger pointed at the chair.

"What? I know saying sorry is lame, but what else can I do?"

Then her voice fills my mind. *Lift*.

Oh geez. That's the last thing I want to do. Have Mira show me up again. Oh well, payback stinks.

I point my gloves at the chair and feel the connection. I

focus on the chair and will it to lift. The metal legs wobble on the ground for a few seconds, and then the chair slowly lifts until it hovers a few centimeters above the ground.

Mira places her hands on my shoulders. At first that's all there is—the physical connection. It makes me feel weird, like I did in the ball pit when our legs touched or in the suction chute when we were all tied up in each other's space. Then something happens. Slow at first. A slow infusion of energy into my neural stream. My gloves' power increases, and the chair begins to lift.

She feeds it to me gradually so I'm not overwhelmed. But soon the chair hovers near the ceiling, and an immense power unlike anything I've ever known radiates from my fingertips. She linked with me. And together our power is amplified.

Without warning, Mira takes her hands off my shoulders. I lose focus, and the chair falls to the floor.

I flip around to face her. "That was amazing!" We were more forceful together than I could ever be alone. "How did you do that?"

Mira pushes herself up, retrieves her blast pack, and waltzes over to Gedney to collect her new straps.

I CAN'T WAIT TO RACE REGIS WITH THE
new blast pack straps. I won't shut up about it. I talk about
it straight through dinner. I talk about it on the way back to
the dormitory. And I want to talk about it some more before
curfew, but I can't find Cole or Marco anywhere.

Eventually, I spy them crouched together on Marco's bunk.

"What are you guys doing?" I ask.

"We're working out the plan," Cole says. He sounds peeved,
like I'm interrupting him or something.

"For tomorrow's Mobility class?" I ask.

"No, Ace," Marco says. "Can't you give that a rest? Home

leave starts in five days, which means we only have three days left to break into the cellblock and find the alien." Marco flashes something silver at me. He's stolen a classified tablet again.

Cole grabs the tablet and glides his fingers across its face. "I'm more convinced than ever that the alien has something to do with the Incident at Bounding Base 51. Have you noticed the security around here has practically doubled?"

Cole's words jar my memory. I've been so distracted with my blast pack problems and the rumors about me and Mira, I completely forgot to fill Cole and Marco in on Waters's conversation with Admiral Eames.

"They've raised the security level to orange," I say. "Waters wanted it raised to red." I tell them about the night I was caught with Mira, leaving out the music room.

"You've known about this for almost a week and didn't tell us?" Cole says.

I shrug. "Sorry." I've been saying that a lot lately.

"Yeah, you suck, Jasper," Marco says. "But now I get where the rumors about you and Queenie got started. You do look awfully cute together."

I punch Marco in the shoulder. He pins me in a headlock before I can even get my fists back up to defend myself.

"Call it." Marco's forearm presses against my windpipe.

"I give up," I grunt. "You win, dude."

Marco releases me. I rub my throat. Marco's reflexes are out of this world. It sure wasn't the first time he had to fight someone off. I wonder if his older brother used to beat him up. When Marco talked about him in pod session, his brother sounded like a bully. It's probably best not to mention it.

I nod at the tablet. "Cole, get back to work. We've got to get into that cellblock."

We spend the next twenty minutes hammering out the plan.

"I think the best option is to use my lens signature," Cole says.

"Great option if you want to get caught," I say. "They'd know it was you!"

"Yeah, not your best, Brainiac," Marco says.

"Don't insult my intelligence," Cole says. "They use a right-eye lens signature here. I'll scan my left eye. And, either way, I'll program it as a temporary file to delete after a one-time use."

"Fine. Whatever works," I say. "Just do it."

Marco stands lookout while Cole leans close to the tablet and scans in his left lens signature. I hold my breath as the system uploads the data, but Cole doesn't seem too worried.

When Ridders yells lights out, Marco slips the classified tablet back into his pack.

"So it's settled," he says. "The day after tomorrow we'll break into the cellblock after curfew."

We clasp hands in a three-way shake to seal the deal.

As Cole and I head for the front bunks, Marco whispers after us. "Hey, J-Bird, don't get so jacked about the pack that you wind up back in the med room. We're counting on you."

· Ƒ ·

"Let's go." Lucy gathers her trash from lunch and lifts her tray. "Time for Mobility."

I kick my feet up on an empty chair. "Why rush?"

Lucy fixes me with her evil glare. "What's the deal, Jasper? I thought you were counting the minutes until you could show off your new moves."

"No need to be hasty," I say. "We might as well let Regis and his gang wait it out."

"Oh, I get it," she says. "You want to come in late so he'll think you're scared and then surprise him with the new grips. Am I right?"

I shrug. Leave it to Lucy to figure it all out.

"Jasper, you're exhausting. Get your tray and let's go."

Me? Exhausting? Coming from Miss Chatterbox?

The others rise and follow Lucy out the door of the mess hall.

Who cares what they think? This is my moment. I slurp down what's left of my milk and chew on an apple.

I take the long route to the hangar. When I arrive, Regis

and his pod mates are already in the air, hovering near the seal gates. As soon as I walk in, they burst out laughing.

Today the joke's on you, Regis.

I convinced the others to give me the last leg in the relay. Regis always closes for his pod, so we'll go head-to-head.

Marco leads off, and he pulls out in front.

I'm so focused on the race, I don't notice Regis step up beside me. "Are we in for a show today, Jasper? How 'bout you get stuck in the rafters again? Make your buddy come get you."

"Shut up, Regis. I'm flying the last leg today."

"Ha!" Regis cracks up and slaps me on the back. "Priceless. See you in the air. Or not."

I bite down on my lip to stop from going off. Cool it, Jasper. Don't ruin the surprise.

Marco makes it back to the start, and Lucy and Mira push to hold the lead. If anyone notices they're wearing their gloves or using new handgrips, they don't say anything.

Lucy tags Cole, and he takes off. He zigzags across the hangar. Regis's pod mate passes him early in the lap.

"I should have guessed Cole wouldn't be nearly as good with the new grips," I say to Lucy.

"Quiet," she says. "Unless you want everyone to hear. Isn't your whole plan based on stealth?"

Cole makes the turn, soars over the beams, circles the

barrels (nearly knocking one of them down with his foot), and ducks beneath the launch platform. Three pods pass him before he tags me. Regis is already a quarter of the way to the seal door.

I shoot from the hangar floor. My intentions are laser sharp. Rise. Fly. Fast. I'm focused on the course. I'm focused on Regis.

I pass him on the turn. As I zip forward, I call over my shoulder. "See you at the finish line. Or not."

Okay, so I shouldn't have been cocky. I should have let a victory speak for itself. Because when I gloat, I let my focus slip, and I slow just enough to bring Regis in range. He grabs my ankles, and we tumble for the floor.

I kick wildly, trying to slow our descent. "Get off me! Let go, B-wad!"

Regis swings his legs forward and nails me in the stomach. We drop. Half-a-meter from the floor, I regain control and fly for the ceiling.

Regis clings to my ankles. "You think you're something special, don't you?" he hollers.

"A heck of a lot more special than you!" I crisscross the hangar, dragging Regis behind me. Voices rise from below, but I can't make out what they're saying. I'm too focused on flying. And I'm too angry at Regis.

The beam I got stuck on during one of our early pack

lessons is straight ahead. As I race for it, I have an idea. It's risky, but it could work. Since Regis has me by the ankles, he probably isn't holding his straps.

I fly directly for the beam. Regis hangs below me, his fingers digging into my skin. When we're nearly there, Regis's scream confirms my hunch. He has two choices. Let go and drop thirty meters to the floor—or slam into the beam. My part's tricky. I have to avoid getting hung up with Regis on the beam.

I cut low over the beam. Regis collides with the metal in a loud thud. At the exact moment of impact, I point my toes.

I slip right out of my shoes and soar off, leaving Regis bent over the beam, one of my shoes in each of his hands.

Priceless.

I lower myself to the hangar floor, laughing out loud. Take that, Regis. I can't wait to watch Hakim and Randall try to get him off that beam.

When I land, an unexpected guest is waiting. Waters is in the hangar, and he doesn't look amused.

This is not going to be good.

In five long strides, Waters crosses to where I stand. "What's going on, Jasper?"

My mouth hinges open, but no words come out. I have zero idea what to say.

"This is the second time I've caught you violating rules,"

Waters continues. "And both times I find you in a dispute with this boy, Regis."

Bad Breath pipes in. "Jasper's been disruptive in class since the beginning."

Disruptive? If you call being unable to fly disruptive, then fine. But that's not the same thing as violating rules.

"I'm sorry," I say. "It won't happen again."

"I'm sure it won't," Waters says, "or we'll be talking permanent consequences. And that will affect your entire pod. Understood?"

My pod mates stand behind Waters, close enough to hear what he said. Lucy's face is scrunched up, and her arms are crossed tightly against her chest.

"Understood," I say, and drop my head.

Waters must follow my gaze, because he spots the new straps. "I see I need to have a word with Gedney as well."

Waters turns to Bad Breath. "I had to walk by the hangar on my way to the briefing, so I thought I'd check in on your class."

"Briefing?" Bad Breath says.

"Yes," Waters says. "Didn't you hear the beacon?"

Bad Breath presses his pockets. He must have forgotten his com pin. And he yells at us because we can't get into our uniforms fast enough? What a hypocrite.

"If I need to be at the briefing, what am I am supposed to do with these clowns?" Bad Breath says. "The relay was a bust, and they need these scores for the rankings to be tabulated."

"They're cadets, Auxiliary Officer. Not clowns. Not B-wads. You're to refer to them as cadets." Waters glares until Bad Breath crumbles. "Today's scores will need to be voided," he continues. "The briefing can't wait."

Waters heads to the door, Bad Breath on his heels. Before he steps out, he looks up at Regis, still clinging to the rafters. "And someone bring him down, for earth's sake."

· E_F ·

Waters's interruption meant Mobility ended thirty minutes early. We were lucky. It gave us more time to plan our mission to the cellblock for tomorrow night. But not everything is rosy with the pod. Lucy holds a grudge against me. Even though I apologized before we left the hangar, she hasn't looked at me or spoken to me directly.

As we make our way from Technology class to the mess hall, she hangs back, arms crossed in front of her chest. I can feel her ice-cold stare on my back.

"Are you coming or not, Jennifer Lawrence?" Marco calls over his shoulder.

"Who's Jennifer Lawrence?" Cole asks.

"Twenty-first century? Famous Actress? *Hunger Games*?" When Cole stares blankly back, Marco just shakes his head. "Forget it."

"Please tell Jasper he could have gotten all of us in big trouble," Lucy says.

I stop in my tracks and throw up my arms. "Enough of the go-between talk." I turn around to face Lucy. "We've been through this already. I'm sorry. What else can I say? And what exactly was I supposed to do? He grabbed me."

She fixes me with her wide-eyed glare. "How about spending less time worrying about what Regis and everyone else thinks of you and more time focused on your pod?"

That's easy for her to say. She hasn't spent the whole tour being teased. Though, come to think of it, no one has said a single negative word to me since Mobility. Nobody but Lucy. Certainly not Regis. Mission accomplished.

I don't have anything else to say to Lucy, but there she stands, her arms still crossed, waiting. She reminds me of Addy when she's mad. That means a lecture about my horrible communication skills is coming next. Thankfully, I'm saved by a mini Spider Crawler.

Beep! Beep! Beep!

Lucy jumps. "I hate those things!"

"That's because you aren't thinking creatively." Marco crouches low, and just as the Spider speeds by, he springs, landing right on top of the black box. "Woo-hoo!"

Yes! We sprint to keep up with Marco as he clings to the robot.

"This is *awwwe*-some!" he shouts. "You're next, J! Run alongside!"

I keep pace with the robot. At the corner, Marco leaps off and I jump on. My left leg lands its target, but my right leg misses. I grab for the front of the speeding box and somehow manage to hold on and right myself. "Woot! Woot!" I barrel down the ramped hallway like a car on a roller-coaster track.

"Who's next?" I shout.

"Get off!" Lucy yells. "Or are you trying to get us in even more trouble?"

I hop off the robot at the next corner, two turns from the mess hall. "Come on, Lucy, that was fun. You would have loved it!" Lucy's face doesn't soften. "Look, I'm sorry. Let's finalize our plan to find the alien." When we told the girls we wanted to break into the cellblock, Lucy seemed excited, especially when she learned the whole plan hinged on her acting skills.

"I'm not so sure about that anymore, Jasper," Lucy fumes. "It seems like everywhere you go, there's trouble."

"Cool it, Florine Wannabe," Marco says as we enter the mess hall. "The blast pack high jinks are over, okay? Jasper's moved on. You should, too."

"Since when are you the voice of reason? And speaking of reason"—Lucy lowers her voice as we sit down at our regular table—"what exactly is our reason for visiting the alien? If I decide to help you, what are we going to do once we break in?"

Marco and I exchange glances. It's a fair question, but I haven't really thought that far ahead.

"We have evidence tying him to the Incident at Bounding Base 51," Cole says. "We're going to interrogate him."

We all stare at Cole. Interrogate him? Really? We're not even sure he talks, let alone speaks the same language we do.

"Yeah," I say, "what Cole said."

Marco smiles, turning up the charm factor. "Think about it, Lucy. You're curious, aren't you? Just getting a better look at Green Lantern might give us more information."

Lucy scrunches up her face like she's thinking. "Fine."

"Good, we've got a plan," I say.

Marco nods to the porthole on the far side of the mess hall. "Mira's the real wild card in all this, you know."

Mira's been better about sticking with the pod, but you can tell it takes a toll on her. She needs space.

"Maybe we should just leave her behind," Lucy says.

"No," I say. "We're doing this as a pod."

How many times do we need to have the same discussion about Mira? For better or worse, she's one of us. And as far as the bounding rankings go, she's carrying us.

So it's settled. The plan will go down tomorrow night. We'll sneak out after curfew. Lucy will run a diversion with the guard. Then we'll break into the cellblock, find the alien, ask some questions, and get out before the guard returns. We should be back in our beds with plenty of time to rest up for our big end-of-tour field trip to the Paleo Planet.

Everything just has to go as planned.

18

AS SOON AS I STEP INTO THE DORM, SOME-thing slams into my ribs and knocks me onto my back. I'm winded. As I gasp for breath, I see things flying above me in the air. I must have hit my head.

My vision comes into focus. I didn't hit my head, and I'm not seeing things. It's Regis, Hakim, and Randall soaring across the dorm in their blast packs. When I try to prop up, Regis lands at my feet and shoves me back down.

"What do you have to say about these, B-wad?" Regis shakes his hands. He wears his gloves, and he grips the new silver pack straps.

"You cheated!" Hakim yells.

"We knew it was fixed!" Randall shouts. He hovers over me alongside Regis and Hakim.

Regis kicks me in the stomach. Then he crouches down inches from my face. "You think you can humiliate me again, B-wad? You won't walk out of here. They'll have to wheel you to the med room."

Out of the corner of my eye, I spy Marco skipping along the tabletop, his hands glowing with the light of his gloves.

"Regis?" I whisper.

He leans even closer. "Yeah, B-wad?"

"You stink. You smell worse than Bad Breath. Are you training to be an auxiliary officer?"

I laugh and then brace, waiting for the next blow. Marco raises his hands in the air. Behind him, Cole stretches his arms to the side. Then twenty pillows fly across the room and hit Regis and his sidekicks in the head, knocking them off balance.

I jump to my feet and whip my gloves from my pack. I hop up next to Marco. A dozen other cadets have climbed onto the table, too. Marco must have clued them in on some of the gloves' bonus functions. They lift the fallen pillows from the floor and fling them at Regis. Cole, the master *Evolution* strategist, shouts directions, and we stage a coordinated attack on the enemy. Half the cadets launch an assault from their stationary positions on the table. The other half suit up in their blast packs and dive-bomb the bullies.

Regis, Randall, and Hakim dodge about aimlessly. Fear colors their faces. They can't figure out what's making the pillows fly.

I direct my gloves at a pile of shoes by the door. One by one I hurl them at Regis. When the final shoe hits him in the head, he runs for his bunk and hides beneath his blanket.

Once we've defeated Regis and his foot soldiers, the master offensive disintegrates into the biggest pillow fight ever waged at the EarthBound Academy. Cole gets me good with a pillow to the face, but I surprise Marco with a triple-pillow combination from behind. Ryan and the other guys in Sheek's pod annihilate me with a coordinated strike. I can't even defend myself, I'm laughing so hard.

We know Ridders will show up eventually with his whistle. When he does, I hop down from the table, grab the closest pillow, and climb up to my bunk.

Before burrowing beneath the covers, I run my hand along my clarinet case. I can't believe our first tour of duty is almost over. This place isn't so bad after all. I'm a Bounder. I belong here. I'm excited to go home in a few days, but I'll be psyched to come back for our second tour. And I can't wait until next year when I can show Addy the suction chutes and the bounding ships and the Ezone. But most of all I'm excited to introduce her to all my friends at the EarthBound Academy.

· EF ·

The next night the kitchen pulls out all the stops in honor of the final rankings. They toss salads with the fresh romaine and tomatoes we grew in Subsistence. They dish out huge ladles of hot, gooey macaroni and cheese (the noodles might be tofu, but they're drowning in cheese, so I try not to think about it). The dessert is awesome—butterscotch squeezy tubes. Marco and I keep grabbing more when the cook's head is turned. I have five.

Nothing can undo the damage of the twenty-one meals of tofu dogs we've had since arriving at the Academy (fourteen lunches and seven dinners, but who's counting?), not to mention the thirteen servings of tofu strings, eighteen fluffed tofu breakfasts, seven lunches' worth of tofu nuggets, and last Saturday night's special, Tofu Surprise (don't ask), but it's nice to finish a meal without feeling hungry for once.

All the cadets sit with their pods. The mess hall hums with laughter and chatter. But the chatter has a sharp edge, because final rankings post after dinner.

Bad Breath held a Mobility make-up class this morning. By now everyone knows about the glove grips and has practiced with them in the Ezone. For the final relay, cadets got to choose which grips they wanted to use. Of course, I used the glove grips. Our pod won the relay fair and square. Not even Regis could come up with a complaint. Thank goodness those scores made it in for the final tabulation. We still have a shot at winning the competition.

After dinner the five of us huddle around our orange table. "Can you believe the first tour is almost over?" Lucy asks. "Only two days until our field trip to the Paleo Planet, and in three days we'll be back on Earth. It's flown by. Really, it has. I can't wait to get back home, but I'm bummed to go. I'm gonna miss all of you so much. It feels like I've known you forever." Her voice cracks at the end of her speech.

"You'd win an award for that performance, Drama Queen," Marco says.

Lucy smirks. "Aren't you a bunch of lucky boys? You have the Drama Queen and the Dancing Queen in your pod!" She pats Mira's hand. "I'm just teasing, sweetie." Mira stares in the direction of the porthole. Did she even hear Lucy?

Lucy's a drama queen, but she's right. It will be hard to say good-bye. We won't see one another until the next tour of duty more than four months away. Cole and I talked about hanging out on Earth. We are only a few hours apart by rail in Americana East. But I don't really think it will happen. We'll be busy making up schoolwork, spending time with our families, and preparing to head back for our next tour this fall.

"I can't wait to see Earth again from space," Cole says. "Maybe we'll make a polar approach so we can see what's left of the ice caps."

"Don't know, Wiki," Marco says, "but I call your seat for the return trip."

"Ohhh, yes, I get Jasper's!" Lucy says.

"No," Cole says in a flat tone. "We'll want the front seats for reentry."

I'm about to stake my verbal claim on the front row when the admiral's honor guard enters the mess hall. A moment later Ridders appears with the rankings poster, and all the pod leaders march in after him. Even Florine Statton, who has kept a lower profile since the tofu strings episode, shows up.

"Admiral on deck!" Bad Breath shouts.

Chairs scrape against the floor as all one hundred and thirty cadets stand at attention.

Admiral Eames crosses the mess hall, letting her gaze fall on each of us as she passes, just like she did when we took the Earth Force oath. "Good evening, cadets," she says when she reaches the middle of the room. "I've been keeping track of your progress through regular meetings with your pod leaders and review of your scores. You're an impressive bunch. All of you. You should be proud. You've truly exceeded our every expectation when we started the Bounder Baby Breeding Program and made plans for the EarthBound Academy. I applaud you."

When the admiral claps, we join in. The energy in the mess hall is thick. Our claps and hoots and hollers swell to a roar.

She waves her hands to quiet us down. "Let's get to the results. Please be seated."

We settle at our tables, still whirling with excitement and anticipation.

"Of course, there can only be one first-place pod," she continues, making her way back to Ridders's side. "And, as you know, the winners will free-bound at our closing ceremony two days from now, after your field trip to the Paleo Planet."

Marco kicks me under the table. Lucy squeezes my hand. Did we pull it off? Or did my Mobility performance during most of the tour keep us from first place? I cross the fingers on my free hand.

Ridders leans close to the admiral and whispers in her ear. The admiral searches the crowd. Maybe I'm wrong, but I swear her eyes zero in on Mira.

"Placing first in the rankings," the admiral says, "is Jon Waters's pod."

Wow! We did it!

Marco and I leap from our chairs and slap a high five. Lucy spins around in an impromptu dance. We lean forward into the center of the orange circle, pulling Cole and Mira along with us, and clasp arms as a pod. We did it! We really did it!

274

At the front of the mess hall, Waters shakes the admiral's hand. He waves back at the crowd of officers. They split apart and let Gedney step through their ranks. He hobbles over to Admiral Eames and Waters.

Friends from other pods gather at our table to say congratulations.

Meggi hugs me. "Way to go, Jasper. To be honest, I didn't care much who won as long as it wasn't Regis. There'll be plenty of time to bound next tour."

Ridders posts the rankings. The other cadets crowd around the poster to find out their final rank. Regis, Hakim, and Randall try to sneak out the back, but Han runs after them and herds them to their table where he stands guard. That's right, Regis. *Ultio.*

Admiral Eames walks over to our table, Waters and Gedney at her sides. She takes a moment with each of us, shaking our hands and praising our win.

"Jasper Adams?" she asks when she reaches me. She knows my name? I nod and smile so big, I worry my face might get stuck that way.

"Congratulations," she says. "You deserve this win. Now do me a favor, okay?"

I nod again, not sure I can speak.

The admiral laughs. "Enjoy your home leave. We have a lot of work to do when you come back for your next tour of duty in the fall. You're important to us. Earth Force is counting on you, Jasper. I'm counting on you."

"Yes, Admiral," I choke out.

She stares at me for a long moment. A slow smile blossoms on her lips, and she tousles my hair. "Sometimes I forget you're just kids. Now, if you'll excuse me, I have some important business to get back to." She shakes Waters's hand, nods at Gedney, and leaves the mess hall.

Waters and Gedney pull up chairs. Waters stretches his long legs in front of him and grabs a butterscotch squeezy. "These things are good," he says. "Just steer clear of the tofu dogs."

"Uhhh, yeah," Marco says, "we figured that out on day one."

"How do you like the tofu strings, Marco?" Waters asks with his *I've got a secret* grin plastered on his face.

Does he know about the prank?

Marco shrugs as the color drains from his face.

Waters laughs and claps a hand on Marco's shoulder. "The admiral's right. You kids should be really proud. I'm really proud of you. You've done a great job this tour. Now you'll get some downtime with your families, and we'll be back together in a few months for your second tour of duty."

"Yes, yes, you've done well," Gedney says. "You picked up the gloves very quickly."

That's Gedney, always wanting us to be quick. I'm glad he thinks we're fast learners.

Cole hasn't said much. And he hasn't touched the second butterscotch squeezy I grabbed for him in the kitchen.

"You okay, Cole?" Waters asks.

"Yes, it's just . . . I'm worried about the free-bound."

Waters switches his grip to Cole's shoulder. "You'll do fine, Cole. Don't worry. Your percentages have been high. We'll practice again before the bound."

Cole nods.

"I wish we could stay," Waters says, "but we have a briefing. Let's get going, Gedney." They rise and head for the door. Most of the officers have already left the hall.

"We did it," I say to my pod mates.

"As if there were ever any doubt . . . ," Lucy says.

We sit for a minute, basking in our win, sucking down a few more squeezies. There's nothing I like better than hanging out at this orange table with my pod mates. Back on Earth, I always felt like I stood outside the circle, looking in. With my pod, though, I'm part of the circle. We all are.

Marco slams his hand down on the table. "Okay, Bounders, we got the win. I'll put a check in that column. Now on to the next adventure. Tonight we have a date with an alien."

"ALL CLEAR," MARCO SAYS. HE STEPS
into the hall, and Cole and I are on his heels. We dart for the
chute cube.

As soon as I pull the cube handle, Lucy peeks out of the
arrival chute. "Nice of you to be on time."

"We're here, okay? Is Mira with you?"

"Ummm, yeah. We're basically on top of each other in
here. I'll write it up as girl bonding."

"Whatever. I'm pushing the button, so be ready." The
girls crawl out of the arrival trough. The chute hums when
I activate the system. Marco jumps onto the grate and is

sucked into the chute. Lucy grabs Marco's ankles, and Cole grabs Lucy. I make sure Mira's in next, and I sail in behind her.

As I whip around the last corner, I hope the others have cleared out. I'm not looking for a five-cadet pileup. Fortunately, Mira and I glide into an empty trough. I leap off and help her out after me. I straighten and take stock. We all made it. Time to move on to step two.

"Cole, you know how to get to the cellblock, right?" I ask.

He points to his head. "It's all up here."

I nod. "Let's go."

We dash out of the cube and run down the hall. Cole leads us through a series of turns until we reach another chute cube. We soar through the tube to another structure and take off running. We follow the sensor stripe through more turns until Cole pulls up short.

"This is it," he says. "Turn right, and the cellblock branches off from the end of the hallway."

That means the guard is at the end of the hallway, too. I look at Lucy. Her eyes open wide, and she looks like she's holding her breath. "Hey," I say. "You've got this, right?"

She nods and squares her shoulders. "It's not like any of you clowns could do it. Here, take this." She shoves her blast pack into my arms and sprints around the corner.

A loud male voice: "Miss. Excuse me, miss! This is a

restricted area. I'll have to ask you to turn around and return the way you came."

Then Lucy's voice, ragged with sobs: "Oh, thank goodness, I found you. I'm mixed up. I have no idea where I am. See, I'm just so devastated"—sob, choke, sob, cough, sob—"I can't talk about it. Oh, I might as well talk about it. It's Marco . . ."

"Who?" the guard asks, but Lucy bowls right over him.

"I can't believe what that tofu-faced imbecile did," Lucy wails. Next to me, Marco's eyebrows pinch together. "He promised to save me a seat in the mess hall, and I found him talking to *her*."

"Who?"

Oh, that poor guard.

"I came in with my tray, and there she was. She'd pulled her chair up right next to his"—sobs so loud, I want to stick my fingers into my ears—"and she was practically on his lap—"

"Miss. Miss—"

"I didn't know what to do, you know? I mean, do I shout at him for not saving me a seat? And I couldn't anyway because I was just so shocked and so hurt and—"

"Miss. You're going to have to come with me, miss. No, no, no. You can't sit here. I'm sorry about this, miss, but please. You'll have to stand up."

Geez. I feel sorry for the guy. Listening to Lucy makes *me* cringe, and I know it's all a ruse.

Sob, choke, sob, cough. "I can't get up. I just can't. I don't think I can walk. My chest, it hurts. My heart is broken. Or maybe I'm having a heart attack. Oh my goodness, that's it—I'm having a heart attack. He's killed me."

"Listen, miss, is there someone I can get for you? Someone who can help you?"

"Florine. Florine will know what to do."

"Ms. Statton?"

"Yesss!" Sob, cough, wail. "Hurry! Please!"

The sound of the guard's footsteps rattles in the hall. Heading in our direction. Oh no! We didn't think of that. I grab the nearest door handle. Thank goodness, it's unlocked.

"Quick. Inside," I say.

Marco and Mira duck in. I pull Cole by the collar and slip in behind him just as the guard turns the corner. If he weren't so focused on escaping Lucy, he probably would have noticed the door latching shut.

Portholes line the far wall of the room we hide in. The cellblock stretches out behind it at a right angle, so we can see the exterior of the structure through the window. "Hey," Marco says. "Check that out."

The end of the cellblock is aglow with a weird silver light.

"What is that?" I ask.

"That's the occludium shield," Cole says. "The alien has to be in that cell."

"That's not all," Marco says, pointing at the porthole. "The alien's got company."

Out the window, a couple hundred meters from the space station, a fully manned gunship hovers.

"Whoa," I say, "that's some serious artillery." Something heavy fills my belly. Whatever the deal is with the alien, Earth Force has brought out the big guns. Literally. Maybe we should call it off. . . . No, we've come this far. But we need to stay focused. "We've gotta go. Lucy's waiting."

The others follow me out of the room and around the corner. Lucy stands anxiously by the bioscanner leading to the cellblock.

"What took you so long?" she asks.

"I don't have a tofu face," Marco says.

"Actually, you kind of do." Lucy's lips curl. She probably planned that just to take Marco's ego down a few notches.

"Save it for later," I say, and turn to Cole. "Ready?"

Cole's face has lost a few shades of color, but he doesn't chicken out. He leans into the scanner and doesn't flinch as the laser reads his left lens signature. A few nervous seconds pass before the door buzzes, admitting us to the cellblock.

I toss Lucy her pack. "Okay, here we go. Put on your gloves and make sure you can reach your straps just in case."

"In case what?" Marco asks. "Cole said this was a dead end. If we're caught, we're caught."

"Just do it," I say.

I pull on my gloves and start down the dark hallway lined with empty cells. At the end of the hall, the same silver glow we saw through the portholes casts a crescent beam of light onto the floor in front of the last cell. As we close in, an invisible cord tightens around my neck. I suck in air. A strange metallic scent stings my throat.

Our speed drops off the closer we get to the alien's cell. We grind to a halt at the edge of the silver light.

Even Marco looks scared. "Is that the occludium shield?" he asks.

"Yeah," I whisper. "We can walk right through it. The shield only prevents bounding."

Marco takes a sharp breath. "It's what we came for, right?"

I nod, but I can't take that last step.

Mira crosses from the darkness into the sphere of silver. Her eyes—usually so completely disengaged—open wide. I step in after her.

The cell is dark. Darker even than the dimly lit hallway. But the silver glow gives enough light to see. It's a small space. Maybe two by three meters. A raised metal bench lines one wall. A bed, I guess, although not much of one.

On the bed lies the alien. He is stretched out, his feet pointed toward us, his head against the rear wall. Lying there, spread out like he is, he doesn't look that different from one of us. I mean, sure, he looks totally different. But not really. He's resting. Probably dreaming. Dreaming of a better place that isn't dark, that isn't guarded by an occludium shield. Or maybe he's having a nightmare. A nightmare about that gunship hovering a hundred meters away.

Then a stirring. A shifting. And a horrible noise—higher and louder than anything I've ever heard. The noise fills my brain and beats against by eardrums. I half collapse and throw my hands over my ears to block it. But the noise isn't coming from outside. It's coming from inside.

And then it's coming from outside, too. A second noise. An alarm.

The others are bent over like me. Shielding their ears and trying to escape the noise. And then the noise fades—not the alarm, that keeps ringing—but the other noise. The inner noise.

I lift my head and turn toward the cell. The alien rises. He is on his feet. He is walking to the door of the cell. And I know, as certainly as I've known anything in my life, that the noise came from him.

Mira steps closer to the cell glass. Every instinct in me screams to pull her back, but I can't. I'm frozen. Frozen in fear and completely mesmerized and immobilized by the green manlike figure walking toward us. The figure who, despite

MONICA TESLER

being locked behind a reinforced glass door and guarded by an occludium shield, just invaded my brain.

He reaches the glass. He tips his large, bulbous head to the side, like he's considering us. The moment stretches on and on.

And the alarm keeps ringing. We'll be busted in seconds. We aren't even trying to get away.

Mira lifts her gloved hand—slowly, like she's pulling it up through fast-moving water—until it lies flat against the thick glass wall separating her from the alien. Then the alien raises his wide, green, pulsing palm. He places it against the glass.

Mira's glove glows. Streams of light race to her fingers and pulse to the rhythm of the alien's hand. Their eyes lock.

They are communicating.

Mira's face colors pink, and her eyes gleam as she communes with the alien. I've never seen her so engaged. She's beautiful. I can't tear my eyes from her.

Shouts erupt from the end of the hall and shake me from my trance.

I blink hard and turn to the others. "We need to go! Now! Use your packs!"

"This way," Cole says. He soars down an adjacent hallway. Marco and Lucy jet after him.

Mira doesn't move. I yank her free hand. "Mira! Snap out of it. We're going." I shove her down the hallway. "Fly!"

She takes off, and I follow. We quickly catch up to the

others. Marco is in the lead. He zooms around corners and soars through the halls until we come to a wall.

"What now?" he asks, looking at me.

"Backtrack?" I suggest. "Take another turn?"

Cole shakes his head. "No good. I've reviewed the blueprint, remember? Marco was right. There's only one way in and one way out. This is a dead end."

"Find a place to hide," I say. I start back down the hallway, searching for an unlocked door.

"No dice," Marco says. "These are all cells. See-through glass. Face it, Ace. We're busted."

Everyone stares at me. But I don't have any ideas. And who made me the leader anyway? I crouch down and cover my head. I have to think. There has to be a way out.

The shouts in the hall intensify. They'll be on us in a minute. That's it. We're cooked.

Mira stands a few meters away. In her own space, as usual. I don't pay any attention to her. None of us do. It's not like any of us think she'll offer up a great idea for escape.

But a glimmer catches my eye, and I turn. A ball of light emerges in the air before Mira. And—*bam!*—she's gone.

"That's it!" I yell.

"What?" Cole says.

"Ummm . . . where's Mira?" Lucy asks.

"She bounded!" I say.

"No really. Where'd she run off to?" Lucy says.

"I told you. She bounded. And we have to, too!"

"You're serious?" Marco asks.

"Yes. Do it now. Gather your atoms. Then bound. We don't have much time."

"Where do we bound to?" Lucy asks.

"The Ezone. That's the only place we all know how to get to. Quick! Do it!" The shouts sharpen. The officers are nearly on us.

Marco and Lucy gather their atoms.

"I can't do it," Cole says.

"You can."

Cole shakes his head. "No, Jasper. I can't. I'll disappear. Disintegrate. I've never gotten one hundred percent. Not even in drills. I can't do it."

I take Cole by the shoulders and dodge my head around so he's forced to look me in the eyes. "Trust me. You can do this. You have to take a leap of faith." In my peripheral vision, Marco and Lucy vanish.

Cole nods. He scrunches up his face and bites his lip. Then he waves his gloves through the air, gathering up the building blocks he needs to bound.

I do the same—scooping and pulling atoms. Cole looks at me one last time. His ball of light hovers before him.

One, two, three . . . , I mouth.

Then I bound.

MY WHOLE BODY TINGLES WITH CREEPY-
crawlies, and my shoulder hits the ground hard. *Ouch.* I open my
eyes. Darkness. But a familiar darkness. I made it to the Ezone.

"Jasper the Bounder has arrived," Marco says.

"Cole?" I ask.

"He's over here," Lucy calls. "And Mira's here, too."

Relief floods through me. We all made it. We actually
bounded.

"Thank goodness we had our gloves with us," Lucy says.

Thank goodness is right. I'm not going anywhere without
my gloves anymore.

"Well, now, what have we here?" a familiar voice asks.

Oh no. Gedney.

"Finally decided to hurry, did we?" Gedney asks.

Gedney has that wacky professor vibe, so I kind of expect him to be all flustered that the five of us suddenly popped into the Ezone. Nope. Cool and calculating Gedney showed up to the party. I can't tell at first whether he's going to be an ally or the one to sell us down the river.

And cool and calculating Jasper definitely did not show up to the party. I barely have the energy to think. None of us do. We're scattered around the Ezone floor. Only Mira moved from her landing spot. She sits in her lonely corner, rocking.

No one says anything, and I realize they're all looking at me. Again, people, who made me the spokesperson?

"That's right," I say. He knows we bounded, so the best we can hope for is spin. "We wanted to put everything you've taught us into practice."

"I see," Gedney says.

I brace myself for all the obvious follow-ups: you're not supposed to bound on your own; you're not supposed to be out of the dorms; you're not supposed to be in the Ezone without supervision (which I guess, technically, we're not). And those don't even touch the most incriminating questions: Where on earth were you bounding from? And why?

Gedney skips over all of that. "How was it?" he asks.

"What?" He lost me. What are we talking about?

"It was your first bound," he says. "I want to know how you liked it."

"Oh," I say. Bounding was awesome, but how do I describe it?

"Tickly," Lucy says.

Gedney laughs. "Yes, I suppose so. Marco, what did you think?"

"No words, Geds," Marco says, "except that I swallowed my stomach and thought I might explode. When can we do it again?"

Gedney smiles and turns to Cole. "Good work, son. *I* knew you could do it. But I didn't think *you* knew. What changed?"

"Ummm . . . ," Cole starts.

Cole is the worst liar. Ever. He's seconds away from blowing our cover.

Someone else is a second ahead of him. The door to the Ezone blasts open. The florescent light from the corridor pours in.

Silhouetted by the light, Bad Breath steps over the threshold.

An acidy taste rises in my throat. He does not belong in the Ezone. He must be here for us.

"Can I help you?" Gedney asks.

"No, old man," Bad Breath says. "I've found what I'm

looking for." He marches into the Ezone and yanks Marco up by the shirt collar. "Busted, wise guy."

A million thoughts race through my brain. Should I say something? Try to defend Marco? Offer myself up? Spit out an admission so we get a few extra points for honesty?

"Take your hand off him," Gedney says. His voice rings with a steely confidence I've never heard him use.

"What's it to you, gramps?" Bad Breath says. "We're looking for a group of five who broke into the cellblock. This crew was missing from the dormitories. The shoe fits. It's a bust."

"The cellblock, you say?" Gedney's eyes lock with mine. "You have the wrong group. These kids have been with me all night. We've been running extra drills."

Bad Breath hesitates but doesn't let go of Marco's collar. "Drills? There's no record of that. These kids are supposed to be in the dorms. They're not."

Gedney elbows in front of Marco, breaking Bad Breath's hold. "No record? My mistake. As I said, we were doing drills. How do you think we got to be the top-ranked pod?"

Bad Breath glares at Gedney. His head twitches. Even in the dark Ezone, I can see his cheeks swell. He knows Gedney's lying. And he knows there's nothing he can do about it. He shifts his gaze to me—his eyes brimming with threats—and then stomps out of the Ezone.

Marco backs away from Gedney and smooths his shirt.

"Thanks, Geds." Marco looks at me and raises his eyebrows. What are we going to tell Gedney about the cellblock?

I have no clue. If we spin some tale that doesn't involve the alien, will he buy it? Probably not. His nickname isn't Einstein for nothing.

Gedney saves me the trouble of deciding what to do. "How did you know he was in the cellblock? How did you know about him at all?" he asks.

Whoa. I guess cool and calculating Gedney is not going to waste time.

I glance back at Marco. We might as well go with the truth. It's less confusing, and I'm too tired to think up a plausible cover story. "We saw him on the first night," I say. "In the med room."

"Ahhh." Gedney shakes his head. "Everything happened so fast that night. And half the staff was busy with the kickoff for the EarthBound Academy. There wasn't time to take the necessary precautions. Other than the shield, of course."

"The alien just got here?" Cole asks. "So he didn't cause the Incident at Bounding Base 51?"

"Oh, you kids. You've put a lot together, haven't you?" Gedney shuffles across the floor of the Ezone and lowers himself onto the chair we practiced lifting. One of its legs is broken from Mira's throw, so it wobbles whenever Gedney shifts his weight. "No, of course he didn't cause the Incident. He's just one man. The Incident at Bounding Base 51 was a highly orchestrated military event. And he was probably about your age when it occurred."

"A man?" Lucy says. "All I saw in that room was a green creature with glowing hands and a big pulsing brain."

"Then perhaps you weren't looking closely enough," Gedney says. "Is he a human like you and me? No. But how different is he really?"

"But his race. His kind. Whatever you call it," I say. "They did cause the Incident at Bounding Base 51, right?"

Gedney nods. "We've been at war with his kind for thirteen years."

I can't believe what Gedney is saying. We've been at war all this time—thirteen years—and no one knew? How is that possible? How could they justify keeping that secret from the billions of people on Earth?

"The alien's a prisoner of war?" Lucy asks.

Gedney nods again.

"We have their man," Cole says. "They're the ones who'll be looking for revenge now."

"Oh, I suspect so," Gedney says.

My breath comes fast, and a low-simmered rage brews in my blood. "If the alien's a war prisoner, what does that make us?"

Gedney doesn't answer. He stands and walks away from our group, hunching more and more with each step.

"I said, what does that make us?" I shout. "Soldiers in your war?"

"It's not my war," Gedney says. He keeps his eyes fixed on the floor.

What's that supposed to mean? Not his war. Well, it sure is somebody's war. "All this time you've stuck with the story that Bounders have a special gift at space travel. And all the while you've been breeding soldiers!"

I feel like my brain might explode. My body still feels like jelly from the bound, and now Gedney is serving up one nugget of classified planetary security after the next. I squeeze my eyes shut and try to force everything out. When I clear away most of my thoughts, I'm left with one stark image: Mira's glove pressed against the glass, pulsing to the rhythm of the alien's hand. Then it dawns on me. The alien's hands. Gedney's gloves.

"The gloves," I say. "They're the aliens' technology. We stole it from them. Didn't we?"

Gedney deflates. He braces himself against the Ezone wall. He won't look any of us in the eye. "You'll have to talk to Waters. I've said enough tonight. It's late, and you have a busy few days before you return to Earth."

· *EF* ·

The morning pod session is canceled. Waters, Gedney, and the other pod leaders were called to an emergency briefing with Admiral Eames.

　　　　　　　　　　MONICA TESLER

"Perfect," Marco says. "They have to talk strategy about how to defeat the little green men."

"He wasn't that little," Cole says.

We have an hour to kill before our last lecture, so we con a plebe into letting us into our pod room. We sprawl on the beanbags and stare at the starlit ceiling. I drag my fingers along the carpet. I want to talk about what happened, and what it all means for us, but I don't know where to start.

"Do you think Waters knows we bounded?" Cole asks.

"I'm not sure," I say. "I actually think Gedney might keep our secret."

"Why do you care?" Marco says. "An alien war is a much bigger deal than us breaking their silly rules."

"What do you think they want from us?" I ask. "How do we fit into the war?"

"I don't even want to know," Lucy says. "I just want to get home and see my family and my friends and go back to drama class and paint my nails and tie my hair in whatever ribbons I want and forget I ever came to this place." Lucy's voice cracks, and this time it's not an act.

"Come on, Lucy," I say, "you don't mean that. We've got one another now."

"You're right," Lucy says. "It's just . . . scary . . . you know?"

Yeah, I know. I'm super scared. I can bound, and I'm decent at *Evolution*, but I'm not a soldier. Even the gloves scare me. Now that I know what they are and how little we actually know about them, I realize how dangerous they'd be in the wrong hands. Wrong hands, get it? Yeah, it's not funny. Nothing about stolen alien technology is funny.

"I'm not scared," Marco says. "I'm mad. They want us to be soldiers in their war, and they never mention it? They don't even tell the people of the planet they're fighting a war? How does that fly?"

"Simple," Cole says. "If they told, there never would have been any Bounders. The people approved breeding kids for space exploration, not for battle."

"Maybe that's true," I say, "but there's still a lot we don't know."

"And a lot we're not going to know," Cole says. "Let's face it. They're not giving us these answers in the next two days. I read everything I could about Earth Force, and there wasn't a hint of this. Someone's gone to great lengths to keep it secret."

"You're right about that, Wiki," Marco says.

We're quiet. Marco plays with the lava lamps. I run my fingers through the shag carpet.

"Let's make a pact," Lucy says. "We don't have all the answers, and we don't have many choices, but let's enjoy the next two days as a pod. Enjoy the field trip to the Paleo Planet. Enjoy being kids. Who knows how much longer we have to do that?"

Marco, Cole, and I nod our agreement.

Mira slips her hands into her gloves. She tips her fingers toward the starry ceiling and fills the air above us with a thousand lights that blink in an intricate pattern. Lucy pulls on her gloves and adds to Mira's picture. The rest of us follow. A million lights twinkle beneath the ceiling stars of our pod room.

Mira flutters her gloved fingers, and a soft sound like the tinkling of piano keys fills the air. I don't know where the sound is coming from, but I know enough not to ask.

Then Mira rises and dances in the starlight. One by one, we join her.

· E_F ·

As I set my tablet down next to Marco and Cole, I wonder which famous poster-worthy aeronaut will lead our last lecture.

A ripple of whispers makes its way from the rear of the hall. Marco jabs me in the ribs and points. A Tunneler walks down the aisle. When he reaches the podium, he steps onto a stool and plugs his voice-translation box into the projection system.

Grunts and clicks and stutters blast through the speakers. Then the voice box translates: "Good afternoon, cadets. It's a real honor to speak with you today. My name is Boreeken— Bo, for short. I'm from the planet Gulaga, or P37, as you usually say. The admiral asked me to talk about my home planet and also about the one I just visited, the Paleo Planet. Is everyone excited for the end-of-tour field trip tomorrow?"

All the cadets clap. I can't believe tomorrow we'll be on the Paleo Planet.

"As most of you know," Bo continues through the translator, "the climate on Gulaga is much colder and less hospitable than on your Earth. That's why we spend most of our lives underground. Our towns and infrastructure are all subterranean. The only common surface endeavors are agriculture and transport."

Bo explains his planet's geography and his civilization's history. He talks about the advanced mining technology the Tunnelers developed after generations of living underground. I try hard to focus. No matter how awesome I am with the gloves, paying attention still isn't my thing. And I definitely want to hear what Bo has to say, especially when he starts talking about first contact.

"You Earthlings were searching for veins of occludium in our planetary system," he says. "When we first spotted your ships in the starlit sky, all the Gulagans came above ground. It was the first time our species had been on the surface in those numbers in our recorded history. We didn't know what was happening. Strange beings appearing in the sky? Many believed it was the day of judgment. That the gods had arrived."

MONICA TESLER

Bo skips over the early years of Earth relations and the details of the diplomatic envoy. He jumps right to the end: Gulaga signed a treaty with Earth to let us extract occludium in exchange for a technology transfer. They gave us occludium and showed us how to mine it. We gave them technology, including quantum space travel.

"The Paleo Planet was also discovered during one of your ore searches," Bo says. "Yes, the planet contains rich stores of occludium, but I think the biggest draw for you Earthlings is the Paleo Planet's close resemblance to your planet in its infant stage."

That's true. Paleo Planet is the name Earth Force dreamed up for P63 to promote the tourism initiative that's slotted to begin later this year. With all the pics and vids on the webs of the green valleys and dense forests and sparkling blue lakes, everyone I know is dying to go there. I can't count how many times I've watched the vids of the wildeboars and the saber cats and the giant hairy beasts that look just like woolly mammoths. The only reason the Tunnelers are linked to the Paleo Planet is because their species run the occludium mines.

When Bo wraps up his speech, the lecture hall bubbles with excitement. We're leaving for the Paleo Planet tomorrow morning, and we can't wait!

THE HANGAR DOORS RETRACT AS THE
captain initiates the countdown. My stomach lurches. Something about seeing the vast expanse of open space makes me queasy.

We left breakfast early to be first in line for seats. Our pod scored the front row, which, according to Cole, is the best spot for the Paleo Planet approach. But right about now, it's also the best spot for nausea, at least for me.

Cole taps me on the shoulder. "Check it out." He points to the edge of the hangar doors, where rows of gunmen stand at the ready.

"More than when we arrived," I say.

"You guys weren't kidding about the security," Marco says. "I can't believe I missed it before."

"There's more," Cole says. "Look!" He points out the hangar door. Ships like the one we spied near the cellblock hover on either edge of the hangar, and a half dozen more are visible a mile out. I bet they're going to escort us to the Paleo Planet.

"They need those gunners," I say. "They're transporting precious cargo. All their trained free-bounders are here in this craft. We were born to be the front line in their alien war, so they better keep us safe."

"Shhh!" Lucy swats her hand at us. "Can we give it a rest? All I've thought about since we left the Ezone two nights ago is you-know-what, and I need a break. We made a pact, remember? Can't we talk about the Paleo Planet and all the amazing things we're going to see there, like the saber cats and the wildeboars and maybe even an amphidile? And all the flora and fauna. And the Tunnelers, of course. Maybe they'll even give us a tour of the occludium mines, and—"

"Why did I agree to sit next to you?" Marco asks. "Do you plan to talk the whole flight?"

"Yes, if it makes you stop talking about the other stuff."

"I'll shut up if you will. Deal?"

"Oh, fine, I guess," Lucy says. "I'll go find Meggi and Annette once we're allowed to move around." She pulls purple ribbons from her pack and twists them through her hair.

Marco and Cole take out their tablets. I lean back on the headrest and close my eyes.

Lucy has a point. We all need a mental break. Maybe we'll actually have fun on the field trip. We've been psyched to go to the Paleo Planet for months. The trip was announced long before we departed for the space station.

Mira sits next to me. The others will forget she's even here, but I never can. It's like we're connected by an invisible tether. Sometimes it stretches, and Mira is little more than a dull touch at the edge of my mind. Other times the tether yanks, and Mira is right on top of me, filling my brain.

I peek over at her and quickly turn away. I don't know what I'm nervous about. It's not like she'd notice if I looked at her, and I doubt Regis would catch me. Still, my chest feels like a full glass of water, like I have to sit up really straight so the water won't slop over the side. I glance again. Her long fingers lie in her lap. Her nails are cut short, and her skin is pink. I know if I grasp her hand, it'll be cold. Her thick braid hangs over her left shoulder. Gold flyaway hairs fall around her face like a wreath. A breeze would lift them, but in the air-controlled ship, they're still. Mira is still, her eyes clouded over like usual.

I wish Mira would talk. I don't expect her to, of course, but she knows more than anyone about the alien. She has to. She communicated with him. The others laughed it off when I told them, but it's true.

I press my fingers to my forehead and concentrate. *Mira, can you hear me?* I picture an open door and will Mira to walk through it. *Mira? Answer me. Mira?* It's no use. I'm basically having a conversation with myself.

Which is pretty boring. And ridiculously pathetic.

· *EF* ·

"Cadets, this is your captain. We are disengaging FTL. Once we stabilize gravity, take a look out the front. The Paleo Planet will be in full view."

I must have fallen asleep, because the last thing I remember was trying to get Mira to respond to my lame attempts at ESP. Cool, Jasper. Real cool.

The ship jerks out of FTL. My body lifts and pulls against the restraint. A bunch of cadets burst out laughing. A few rows behind us, Hakim floats up and over the seats. Guess he forgot to fasten his harness. Busted. Maybe he'll have to sit out the field trip.

The ship glides forward, and soon the whole front windows are filled with the image of an enormous planet. The Paleo Planet.

"Whoa," Marco says, "that thing is massive."

The planet is veiled in a shimmery light so it seems like we're looking through gauze.

"What is that haze?" Lucy asks. "Could there be clouds up this high? Are we already in the atmosphere?"

"No," Cole says.

We look at him, hoping he'll elaborate. But in classic Cole fashion, he doesn't.

"Come on, man." Marco shakes his head and turns back to the window. "Wait . . ."

The gauze is gone.

"What happened? Did we pass through it?" Marco asks.

"They lowered the shields," Cole says.

"Seriously?" I ask. "The entire planet is shielded?"

Cole nods. "Occludium shields. They're probably tethered to a standard force field they deactivated for us to pass through. I bet they have them on Earth, too. They probably kept them lowered until we shifted to FTL the day we left the planet."

"Yeah, and we had no clue we needed them then," Marco says.

"Wait, wait, wait a second," Lucy says. "Let me remind you again. Today we are supposed to be free from all talk about you-know-what."

"I guess this is just reality, Lucy," I say. "Gunner ships, occludium shields . . . Welcome to the world beyond the secrets."

"Maybe the secrets weren't so bad after all," she says.

"Listen up, Scaredy-Cats," Marco says. "Things are the way they are, okay? And while you guys are busy debating what we do or don't know, I'm looking at that." He points out the window.

The Paleo Planet is now on clear display. Cobalt blue oceans merge into lush land formations. Swirls of white are dissected by peeks of mountain ranges. Bits of brown and black and silver blend into the vibrant hues.

"It's incredible," I say, "it looks just like the old pictures of Earth."

"Yeah," Marco says. "Earth with a lot more green."

The ship shakes as we enter the atmosphere. When we fall below the cloud line, the landscape comes into view.

Mira takes my hand. She stares out the window, smiling.

"It's so gorgeous," Lucy whispers.

High mountains rise at near ninety-degree angles from the land, and waterfalls a kilometer high cascade off cliffs. Trees the size of skyscrapers burst with a thousand colors of flowers. Wide lakes with lines of whitecaps stretch between the peaks like an open mouth between jagged rows of teeth. We clear the range, and a vast valley spreads beneath us. As we descend, someone yells, "Look! Animals!"

Sure enough, a herd of wildeboars grazes in the valley. Cole points toward the range. Hairy beasts that look like woolly mammoths munch leaves at the tree line.

"Those things are huge," Marco says. "I wouldn't want to get in their way."

The ship flies low over the grass and flushes up a flock of fuchsia birds. There are thousands of them, tens of thousands. They lift off the plain and break into an intricate formation to avoid our craft, then merge together again on the other side.

A lone saber cat chases the flock. He dashes after the birds at blinding speed. When he reaches a wide brook, he leaps and splays his legs to the side, gliding across the gap on his furred flaps of skin.

"A winged cat!" Lucy says. "I never thought we'd actually see one!"

Florine emerges from somewhere and morphs into a tour guide. She names the animals and plants we pass and points out landmarks. "And over this next range we'll see the mines."

We clear the line of spiky peaks and dive back down. At the edge of the range, a cluster of metal buildings hugs the ground. They are wide and flat with odd angled sides. From above, they look like honeycomb.

The buildings surround a stretch of pavement buzzing with Tunnelers. Metal tubes lead from the pavement into the ground, heading in the direction of the range. Every few moments a strange treaded vehicle, the shape of an egg, emerges from one of the tunnels. The exiting vehicles steer to a conveyer belt that lifts the egg from its treads, cracks it open, and empties its contents onto the belt. The egg is returned to its treads, and a Tunneler pilots the empty egg to an inbound tube.

Our craft sets down on a landing strip adjacent to the mining operations. Dozens of Tunnelers line up to greet us. They're all bunched together, hairy and stooped. Six weeks ago I'd never seen a single Tunneler, and here I am staring at fifty of them.

"It's strange, right?" Lucy says. "Cool, but strange."

"There's just so many of them," I say.

"This must be what it feels like to be an Earthling on their planet," she says. "We're the ones who don't fit."

"They don't fit here either," Cole says. "This isn't their planet. We brought them here to mine, remember?"

Marco laughs. "Are we going to talk? Or are we going to explore? Let's go." He leads the way as we push to the front of the boarding ramp.

As soon as I step off the craft, I'm blinded. I have to squint just to see where to put my feet. The star that warms the Paleo Planet's system is both closer and weaker than Earth's sun. It creates basically the same conditions for life, but it's a bit brighter. The Tunnelers must hate it. Even Earth is too bright for them.

At the end of the boarding ramp, two Tunnelers hand out sunglasses from large bins.

Kleek. Kleek. Argakreek.

"For your comfort and protection."

They repeat it over and over, resulting in a hysterical mash-up of grunts and mechanical voice-overs.

Marco slips on the glasses and stoops over. "For your comfort and protection," he says in a robotic voice.

Lucy slaps him. "Cut it out. I thought you were more sensitive."

"Come on!" he says. "It's funny."

I'll tell you what's funny—how ridiculous we look in the glasses. They were obviously not made for kids. They look like giant bug eyes, particularly on Cole and Lucy. They're only partially shaded, so you can still see our eyes.

"Looking good," I say to Cole.

"They're not for fashion, Jasper. They're protective eyewear."

"Right," I say. "Comfort and protection."

"Please," Lucy says. "Let's go."

We join the rest of the group and head for the center of the pavement, where the largest crowd of Tunnelers is gathered.

"Welcome, visitors," one of the Tunnelers says through his translator box when we're all assembled. "My name is Norideek, and I am Chief Engineer of Earth Force Industries Occludium Mines at Paleo Planet. We have a very special tour planned for you. But first let us show you around the

308   MONICA TESLER

mines. Please break into small groups and proceed with one of our fine guides." He gestures to a row of Tunnelers standing behind him.

We match up with our pod leaders—it's weird to see Waters outside the space station—and then meet our tour guides. Our Tunneler guide introduces herself as Charkeera and leads us to the egg-cracking conveyer belt I saw from the craft.

Arrrgh. Arrrgh. Awwwk. Kleek.

"Most Earthlings don't know this," she says, "but occludium stays in liquid form throughout the mining process. These specially designed transport vehicles keep the occludium at the ideal temperature and allow it to flow feely in the rounded container until it's processed for transport."

The egg-shaped vehicles are sleek and seamless. I can't even spot the hinge where they separate to unload until the crane lifts and tips one of the eggs. The coolest thing about them, though, is the steering compartment in front. There's only enough room for the Tunneler driver. In other words, they're kid-size. Not many grown-ups would fit inside an eggmobile.

"Any chance we can take one for a spin?" Marco asks, taking a step toward a vacant transport.

"Did you bring your driver's license?" Charkeera asks.

"Ummm . . . ," Marco says.

Klarrr. Klarrr. Klarrr.

"Ha! Ha! Ha!"

Tunneler, one. Marco, zero.

"These transports are for mining purposes only," Charkeera continues. "They require special training."

Waters inserts himself between Marco and the egg. He knows Marco's impulsive streak all too well.

Charkeera keeps talking about the mining process, the tunnel systems, and the shipping of occludium off the planet, but I'm barely listening. I tip my head and warm my cheeks. I don't stare directly at the star, but I peek at its corners, mesmerized by the enormous disk in the sky, three times as large to the eye as our Earth sun. It bathes the Paleo Planet in golden light.

Cool damp air rolls off the range that looms over the mines. The peaks are high and steep. You could fall right off if you weren't careful. Once the monster sun crosses the horizon, the entire mine will be swallowed in the shadow of the mountain.

After being cooped up at the space station, everything seems so fresh. I inhale the scent of flowers and loam and . . . something metallic?

"What's that odd smell?" I whisper to Cole.

"The occludium," Cole says.

Charkeera must have heard us, because she shuffles in our direction and grunts. "The occludium has a much stronger odor here at the mining site where we're scraping the ore, but it will retain a faint metallic smell even when processed."

Cole asks follow-up questions about mining technique and ore composition I don't begin to understand. From the confused look on Marco's face, neither does he.

After a few more questions, mostly from Cole, Charkeera leads us to our next stop. When we've finished our tour of the mines, we head back to the landing strip, where most of the other Bounders are already waiting. A line of open-air hovercrafts is stationed at the far end of the strip. Tunnelers are hustling from a nearby building carrying bags and rolling barrels to load onto the hovers.

"I see they've packed lunch," Waters says.

"What's in the barrels?" Lucy asks.

"Pomagranana Punch," Charkeera says. "It's manufactured here on the planet from a native tree. They're planning to sell it on Earth to generate buzz for planet tourism."

"I've tried the punch," Waters says. "Delicious. But don't drink too much. It causes flatulence."

"Flatulence?" I ask.

"Gas," Cole says.

"Oh." I laugh. "Well, then let's slip Marco a second cup when he's not looking."

"Ha-ha, Jasper the Joker." Marco nods at the hovers. "Those don't look like punch." Now the Tunnelers' arms are loaded with metal machinery, and they have guns strapped across their backs.

"Indeed not." Waters's lips pinch in a weird blend of curiosity and concern.

A whiff of roses brings a two-second warning Florine is approaching.

"Good after*noooon*," she says in her signature, drag-out-the-vowel way. "Who is excited for the tour of the Paleo Planet? I know I am. This is the official kickoff of the tourism initiative. And because it's such a special day, I'll let you keep those ribbons in your hair, Lucy, dear. Just this once."

"What a snoot," Lucy whispers as Florine leaves to speak with an aeronaut. Once Florine started holding on to Lucy's ribbons for safekeeping—and never returning them—Lucy's fondness quickly evaporated. Of course, she still mines her for gossip.

"Why the cameras?" Marco asks. Tunnelers load video equipment and position a camera in front of the hovers.

"Oh my goodness!" Lucy shouts. "They're filming for EFAN! We're going to be on the webs!"

"Really?" So Florine got her wish. I knew I'd eventually make EFAN as part of Earth Force, but with the communication ban, not to mention all the top-secret info floating around, I figured Florine wouldn't pull enough strings to make it happen during our tour.

Florine speaks with the Tunneler manning the camera and then steps to the front. At the cameraman's signal, she flashes her teeth and spreads her arms wide. "Bounders, Tunnelers, esteemed officers of Earth Force, welcome to the Paleo Planet." She waves her right hand in a flourish. "With great pleasure I invite you to board the hovercrafts as we prepare to commence our inaugural tour. Please, proceed this way."

22

A TUNNELER WITH A TABLET STEPS FOR-ward and directs us to our assigned hovers—two pods per hover, plus two Tunnelers, one to drive and one to film. Charkeera is assigned as our driver. And, lucky us, we're paired with Maximilian Sheek's pod.

Our hover looks like a cross between a yacht and an old-fashioned school bus with its top cut off. We climb up and score spots at the bow. Ryan sits with Marco, Cole, and me. Lucy hangs back with Meggi and Annette. Mira positions herself at the very helm of the hover.

Sheek is dressed like he's going to a movie premiere—black

shirt, silver jacket, mirrored sunglasses, bouffant hair. I wonder if his windblown style will actually survive being windblown.

He boards last, of course. First he shakes hands with all the Tunnelers, making sure the camera is following his every move. Next he saunters over to the boarding steps, stops to pose with a hand on the bow, and then hoists himself up in a ridiculous yet graceful leap.

"Jon Waters," Sheek says once aboard, staring down at our pod leader.

Waters nods. "Max."

"It's Sheek."

Waters doesn't respond, which leads to an uncomfortably long silence. Finally Charkeera revs the engine, and Sheek takes the cue to find a seat with his pod.

We pull away from the mining camp and glide across a flat plain. The grass is yellow-green with saffron shoots sticking up like husks of wheat. Giant crimson flowers flop in the draft of the hovercraft and pop back up when we pass, like they're waving at us.

Even with the special sunglasses, the sky is bright, almost blinding. And the blue is endless. Without any buildings obstructing the view, it's epic.

Mira perches at the front of the hovercraft. The wind pulls the hair from her braid and whips it around. Waters stands beside her. It's his first trip to the Paleo Planet, too, and he looks like he's having as much fun as the rest of us.

"Why haven't you visited before, Boss?" Marco asks Waters.

He shrugs. "I haven't had the time. Gedney and I rotate between the space station and our home labs on Earth. The Force's focus with the Paleo Planet has been mining and tourism. My focus has been . . . elsewhere."

Marco shoots me a knowing stare. Waters's focus has been plotting how to defeat the green guys.

The hovers fly along the edge of the bordering range. I can't believe how angular the landscape is. On one side, plains; on the other side, cliffs.

"Check it out!" Marco says.

Up ahead, the ground looks greener, and the shrubs grow higher. A waterfall plunges from a high peak.

Behind me, Meggi shrieks, "Birds!"

"On both sides!" Lucy says.

I spin around. Some of the fuchsia birds we saw from the ship chase the hovercraft. But they're not alone. Soaring above them are enormous orange things covered in fur with large leathery wings.

"Are those birds, too?" I ask.

"Those are kite bats," Charkeera says, "native to the planet, obviously. They roost in the pomagranana trees."

Soon the kite bats overtake the hover. They dive low, and

we duck. Meggi screams, then Lucy screams, then pretty soon we're all screaming.

"Stay calm," Charkeera says. "They won't attack. They're just getting a closer look."

"Easy for her to say," I whisper to Cole. "She's all fur, too. Who knows if they'll be so friendly to a bunch of humans?"

One of the bats swoops close, and Marco strokes its belly. The bat screeches and soars straight into the air.

"What the heck?" I say. "Are you trying to provoke it?"

"I couldn't help myself," he says. "And by the way, it felt like puppy fur."

"Marco!" Waters says. "Keep your hands off the wildlife."

"Yes, sir."

"What did I tell you about calling me sir?"

"Sorry. I'll try not to touch the wildlife again, Mr. Waters."

Meanwhile, we've closed the gap to the waterfall. The water plummets from a peak higher than my apartment building and cascades to a deep, turquoise pool below. Next to the pool is a vast grove of trees bursting with plump purple fruit and lavender flowers. The trees don't have trunks—just a huge mass of branches that sprout from the ground. They look like the prickly disco lights in our pod room.

The hovers pull to a stop about a hundred meters from the trees. The kite bats soar past us and into the grove.

"We'll be picnicking here," Charkeera says. "Follow your

fellow Earthlings over to that clearing next to the poma-granana grove."

I hop off the hover after Cole and Marco, and then help Mira down behind me. As we make our way to the clearing, kissing noises smack from behind. Geez. Regis can't even give it a rest today.

Marco looks at me and raises his eyebrows.

Ignore them, I mouth, taking Mira's hand. So there, Regis. See how much I care.

Marco spins around, now walking backward toward the clearing. I should have known the silent treatment was not in his repertoire.

"Hey, Regis," he says. "Do you have any idea what's in those barrels?"

Back at the hovers, the Tunnelers are unloading the kegs of pomagranana juice.

"Is this a quiz?" Regis says. "Or are you just making con-versation so you don't have to talk with the king and queen of freaks?"

"It's pomagranana juice," Marco says. "Florine said it has an immediate effect on your muscles. It wears off, but it temporarily makes you twice as strong. How about we drink some and have an arm-wrestling match? Settle this beef with our pods once and for all?"

"I'm not settling anything with you losers."

"Suit yourself."

We stop and let Regis and his buddies pass us.

"That's not true," Cole says.

"Of course not," Marco says. "But it's true it gives you gas. So those clowns are in for a real surprise."

"Yeah, and we're in for a stinky ride back to the space station," I say.

"Victory will never smell so good, or bad, if you know what I mean."

We settle on blankets next to the pomagranana grove. The kite bats nest deep in the branches. The trees have that sweet, pungent smell berries get right before they rot. The fruit is bigger than my head, kind of like giant eggplants, but with spiky skin.

The Tunnelers pass out sandwiches, which are more like flat crackers spread with gray goop that looks gross but is actually delicious. It tastes earthy with hints of walnut and maple. Charkeera explains that the spread is made from groundnuts found on the planet. They also serve up carrots and cucumber slices grown in a hydroponic farm near the mines. Finally we each get a cup of pomagranana juice.

The juice is purple and smells kind of like raspberry lemonade.

"What are you waiting for, Ace?" Marco asks. "This stuff is delicious."

I sip the juice. My mouth puckers at the extreme tartness.

I'm not sure I can swallow. But the tartness is quickly replaced by sweetness, like sour candy with a red licorice aftertaste.

"Yum! Can we have seconds?"

"Careful, Jasper," Lucy says. "Remember what Mr. Waters said." She whispers to Meggi and Annette, presumably about the gas.

I wouldn't want to stink everyone out on the way home. One cup is enough.

"It looks like someone didn't get the memo." Lucy points at Regis, Randall, and Hakim, who are sneaking refills from the pomagranana keg. The girls burst out laughing.

"You can thank *me* for that," Marco says.

"Oh, Marco," Lucy says, "always the prankster."

Meggi turns almost as purple as the pomagrananas. Is she ever going to get over the tofu strings?

"Cadets!" Edgar Han crosses to the center of our group.

We all stand. "Yes, sir!"

"At ease," he says, "no need for formality. You've worked hard this tour, and now it's time for recreation. We thought it would be fun for you to try out your blast packs by flying around the waterfall."

Ummm, yes please!

I throw on my pack and dash for the cliff. As I run, I slip on my gloves and unzip my grips. A squeeze of my hands, and I lift off.

"Jasper! Wait!" Cole shouts.

I ease up just a bit, letting him close in. A grin the size of a pomagranana stretches across his face. Instead of stopping, he flies right past.

"Beat you!" he shouts.

No fair! I chase Cole. We fly close to the waterfall, and the spray spritzes my face.

Cole shoots straight up, tracking the trajectory of the falls. "This way!" He crosses in front and ducks out of sight.

I follow him to the other side, but he's nowhere to be seen. Did he fall? I squeeze the grips and bring my body to a standstill in the air. As my legs sway, I scan the ground beneath me for Cole.

"Over here!"

I crane my neck but still can't see Cole. Wait a second. . . . Is that him . . . through the waterfall?

I fly forward and curve close to the cliff. Sure enough, Cole is sitting on a small ledge behind the waterfall. I coast in beside him. We have our own private hideaway behind the wall of water.

The light snakes through the falls, flickering in tiny rainbows on our skin. Every few seconds we catch a glimpse of another Bounder flying in front of the water or rising from the ground.

"I didn't think it was possible," Cole says, "but I actually managed to forget about the alien for a minute."

"Me too, until you went and brought him up," I say.

"Want to forget again?" Cole asks. "I'll race you to the ground."

· $\mathcal{EF}$ ·

We load back into the hovers, full from lunch, bloated with pomagranana juice, and exhausted from flying our blast packs. I stretch out, plop my feet on the bench in front of me, and take in the amazing sights of the Paleo Planet. This place will be the ultimate gold mine. They'll pack them in by the thousands. Forget Disney World. They should build an amusement park here. Or a water park with a log ride off one of those awesome waterfalls. I can't believe how lucky I am to come here first. The kids at home will be so jealous. Will Stevens will finally shut up.

That's right, Will. I'm a B-wad. A B-wad who just blew by you in my blast pack.

Our hover leads the others across the vast landscape. Our cameraman pans his lens across the plains. At the controls behind me, Charkeera grunts and clicks. "We're approaching a watering hole. You'll see lots of native animals in this area. Over by the ridgeline, the wildeboars graze. We count their herd as more than a million strong. And don't miss the mammoths. They're slowly making their way to the water."

A thin river snakes across the valley and widens into a basin. Animals are everywhere. Birds covered with a rainbow of feathers bathe and fish in the water. Small rodents with four pairs of legs pop out of holes near the bank. A saber cat limbers over. The other animals give him a wide berth as he bends to drink.

"This is unbelievable!" Ryan says. "Like an intergalactic safari!"

"No kidding," I say. "Get a look at that cat!"

"He's gorgeous," Lucy says. "Check out his muscles. We better not get too close."

"What on earth are those?" Marco asks.

A group of creatures walk in a cluster toward the watering hole. I can't tell for sure, but from this distance they appear to be walking on two feet. I had no idea there were any bipedal animals on the Paleo Planet.

Charkeera makes a loud noise, a bark I've never heard before. She grunts and clicks into her com pin. Her translator box stays silent. She must have turned it off. The Tunneler manning the camera stands and shouts at Charkeera. Shouldn't he be catching this on film?

Sheek pushes past us to the helm of the hover. He lifts a hand to his forehead to cut the glare. "And I thought it was a rumor!" he says. "You are in for a real treat, kids! We've encountered some humanoids!"

Humanoids? As in humanlike aliens? Is he serious? Did we even know there were humanoids on the Paleo Planet? Did I zone out during that part of the lecture? I lean over to Marco. "Did you know there were humanoids?"

Marco shakes his head. I'm about to ask Waters, but stop cold. Something about him makes me shudder. A gray curtain has fallen across his face, and deep lines crease his forehead.

THE HOVER SLOWS. CHARKEERA REACTI·
vates her translator. "We'll stop here for a minute, then return
to the base."

"No, no, no," Sheek says. "Bring us in closer. I am not
going to miss this."

Charkeera speaks privately into her com again. She shifts
her weight from foot to foot, and the pitch of her voice rises
with each grunt. If I had to guess, she seems nervous.

"Take us in for a better look," Sheek says. "That's an order."

Charkeera grimly nods and eases the hover forward.

Up ahead, a cluster of humanoids approaches the riverbank.

They wear hide bags slung across their chests for carrying water. Another group stands together, bending and straightening. They carry woven baskets on their backs.

"What are they doing?" Cole asks.

"Gathering food," Charkeera says. "We believe ground nuts are a staple of their diets."

"Like the ones we had for lunch?" Lucy asks.

Charkeera says yes, and then explains a bit about the humanoids. They used to see them a lot more on the planet, but now they keep to themselves. They live in caves deep in the mountain ranges. As she talks, she extracts her gun from a side storage compartment, straps it across her chest, and disengages the safety.

As our hovercrafts approach, some of the humanoids point at us. Many fall to their knees and drape their arms on the grass.

"What are they doing?" I ask.

"They're bowing," Waters says. His voice is low and laced with something furious. "They must think we're gods."

"Gods?" I gasp and burst out laughing.

Waters glares at me. His face is so clenched, he looks like he might explode. Or punch me in the nose.

I bite my lip to stop from laughing. A memory tickles the edge of my brain. Bo, the Tunneler who led our last lecture, said something similar. When Earth Force arrived in the skies over Gulaga, the Tunnelers all thought we were gods, too.

Our caravan glides forward and parks in a long line of hovers perpendicular to the watering hole.

"We can cover the rest of the ground on foot," Sheek says.

A sputter of high-pitched grunts erupts from Charkeera. "No! That isn't safe! Think of the children! We must stay aboard the hovers!"

"Oh, please." Sheek strides to the edge of the hover and hops off, dropping gracefully to the ground. "A few animals won't hurt us. The kids can fly away in their blast packs if there's a problem. And you have your weapons, of course."

He's already striding toward the humanoids when he calls over his shoulder. "Come on, Bounders. Don't let the saber cat scare you! And bring that EFAN camera along!"

"Let's go!" Edgar Han shouts from his hover. He has his own equipment strapped across his chest—an old-fashioned camera with a huge zoom lens.

Marco hops off next. Lucy grabs my arm as I stand. "Something doesn't seem right, Jasper."

I have the same feeling, but what could go wrong? We have our packs. The Tunnelers have guns. And isn't the whole point of the tourism initiative to get an up-close look at the Paleo Planet and its native animals?

I shrug. "Maybe. But don't you want to check things out?"

Lucy's lips stretch in a thin line. At first I think she's going to sit it out on the hover, but she shakes her head and follows me off.

"Everyone, please proceed this way," Florine says. "This is a very special opportunity! Make sure the film is rolling!" She limps through the grass. High heels weren't meant for this kind of terrain.

We walk as a group toward the watering hole. The eight-legged rodents peek their heads out of their holes, then pop back down as we pass.

"Eek!" Meggi says. "I don't like those things!"

"Oh, come on, they're like meerkats," Marco says. "They're friendly, and I bet they're really soft."

"Marco," Waters says, "*do not* touch the wildlife."

"Yes, Mr. Waters."

The closer we get to the humanoids, the better we can see them. It's like we walked into a time machine. The humanoids look just as I picture early man on Earth. Their skin is dark and covered with coarse brown hair. They're short and kind of hunched like the Tunnelers. A few of the women carry babies on their backs.

"Stay together," Charkeera says.

"Yeah, steer clear of the saber cat," Marco whispers.

Right. Maybe it wasn't the brightest idea to leave the

hovers. I stay near Charkeera and her gun and keep an eye on the cat.

Enormous blue bugs buzz above the grass. One flutters near the humanoid children, and they dash after it. The sound of their laughter drifts in the breeze.

"That's close enough," Waters says, throwing his arm out to block us.

"Quit the worrying, Jon," Sheek says. "We're armed."

"I'm not worried, Max," Waters growls. "And I'm not concerned about *our* safety. I'm saying that's close enough. We shouldn't interfere with them." Waters instructs us to stop, then walks over to the next group of cadets and tells them the same.

Things seem safe enough. The saber cat is stretched out on the riverbank, taking a snooze.

I'm about to plop down on the grass myself when a piercing noise punctures my brain. The sound bullets between my ears and balloons until my entire head rings. I buckle at the waist.

Make it stop! My skull is going to explode!

I crouch on the ground and cover my head, hoping to block out the noise, hoping someone helps. When no one comes, I lift up enough to look around.

The other Bounders are collapsed on the ground, clutching their heads. What on earth is happening?

Waters and the other pod leaders dash about. It doesn't

look like the noise affects them, but they know something's wrong with the Bounders. "What's happening?" Waters yells at Charkeera.

Most of the humanoids by the river seem immune, too. But one of them—a child—covers her ears with her hands.

The noise roars in my brain. Something about it is familiar. Where have I felt this before? The answer is at my grasp, but I can't reach it.

Something smashes the ground a few meters away. A boulder? The air clouds with dust. Another collision. Even closer this time. I've got to get away.

But the noise. It won't stop.

Next to me, Mira straightens. She pulls her gloves from her pocket and fits them onto her hands.

I remember where I've heard this noise.

The alien in the cellblock.

I stand and scan our surroundings. Charkeera swings her gun from her back, points at the nearby ridge, and fires.

My gaze traces her aim up the mountain. At the very top of the ridge there's movement. I shut out the noise as best I can and force my brain to focus.

Oh . . . whoa . . . no.

Five aliens like the one in the cellblock stand atop the ridge. They stretch their arms out by their sides. One of them sweeps his hands through the air, and the next second a giant

MONICA TESLER

ball of light barrels in our direction. It explodes in a blinding burst that radiates heat and ash. When the dust settles, a circle of scorched earth marks the spot of impact.

Marco is beside me. I punch him on the shoulder. "Get your gloves!"

Cole and Lucy are crouched on the ground behind him, covering their ears. I drag them up. "It's the aliens! Quick! Your gloves!" Lucy looks confused, but Cole gets it. He pulls out his gloves and then rips Lucy's from her back pocket.

As I stuff my fingers into my gloves, Waters grabs my wrist. "Jasper, what's going on?"

I don't respond at first. If I tell Waters, it's basically an admission we broke into the cellblock.

I take another step, but Waters tightens his grip around my wrist. "Jasper, I need to know what's happening!"

Most of the cadets still writhe on the ground. They need help. Waters needs to know.

"The aliens!" I shout above the din. "Not the Tunnelers. The other aliens. The ones we're fighting."

His eyes widen, and he releases my arm. "What are you talking about?"

"We saw them on the ridge. This is an attack. On us."

"How do you—"

"There's no time!" I yell. "We need to try to stop them. Get everyone back to the hovers. Go!"

I dash forward. Marco, Cole, and Lucy have their gloves on. They still wince from the brain-invading screech. Mira stands a few meters in front of them, arms raised overhead.

"We've got to get out of here," Marco says.

"No!" I shout. "We need to give the others time to get away."

A giant boulder whizzes by, colliding with the ground just behind us.

"So we can get killed?" Lucy asks.

"I'm not getting killed," Cole says, slipping his handgrips from his blast pack.

"Put those away!" I yell. "If you're flying, you don't have your hands free!"

"Right, we're just sitting ducks for the green guys," Lucy says. "Oh no! They're coming!"

Four of the aliens stand in the valley about eighty meters away. There's no way they could have climbed down that fast. They must have bounded. One alien remains on the ridge, raining boulders and balls of light.

Mira advances, waving her hands. Marco, Cole, and Lucy stand in a cluster, ducking flying boulders and light-balls now aimed at the hovers behind us.

Mira flashes her hands at a boulder, and it stops in midair. She must be wrestling with the alien on the ridge for control of the boulder's atoms.

"Your girlfriend is one of a kind," Marco says.

"Well, right now she's defending us single-handedly, so let's go."

"We need a plan," Marco says. "Five on five is not going to end in our favor."

He's right. Our pod won't be enough. We need to enlist the help of the other Bounders. If anyone can get the word out fast, it's Lucy. Then Cole can outline a defense strategy.

"Lucy, Cole, run back to the other cadets," I say. "Lucy, explain what's happening as quickly as you can! Cole, once Lucy rallies the others, come up with a scaled defense! Pull out your *Evolution* tricks!"

Cole shakes his head. "This isn't a game, Jasper."

"Just do it!"

"Fine," Lucy says. "Come on, Cole!" She grabs his hand and drags him away.

I spin back to Marco.

"What about us?" he says.

I shrug. "Stall them."

Marco holds my stare. I know it's not much to go on, but if anyone knows how to improvise, it's Marco.

He nods, and we instinctively take off in different directions so we flank the four advancing aliens with Mira in the middle. At first I try her strategy—trying to stop the boulders flying through the air—but it's tough. I've never controlled anything as big as a boulder, let alone wrestle with one of the green guys over one.

Distract.

The word appears in my head, and I know it's Mira. I steal a glance in her direction and see she's no longer focused on the boulders and light-balls falling from above. Instead she's throwing whatever she can at the four aliens in the field.

Genius. If the aliens have to deflect our attack—no matter how weak it may be—their hands aren't free to turn on the offense. Or to bound.

I focus on the ground near the aliens' feet and shower them in a cloud of dirt. Mira uproots some bushes behind them and hits the aliens with a sneak attack. Marco catches on and gets creative. He seizes one of the eight-legged rodents from its hole and hurls it at an alien. The rat-faced critter latches on to the green guy's head. He swats and grabs at the little beast, and they both end up on the ground.

Nice one, I mouth to Marco.

Behind me, Cole and Lucy are organizing the others, first by corralling them back to the hovers. By the looks of it, some of the hovers are already damaged.

Our vehicles aren't the only casualties. Han carries a banged-up Bounder over his shoulder. Waters helps a bloody Tunneler onto one of the hovers that's still intact. Two heads pop up from the belly of the next hover. Florine? Sheek? Are they hiding?

Meanwhile, the Tunnelers dodge about, setting up the mysterious machinery we saw them load at the mines. They fit rods together, then stick them into the ground like flagpoles. Once inserted, the tops spring open like metallic umbrellas and silver light cascades down in domes.

Portable occludium shields.

That can only mean one thing. This is not their first encounter with these aliens on the Paleo Planet. No wonder Charkeera was nervous.

Geez. I can't believe they didn't say anything. At least we have the shields. They're not much protection for Marco, Mira, and me, but the rest of the Bounders should be safe from an alien bounding into their space.

The shields also appear to deflect the giant balls of light, but they're useless against the flying boulders. I wince as a huge rock hurtles toward the hovers.

Boom! The boulder explodes, raining rock fragments across the field.

And now we know why the Tunnelers brought their guns.

When I spin back around, there are only two aliens where there used to be four. I still count one at the ridgeline. The others must have bounded.

"Over there!" Marco shouts, pointing at the cluster of humanoids.

In a flash of light Mira bounds, reappearing instantly near

the humanoids. The alien turns to face her as the humanoids dash for the tree line.

I spot the second alien on the other side of the river. It has a clear line to the rest of the Bounders. I grab my straps and zoom toward the group.

"Watch out!" I shout. "Behind you."

I don't slow enough for a proper landing and end up on the ground right by Lucy.

"Graceful," she says.

"Shut up and listen! They're bounding. One of them is advancing from the other side of the river. Tell Cole!"

"Wait! What are you going to do?"

"Bound."

"Jasper, I don't think—"

I tune her out and tap in, mentally gathering the atoms I need to bound. I open my port and—*bam!*—I'm on my feet, sinking into mud on the other side of the riverbank.

The alien is only twenty meters away, but he hasn't spotted me. He's focused on the huge group at the hovers.

Lucy must have gotten the message to Cole. The Bounders circle the perimeter, their backs to the center, their gloves at the ready. Those are smart tactics. This is not a linear engagement. The aliens could bound at any moment. No side is safe.

A wave of water leaps from the river and soaks the alien closest to me. Cole's rolling out the same strategy as Marco,

Mira, and I: keep the alien distracted so he can't launch an offensive. They spray him again, and the green guy backpedals, like he's afraid he's been hit.

Then—*boom!*—a true gunshot.

The alien collapses. Green mucus spurts from his chest.

For a moment I'm back in the space station, gazing down at the med room, watching the alien on the table. Without even thinking, I take a step forward, then another. The alien tips his huge, bulbous head in my direction. His black, bottomless eyes latch on to mine.

He's in my head. It feels familiar, almost like Mira. Almost like Addy.

Leave.

Leave? I don't get it.

Leave.

The air shimmers, and three other aliens are by his side. One waves his arm, and they're shielded inside a dome of light. Another turns to me and lifts his hand. My body is gripped, caught in a suction. The alien is trying to grab my atoms.

"No!" I squeeze my grips and shoot straight into the air, but I can't escape the tugging, now from multiple hands. I have only one choice. I need to bound. But I'm fifty meters high. And directly above the watering hole.

I get one shot at this or I'll be Play-Doh for those aliens.

Once I drop my grips, I'll have seconds to bound. If I don't open my port in time, I'll hit the amphidile-infested waters.

As soon as I drop the grips, gravity steps in. I plummet for the water. Tap in. Sense the atoms. Open the port.

My toes touch the water just as I bound. I land near the ridgeline and take off running in my wet shoes. Mira and Marco are in the middle of the field, trying to hold off the boulders falling from above now that the other aliens are across the river.

"J-Bird, what a relief," Marco says as I skid to a stop beside him. "I was worried you'd been hit."

"Not me," I say. "But a Tunneler took out one of their guys."

"What about the others?" he asks, wildly scanning the surrounding area. "They could be anywhere."

"They bounded to the other side of the river once their guy was shot."

"Is he dead?"

"He was still alive when I last saw him," I say. "But I think he was injured pretty bad."

The remnants of the alien and his message float like a haze in my brain—*Leave.*

A new boulder soars off the ridge.

"Grab that!" Marco says.

I lift my gloves to the monster rock and wrestle with the

alien for control. My energy is nearly drained. There's no way we can keep this up for long. Mira dashes over, and she helps me hold the boulder.

"We've got to make our move while the other aliens are still occupied," I tell them. "Hold him off another minute while I check in with Cole."

I zoom in my blast pack across the field and circle the line of Bounders.

"Get out of the way, Jasper!" Ryan yells as I bend around to the riverside. The Bounders pummel the aliens' shield with everything their gloves can control. The aliens fight back, hurling light-balls at the Bounders. Thank goodness our shields appear to be holding.

"Where's Cole?" I ask.

"At the edge of the river, leading the charge!"

Sure enough, there's Cole. He's shouting directions and waving his arms, coaching the Bounders through the attack.

"What about Lucy?" I ask.

"Last I heard she was shuttling information between the Tunnelers, the aeronauts, and the Bounders. Check the center of the circle."

I step inside the silver light and weave between the wrecked hovers. I finally find Lucy talking urgently with Waters near one of the shield posts.

"Jasper!" She runs over and clasps my hands. "Thank

goodness you're all right. What about Marco? Mira?"

"They're fine, but tired. We can't hold the aliens for much longer. Pretty soon the ones across the river are going to up their attack."

"He's right," Waters says. "Lucy, gather the others. We'll pack into the remaining hovers and retreat. There are better defenses at the mines."

Lucy nods and rushes to find Cole.

"I'll tell Marco and Mira," I say to Waters. "We'll try to stop the boulders. That will give you time to get away."

"We'll come for you. Watch for our hover."

I nod.

Waters grips my shoulder. "And, Jasper . . . thank you."

His eyes are imploring, kind of like the alien's. If I look at him any longer, I might crumble. Instead I spin and fly, dodging through the Bounder offensive and speeding across the field.

By the time I reach them, Marco's face is pale and glazed with sweat. He's exhausted. We have nothing left in us.

"We're falling back," I tell them. "Try to give the others some cover while they load the hovers."

"I can't do it anymore," Marco says. "This guy's too strong. I just have to take him out."

Before I can respond, Marco grabs his pack straps and takes off. He's flying up the cliff face, straight for the alien. Oh no. He's on a kamikaze mission.

"Cover me!" I shout at Mira as I soar after Marco. There's no way he'll be able to take out that alien all by himself.

Marco's above me, flying hard for the summit. Does he even have a plan? Probably not. Marco's more of an act-now-think-later guy. But he's got guts.

He's nearly there. Who knows? Maybe this will actually work.

Then Marco freezes. His body twists at an odd angle. His eyes lock with mine, and I can see his struggle. His fear.

The alien has control of Marco's atoms.

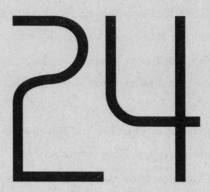

MARCO'S BODY GLIDES IN A WIDE ARC
across the sky. He lands right in the middle of the herd of
mammoths at the watering hole.

"No!" I roar, soaring toward the summit, bracing my brain
for the alien's touch.

I land at the very edge of the cliff. An enormous silver
spaceship is mere paces away. The alien is perched on top,
arms outstretched. Even with my gloves, I am absolutely no
match for this guy.

Leaping onto the spaceship, I tackle him.

As soon as my body touches the alien's damp skin, a wave

of emotion fills me. Surprise . . . confusion . . . anxiety.

These aren't my feelings. They're his. And somehow I have the upper hand. It's like he has no clue how to deal with physical contact.

I slam my fist against his face and knee him in the belly. He struggles beneath me, trying to squirm his way out. Even though he's twice my size, I have the advantage. I press my palms against his wet warm skin and pin his green head to the metal.

Even as I pound him, the connection between us intensifies. We're linking in some way, like Mira and me in the Ezone. My heart beats in sync with his. Our emotions start to blend.

And again I hear the word.

Leave.

No! I will not listen to this guy. This guy who spent the last twenty minutes attacking my friends. This guy who just tossed Marco, probably to his death.

Leave.

"No!" I shout at him. "You leave!"

He vanishes.

Oh no. I didn't mean it that way. He must have bounded. I push myself up and look around. No alien. I stand and scan the area. No aliens across the river or in the valley. No aliens anywhere.

The ground quakes, knocking me off balance.

Wait a second. I'm not standing on the ground.

I'm on a spaceship. And it's lifting.

Oh no. I've got to get out of here.

The ship pitches forward, and I land on my belly. I scramble to the edge and grab on as we glide forward off the cliff.

This was definitely not part of the plan. My throat feels like one of those nasty tofu dogs is lodged inside. There's not enough room to breathe.

The valley spreads beneath me as the ship flies higher.

Think, Jasper. How are you going to get off this ship?

I'll have to bound.

I tap in and begin to gather my atoms.

And then suddenly I can't. I'm blocked. The ship begins to spin. Slowly at first, then faster.

Oh no. They've lifted the shields. They're preparing to bound, which means I can't bound out.

What on earth am I going to do? Even if I survive their bound by clinging to the edge of this ship, who knows where I'll end up? I could be clear across the galaxy with these aliens!

In the fields below, some of the hovers are speeding away. They look like toys from this high up.

I suppose I could jump. I still have my pack, but it's a long way down.

What would Marco do?

I push to stand, squeeze my grips, and run full speed off the edge.

The whirling vortex beneath the ship grabs me and swirls me around. No matter how hard I direct my intention, the force of the motor in my blast pack is no match for the downward spiral of air. And even if I clear the shield, there's no way I can open a quantum port while getting tossed around like this.

The wind stings my skin and pulls at my pack. The ship spins faster every second. At this rate, I'll be torn apart in a matter of moments.

I suck in air but still can't breathe. Maybe the air is too thin this high. No, I'm just panicking. Hyperventilating.

Calm down, Jasper. You can handle this.

The twisting air drills down like the funnel of a tornado. My only shot is to stop fighting and let myself drift along. Hopefully, the spiral's strength will fizzle out as it approaches the ground, and then I can break free. Otherwise, the combination of the spinning air and gravity will bring me to a quick end.

I try to relax and float along with the air current, conserving my energy for the moment I need it. Every few turns I test my pack. I still can't break free.

At least I'm not as high anymore.

The spaceship rises above me—a great disk of spinning

metal both wider and thinner than any ship in the Earth Force fleet.

And then there's me, the enemy soldier falling in its wake.

None of this makes sense. Those aliens have far superior technology. They could have annihilated us.

A single word rings in my mind: *Leave.*

I test my straps. A slight resistance, then a bit more. With all my energy focused on the straps, I force free of the vortex.

Shocked by the sudden switch, I drop several meters before regaining control. The fierce wind fights for my pack. I grit my teeth and push on. The connection with my brain is laser-sharp. Slowly, the animals in the valley grow from miniature to life-size as I continue my descent.

I soar to the field where Mira waits for me. She almost tackles me with the force of her hug. I bury my head in her shoulder. I wish she had some energy to feed into me. But she's just as exhausted as I am.

The spinning vortex of air reaches the ground, clouding the valley with dirt and debris.

Mira and I stand hand in hand and gaze up at the enormous spaceship. The ship blocks the starlight, and the sky is dark with dust. Even though it's afternoon, it feels like twilight.

The ship begins to change. The wide silver circle collapses and folds, shrinking in diameter as it spins, until it is no bigger than one of our own quantum ships. A silver ball in the sky. It's there. And then it's gone.

They bounded. And with their departure, the starlight returns.

Maybe this is over. A glimmer of hope sneaks into my chest. I squeeze Mira's hand, and she squeezes back. We walk toward the remaining hovers, where they're loading the wounded for transport back to the mines.

Then a strange sound fills the valley, and the ground begins to shake. Up ahead, a rolling cloud filled with strange forms tumbles across the land, heading right toward us and the hovers.

The wildeboars. They're charging. All one million of them.

The spaceship must have agitated the herd and incited a stampede. The hovers are in their course. They'll be trampled! I bolt in that direction, but there's not enough time to get the others to safety. The herd will be upon them in seconds.

A sound trickles into my brain. I cringe, bracing for the return of the aliens' high-pitched wail, but this sound is different. An achingly familiar, melancholy note merges with the next note and the next until the entire valley is filled with the most penetrating music I've ever heard.

Mira's hands are raised in the air. She moves her fingers in a pattern that resonates with rhythm and reason. Her chin is lifted to the rays of starlight. Wisps of loose hair crown her head in a halo.

The sounds are emanating from Mira. From her gloves. She's playing music, just like she did in our pod room.

Her face is strained, pulled, as her music grows more complex, the harmonies more sophisticated. We're back in the music room, her delicate body swaying and bending with the emotion of the notes. My heart aches from the sound. I feel like weeping and jumping for joy at the same time. And it's working. The wildeboars come in their cloud of dust, but they're disoriented and sluggish. The music is affecting them, too.

But it's not working fast enough. The wildeboars are still closing the gap to the hovers faster than the Bounders can escape. It isn't any use. There just isn't enough time.

Then I feel her. Mira. Inside my brain.

Play!

Of course. As Mira's music moves through me, I let my own notes rise up and force them through my fingertips. Our music rises together and fills the Paleo Planet.

The wildeboars come, but slower still. New sounds join our chorus. Some of the cadets must have tapped into our song.

I chance a glance back. Most of the hovers have left. A few load their last passengers. And one waits. For us. Waters stands at the helm and waves his arms.

The wildeboars have slowed enough. If we use our packs,

we'll make it before the stampede overtakes us. "Fly for the hovers!" I yell.

I let my notes drop off and pull Mira's hand. "We've done it! Let's go!"

She won't open her eyes. Her music swells again, but her notes are strained. She's so tired. I can't leave her.

Still the herd comes. I peek back at the hovers. All but one have left. And the one that's still here is gliding forward. They're coming for us.

The wildeboars are closing the gap. "Mira, we need to go! Now!"

The hover is nearly here. And so are the wildeboars. I wrap my arms around Mira. I hope I'm strong enough to throw her aboard. The dust cloud reaches us.

And then Mira vanishes. And the music stops.

And all is quiet except the sound of thundering hooves.

"Mira!" I yell.

Waters grabs my arms and yanks me onto the bow of the hover.

"Mira!" My screams scrape against my throat. Waters holds me in a vise grip, but I pull against him. "Mira!"

"She's gone, Jasper," Waters says.

"Nooo!" I can't believe it. She was in my arms seconds before. And I failed. She died for us. All I had to do was pull her onto the hover, and I failed.

I surge again, nearly dragging Waters off the bow with me. Beneath us, the wildeboars pass. Fast. Without the music, there's nothing to subdue them.

"Stop!" Lucy slaps my face. "Snap out of it, Jasper. She bounded, okay? She's not here."

She bounded? I had Mira in my arms, and then she was gone. Could that be it? Could she have gotten away?

Cole grabs my legs and helps Waters haul me into the belly of the hover. I collapse onto the seat next to Lucy.

Waters yells something at the Tunneler, and the hover speeds for the mines.

"You're sure about Mira?"

"Absolutely," Lucy says, squeezing my hand.

I shake uncontrollably. I've never been so exhausted. "What about Marco?"

"He's in bad shape," she says, "but he's alive. Waters sent him back to the mines." She takes my other hand. "We're safe now."

"Safe?" I say. "We're not safe. The aliens may still be out there."

"We heard the report from the base," Cole says. "There is no longer any trace of the aliens in this star system, and they were preparing to raise the shields."

Waters crouches before us. "You kids have some explaining to do, but there's no time now. I promise you, as soon as we get to the mines, you're loading onto the craft and leaving the planet. I have a responsibility to keep you safe." Waters runs a dirty hand through his hair. "Where is Mira?"

No one responds.

"Look, I saw her bound. I need to know where she went."

Still no one responds.

"Now!" Waters shouts.

"We don't know," Lucy says.

"Jasper, think!" Waters says. "Where did Mira go?"

There's only one place she would have bounded, even though it's a galaxy away. "The Ezone."

· EF ·

Waters kept his word. As soon as we reached the mines, they loaded us onto the passenger craft to return to the space station. When Tunnelers wheeled Marco in on a stretcher, I tried to talk to him, but Malaina Suarez waved me back. She directed him into a side room with some other cadets who were injured in the attack.

I join Cole in the back row of the craft and collapse onto the seat next to him. I'm not sure where Lucy is, but I'm too tired to find her anyway. I don't have the energy to talk or even listen to her talk to me.

Once we clear the atmosphere, I flip around in my chair. The Paleo Planet looks just like Earth must have looked millions of years ago. More green. More green because we haven't built any cities or blasted through any mountains or decimated any forests. More green because the temperature is lower and photosynthesis is working and the ground hasn't been peeled back to reach its ore. Or actually, I'm forgetting the occludium mines. I guess that is starting to happen on the Paleo Planet, too.

As we make the shift to FTL, I remember how Earth looked when we took off for the space station. All my nerves about the EarthBound Academy were momentarily replaced with a pure sense of awe at the majesty of our planet. I feel none of that awe gazing down at the Paleo Planet. It is many things: a mine, a future tourist destination, a target for an alien enemy. But nothing that inspires awe. It occurs to me then. When the aliens see Earth, they don't see something awe-inspiring. In fact, with the clutter and waste and ruin, I shudder at what it might look like through their lenses.

The flight back seems to take twice as long, not to mention the craft smells awful. Who thought it was a good idea to trick Regis and his loser friends into drinking tons of pomagranana juice? When we finally glide past the gunmen and coast into the hangar, Gedney and Mira are there to greet us. The knot in my chest unties when I see Mira. Waters had confirmed she'd made it to the Ezone, but I'm happy to see her with my own eyes.

The other cadets head for the dormitories, but I'm too

worried about Marco to sleep. I'm sure Ridders will bust me for skipping out on head count, but I don't care. I head to the med room viewing balcony that Marco and I found on our first night. I sit in the second row and rest my head and hands on the back of the chair in front of me.

In the med room below, Marco lies on a bed in the corner. His head is wrapped in a big bandage, and one of his legs is suspended in a harness. The Tunneler who treated me when I was in the med room checks his vitals. Marco isn't the only patient. The room is filled with cadets injured in the battle.

So this is what happens in war. There are injuries. There are casualties. And in our case, there are kids who are casualties.

I am so not ready for this.

Tomorrow is the last day of the Bounders' first tour of duty. After the closing ceremony, we're leaving the space station. Earth might be scarred, but it's home. And I desperately need to be home.

Maybe Mom will make chocolate chip cookies.

"Jasper." A quiet voice interrupts my food fantasy.

Waters stands in the aisle. His face is flushed, and his hair sticks up at funny angles. He looks more like Gedney than Gedney does sometimes.

"How's he doing?" Waters nods at the glass. Below, the Tunneler hooks Marco up to an IV.

"I'm not sure," I say. "He looks pretty banged up."

Waters slips into the chair beside me and takes a deep breath. The signs are clear. We're headed for a serious talk. I'll probably have to fess up to the whole mess with the alien in the cellblock. I can't muster the energy to be nervous. So much has happened since then.

"Gedney says this is where you first spotted our prisoner," he says.

I can't tell if he's mad or not, so I just nod.

"Relax, Jasper. You're not in trouble. On the contrary, we owe an awful lot to you. You probably saved the lives of all the cadets today. You probably saved my life."

I don't really deserve the credit. Everyone pitched in. "Marco held off the aliens, and Cole and Lucy coordinated with the other Bounders. Mira slowed the wildeboars so the others could escape. If it wasn't for her, we would have been trampled."

"Don't sell yourself short. Mira is special. But you're special, too. She relies on you. And so do the others. Mira alone is nothing compared to Mira and you together. When the whole pod is involved, you kids really are limitless."

I shrug. Maybe Waters is right. The others do rely on me. But I'm a floundering mess where Mira is concerned.

"Mira *is* special," I say. "She communicated with the alien prisoner—you know, brain to brain."

354

Waters runs his fingers through his hair, leaving even more of it sticking up. "Oh, kid, I don't want to know that."

He drops his head. A long moment passes.

"Back up," he says, lifting his eyes to mine. "I really didn't mean that. You should tell me that kind of stuff, Jasper. You *need* to tell me. And you can talk to Gedney. But I don't want you to tell anyone else. That information is very dangerous in the wrong hands."

"So I guess I shouldn't tell anyone that I communicated with the aliens, too."

Waters's eyes open wide. "You did?"

"Yep, on the Paleo Planet, although they didn't make any sense. All they said was 'leave.'"

At first Waters looks confused, then a strange realization crosses his face, and he shakes his head. "That might make more sense than you think. I bet they're not very happy we're mining on the Paleo Planet and disturbing the native human-oids."

"But I thought they attacked the humanoids."

"No," Waters says. "In fact, the whole battle might have been about protecting the humanoids from us."

"Is that why the Tunnelers were so anxious when Sheek made us go in for a closer look at the humanoids? Had the aliens attacked before?"

Waters shrugs. "I'm not sure. The information hasn't all

come out yet. But it seems clear it wasn't the first time the Youli visited the Paleo Planet."

"The who-lee?"

"The Youli. That's what the aliens are called."

The Youli: green bipedal aliens with huge pulsating heads who can penetrate your brain. The prisoner in the cellblock. The guy I tackled on top of the spaceship. The aliens with the advanced technology. Our enemies.

The Youli.

"Can I ask you something?" I say to Waters.

"Of course."

"Why didn't the Youli just kill us? I mean, they must be able to, right?"

Waters stands and crosses to the window with the one-way glass. "There's a lot about the Youli you don't know and I can't share. Let's just say the battle lines are a bit blurred."

Great. More secrets.

We stay silent for a while. In the med room below, a doctor checks on Marco, running scans and inserting medication into his IV line.

"What do you think we should do about the closing ceremony tomorrow?" Waters asks, returning to his chair. "As first-place pod, you're supposed to free-bound in front of the entire Academy, but Marco clearly won't be up to it."

"I think we should wait," I say. "Hopefully, he'll be better when we're back this fall for our next tour."

"Sounds like the right choice. And anyhow, Gedney mentioned something about the winning pod taking the first freebound before we even left for the Paleo Planet." Waters's smile tells me we're not in trouble for breaking into the cellblock.

"I wish things were different, Jasper," he continues. "You kids shouldn't have to bear this burden. And it's only going to get worse. When you return for your next tour of duty, the situation will have escalated. And your responsibilities will be greater. I'm glad this tour is ending. You need a break. We all need a break."

I'm only half listening. My mind has leaped ahead. I'm on the launch platform, running to hug Mom and Dad, finally seeing Addy, taking a bite of a chocolate chip cookie.

Waters shakes my shoulder. "Did you hear me?"

"Huh?"

He laughs. "I said get some rest. Tomorrow you're heading home."

25

"HE'S WAKING UP!" LUCY SHOUTS AS SHE
runs into the mess hall with Mira. All morning we've been
taking shifts sitting with Marco. First we switched off pack-
ing. Cole and I shoved Marco's stuff into his duffels after we'd
stowed away our own. Then the girls had an early breakfast
while we kept watch. They came to relieve us not too long
ago. I shovel a last bite of waffles into my mouth and take off
for the med room.

Sure enough, Marco is sitting up in bed when we enter.
His leg is still suspended, but the head bandage is off. Aside
from a nasty bruise, he doesn't look that bad.

When we walk in, he raises his hand in the air for a high five. "Ace, I heard about your jump off the spaceship. You really are the Red Baron!"

I smile and slap his palm. "I'm glad you're okay, dude. You had me worried. That was one extreme kamikaze mission."

"It worked out, right? I mean, we're here. This isn't a repeat of the Incident at Bounding Base 51."

"Actually," Cole says, "since this conflict involves the same parties, it has a lot of similarities to the Incident at Bounding Base 51."

Lucy laughs. "Yeah, with the key difference being our atoms aren't adrift in space." She gives Marco a gentle hug. "Happy you're safe, Marco."

"Happy we're all safe," he says. "I got lucky. My leg is broken, but that's it. Some of the Bounders are a lot worse off." His voice grows soft. "And two of the Tunnelers didn't make it."

"Is Charkeera okay?" Lucy asks. "I heard she was hit by a boulder."

Marco shakes his head.

Whoa. Charkeera was killed. I don't even know what to think.

Mira covers her face with her hands.

Lucy crosses her arms against her chest. "I hate those horrible aliens."

"The Youli," I say.

"What?" Cole asks.

"That's what they're called. The Youli."

"What kind of ridiculous name is that?" Marco asks.

I shrug. "I think it suits them."

One of the doctors rolls a wheelchair alongside Marco's bed. "Can you kids take him down to the closing ceremony?"

I grin at Marco. "Definitely."

"I don't trust the two of you with that chair for a second," Lucy says. "I'll push."

"Fine," I say.

The doctor helps Marco into the wheelchair, and we walk as a pod to the lecture hall. By the time we arrive, the hall is brimming with cadets, aeronauts, and other Earth Force officers. Ryan waves us over. He saved seats near the front. Lucy parks Marco's wheelchair at the edge of the row, and the rest of us get settled in our chairs.

"Admiral on deck!" Ridders shouts from the front stage.

As the honor guard escorts Admiral Eames to the podium, we all stand at attention. All of us except Marco, that is. I bet he's secretly happy he has an excuse for defying military decorum.

"At ease," she says. "Bounders, this is a momentous day—more momentous, perhaps, than your induction into Earth Force—for today we acknowledge the magnitude of your coming contributions to your planet and its defense."

MONICA TESLER

Here we go. Is she going to disclose the true purpose behind the Bounder Baby Breeding Program? Operation *Ultio*?

"These are perilous times for Earth," she continues. "These aliens—who we've learned are called the Youli—seek to destroy us. But you, Bounders . . . you have stared at the face of our enemy, and you did not cower. You have what it takes to defend your planet. In you, the Youli have met their match. Today we celebrate your first victory in battle!"

The admiral claps, and cadets leap to their feet, peppering the air with hoots and whistles. When the Earth Force officers join in, our pod stands. Even Marco knows to clap. Waters and Gedney slowly rise.

All this feels false, like it's just another piece of Earth Force's grand propaganda machine. How come everyone is so jazzed about fighting a bunch of aliens? Why did the admiral imply that Earth Force just found out about the Youli? And why did she call the battle a victory? That's not exactly how I remember it. I catch Marco's eye, and he shakes his head.

"In a few months," the admiral says, "you will return for your second tour of duty. Be prepared. Your training will intensify. Your obligations will increase. You may again be called to defend your planet. Make no mistake, defending Earth is your birthright."

No joke. We were bred to be soldiers. We were literally born to fight the Youli.

The admiral scans the audience, making eye contact with each cadet. When her eyes reach mine, I hold her gaze. She spreads her arms wide. "Be safe. Be well. We will see you soon."

She gives the podium to Ridders, who reviews our confidentiality obligations and mentions that the first free-bound will be deferred to the second tour. Then each pod leader says a few words about what a great success the first tour of duty was. Waters is grumpy but brief, which is good because all the cadets care about is saying their good-byes and boarding the craft for home.

Finally Florine takes the podium. No one is too interested in what she has to say. I can hardly hear her above the chatter in the lecture hall.

"Quiet!" The microphone screeches with feedback from her scream. "Quiet, puh-*leeeze*." She smooths her black suit and adjusts her sunglasses. "The EarthBound Academy is off to a successful start. And we owe a lot to you, Bounders. However, we owe even more to our aeronauts who taught you everything you know."

Uh, yeah, sure. Sheek was teaching us an awful lot when he hid in the hover during the battle.

"Don't forget to tune in to the next episode of *Chic with Sheek* on EFAN," she continues. "The special guest will be none other than your Director of Bounder Affairs, herself.

Me! Isn't that right, Sheek?" She flashes her teeth at him across the lecture hall.

I bet she's blackmailing Sheek into featuring her on his show. She'll stay quiet about the battle in exchange for a guest spot. If there's one person from the EarthBound Academy who I won't miss, it's Florine Statton.

"If you can make your way to the passenger craft," she says, "your belongings have been loaded, and we are ready to depart."

Now those are the words we've been waiting to hear. I take the handles of Marco's wheelchair and race up the aisle. We're outta here!

· *EF* ·

As soon as the captain disengages FTL on our flight home to Earth, the plebes come through the aisles, collecting our gloves.

"Can't say I'm sad to see these go for a while," Marco says. He sits beside us in the aisle, his foot elevated on his wheelchair.

"I am," Cole says. "I would have liked a chance to practice before our next tour."

"You're fine," I say. "You bounded, remember? That's more than most of these clowns can say." I look at Regis. He's on the other side of the craft, entertaining his groupies with some riveting tale. Probably a lie. "Just enjoy the break."

"You know what I'm going to do on break?" Lucy says. "I've got it all planned. First I'm going shopping with my friends. I have to get caught up on everything I missed while I was gone. Then I'm going for a manicure. Florine shared the name of her favorite pink polish. I'm no fan of Florine, but she has great taste in cosmetics. And then I've got to call my acting coach and try to hit a few auditions. You never know . . ."

Cole rolls his eyes. I laugh. A lot has changed, but a lot hasn't.

"Look!" Marco says. Out the front window, Earth comes into view.

Seeing Earth from space on the day we left for the Academy was probably the coolest thing I've ever done. But somehow it's even more powerful now on the trip home. I know our planet is threatened; I hadn't known that then. And I know I have to defend it. I have no choice about that. It's what I was born to do. But it's a job I would have accepted on my own, even with all the Earth Force secrets.

As the craft touches down at the Earth Force Aeronautical Port, I try to spot my family in the crowd. I think I see Addy jumping up and down, but I can't be sure. It's hard to see out. Everyone is trying to find their families. I'm not the only one relieved to be home.

As soon as the clearance bell sounds, Mira leaps from her seat and slips to the front of the line. So much for good-byes.

Before she steps off the craft, she spins. For a split second her eyes find mine, then she twirls back around and is gone. In my mind I see her dancing in her blue tank top and silver chain, just like the day we left for the EarthBound Academy.

As we wait to disembark, Marco grabs my arm from his wheelchair. "Ace, I'll catch you on the next tour. Be ready for some blast pack races."

I shake Marco's hand, and he pulls me down for a hug. "You, too, Wiki," he says to Cole, dragging him into an awkward three-way hug. Hugs aren't Cole's thing.

Lucy kisses me on the cheek. "Don't do anything silly, Jasper. You know, like throw yourself in front of a herd of charging wildeboars. We're counting on you."

"Good-bye, Lucy," I say. "I'm sure your friends will be psyched to have you back."

"Oh, they will," she says, stepping behind Marco's wheelchair to push him off the craft.

As we inch to the front, I can see the tarmac. Was it only six weeks ago we stood there, waiting to board?

Cole and I fall in line together. "I can't believe it's over," I say.

"I know what you mean."

When we reach the door to the craft, Cole turns to me. "Your sister was right."

"What?"

"She said we'd make good first friends."

"You heard that?"

"I don't miss much," Cole says.

We step onto the ramp. I was right. It was Addy who I saw before. She's jumping up and down, waving her arms. She says something to my parents, and then they're all waving.

I probably imagine it, but I swear I can hear Addy's voice in my mind.

I'm so happy you're home, Jasper!

Me too, Addy. Me too.

Acknowledgments

My name may be on the cover, but a whole team of people helped make *Bounders* a book. I owe deep gratitude to many.

Thank you to my agent, David Dunton, who plucked *Bounders* out of the slush pile and found us the perfect home.

A huge heaping of gratitude goes to my supremely talented editor, Michael Strother. Michael's enthusiasm is contagious, his confidence in me is inspiring, and his vision for *Bounders* was spot-on.

Big thanks to the whole Simon & Schuster/Aladdin team for helping take *Bounders* from acquisition table to bookshelf, including Mara Anastas, Jon Anderson, Mary Marotta, Fiona Simpson, Lucille Rettino, Carolyn Swerdloff, Teresa Ronquillo, Tara Grieco, Anthony Parisi, Candace Greene McManus, Betsy Bloom, Michelle Leo, Christina Pecorale, Victor Iannone, Rio Cortez, Danielle Esposito, Karin Paprocki, Kayley Hoffman, and Ksenia Winnicki.

I am so grateful for my cover illustrator, Antonio Caparo, whose amazing art truly brought my imagination to life.

Thank you to all my writer friends who have helped in so many ways, through critiquing, beta reading, advice giving, and more. A special shout-out to Debbie Blackington,

Julia Flaherty, Erin Fletcher, David Learned, Jen Malone, Lisa Rehfuss, Marilyn Salerno, Melissa Schorr, Neely Simpson, Carissa Taylor, the Yahoo YA/MG Writers Group, the Davis Square Crepes Crew, and the Sweet Sixteens.

An incredible group of young readers gave feedback on *Bounders* before it was acquired. Many thanks to Ella Benjamin, Hannah Dunton, Lillian Gates, Jenna Stowell, Joey Stowell, and Nathan Tesler.

A big cheer goes out to my fabulous friends who get me away from my computer screen, especially Nicole Benjamin, Paula Drake, Liz Fuller, and Joe Stowell who all indulged me in many conversations about *Bounders* and the publication process.

I am blessed with a supportive extended family. Many thanks to my parents, Lynne and Richard Swanson, and to the rest of the Swanson, Ogden, Tesler, and Anderson families.

Finally, the biggest bucket of gratitude goes out to the three guys who keep me going: Jamey, Nathan, and Gabriel. I love and appreciate you so much. Thank you for sticking by my side on this wild ride.

Nathan, my firstborn and first reader, you are a delight and an inspiration. This book is for you.

Don't miss Jasper's next great adventure
in the EarthBound Academy!

AFTER BREAKING INTO PRISON CELLS
and battling aliens, you might think Cole and I would have
no problem with Addy's plan to bust into an apartment
building's mainframe tonight and take its elevator for a
joyride, but you'd be wrong. She's been pestering us ever since
I agreed to let her tag along as I show Cole around our district.

"Jasper says you're an ace hacker." My younger sister narrows her eyes at Cole and pushes into his personal space. Even
though they're about the same size, Addy seems twice as big as
she looms over him on the bench.

"I never said that," Cole stammers. His gaze dodges in every
direction except at Addy. He leans so far back I'm worried

he's going to fall off the bench and land in the grass of the green block where we're killing time before heading back to the apartment.

Cole's not going to be happy with me. He definitely does not like to be called a hacker, although there's really no other way to describe his mad skills at system manipulation. And I doubt being pushed around by my little sister was high on his wish list when he decided to come stay with us for a few days before we leave for our second tour of duty with Earth Force.

"It doesn't matter what you said." Addy transfers her hands to her hips. "It only matters if it's true. This whole plan hinges on you breaking into the lift system. Can you do it or not?"

"How do you know it will work?" Cole asks.

"Do I really have to go through this again?" Addy rolls her eyes, reminding me of our pod mate, Lucy. "Mason's dad works in lift maintenance. He told Eric, who told Larina, who told Molls, who told me. Execute the Lift System Maintenance Protocol and the lift dead drops until the safety tether engages. Easy."

"And we'll free-fall all three hundred floors of the apartment complex," I remind Cole before he chickens out. "Think of the speed! I overheard some older kids talking about it on the rails. It's supposed to be awesome!"

"Fine," Cole sighs. He won't look at Addy, but he shoots me a stern stare.

Yep, he's mad.

"Great!" Addy says, sitting next to Cole on the bench. "Then it's all set. The plan goes down tonight! While we're on the subject, I have a couple other ideas that could use Cole's hacking genius."

I laugh. "You're all about the danger and thrills these days, Ads."

Cole turns his back on Addy. "Speaking of that, Jasper, you better keep your sister away from Marco when she starts at the Academy next spring. They'd make a scary combination."

"No kidding," I say. Our pod mate Marco is the walking definition of thrill seeker. He could teach Addy a thing or two, and from the way Addy's been acting lately, she would definitely go along for the ride.

Addy clears her throat. "Ummm, I can hear you. I'm standing right here. And I can take care of myself at the Academy, thank you very much."

Cole looks at his shoes. He must be struggling to keep his mouth shut, just like I have since I got home from the EarthBound Academy.

This past spring we were part of the first group of Bounders to be sworn in as Earth Force cadets and sent to space for training. Before we were born, Earth Force discovered a link between brain structure and quantum space travel. They reintroduced the Bounder genes into the population and—*Bam!*—twelve years later they had the first group ready to be trained as quantum aeronauts to pilot the ships that can bound across the galaxy in an instant.

We weren't at the space station long before we realized Earth Force wanted the Bounders for more than traditional space travel. They'd stolen biotechnology from an alien race—the Youli—and were convinced the Bounders could master it. And they were right. Now Earth Force is training Bounders to be the front line in their secret war against the Youli. Cole and I have a battle under our belt to prove it.

Addy's completely in the dark. She still thinks the Academy curriculum is learning how to pilot the quantum bounding ships. Cole and I are under strict confidentiality orders to keep it that way. Revealing the truth about the Academy to anyone is a grave violation of the Earth Force Code of Conduct.

Unfortunately Cole's the worst at keeping secrets, and he's about to blow our cover.

"What?" Addy says, ogling us with an evil stare.

Cole and I stay silent.

"Seriously, what?"

"It's just . . . ," Cole starts.

I elbow Cole hard in the ribs. "It's just nothing. Tell us about those other hacking ideas."

"Uh-uh, Jasper." Addy shakes her head. "You know I can

spot a secret from a mile away. What are you guys keeping from me?"

"Like I said, nothing," I spit out quickly so Cole doesn't have a chance to even think about telling the truth.

Addy nods at Cole. "Then why is he squirming around on the bench?"

She kneels in front of Cole and tries to make him look her in the eye.

"Cut it out, Addy," I say. "Leave him alone. It's just Academy stuff we're not supposed to talk about. That's it. You'll find out soon enough."

"You must be joking!" Addy springs to her feet and throws her arms in the air. "I'm a Bounder, too, remember? The whole world knows we're Bounders, J. No more secrets!"

While we've been arguing, the green block has filled with workers on their lunch breaks. And now it seems we're their prime dining entertainment. That is the last thing we need— an accidental announcement to all of Americana East that we're at war with a technologically advanced alien race.

"Go home, Addy!" I shout. "No one asked you to tag along!"

Addy's cheeks color pink like my words slapped her skin. Then the muscles in her face move, morphing from shock to hurt to rage.

I expect her to lash out. Addy is rarely one to give in.

Instead, she spins on her heels and races up the block.

"Why did you do that?" Cole asks.

"Really?" I remember the nosy diners and lower my voice to a whisper. "You were about to spill the beans, that's why!"

"You mean about the—"

Before Cole can say another word, I grab his arm and drag him off the bench. I pull him by the sleeve off the green block and into the thick of pedestrian traffic. After a few twists and turns, I duck into an alleyway and spin to face him.

"What the heck, Cole? What part of *top-level security clearance* don't you understand?"

"I know, but . . ."

"No buts! I've lived in the same apartment with Addy for the last four months! I've kept my mouth shut all that time! Never once did I come as close to caving as you did just then."

"But she's . . ."

"I said no buts! Geez, Cole. Did you tell everyone in your district about the Youli?" As soon as the word slips from my mouth I cringe. Scanning the alleyway, I'm relieved there's not a single person remotely in earshot.

"I didn't tell anyone," Cole says. "I swear! I basically kept to myself the entire time. But something about being here with you . . . and your sister is a Bounder, too . . . and . . ."

"Look, I get it," I say, "but we need to be careful. If word got out, it could be a huge problem."

And now I have another huge problem on my hands: Addy.

"What do we tell your sister?" Cole asks.

"The same thing we should have told her before. Absolutely nothing."

Cole bounces on his toes. He's nervous. He really is the worst at secrets.

"Seriously, Cole. Not a word to Addy about the Academy. If she tries to pry it out of you, bring up *Evolution* or something."

Cole's eyes light with a fire only *Evolution of Combat* can ignite. He's a genius, like a total game master. I've never known anyone who came close to Cole at his *Evolution* skills. All summer we've been syncing up our game modules remotely, and he's been leading the Battle of Berlin. Just last month, we won World War II. It took Cole more than a year to defeat the level.

"You must have made it further than anyone by now," I continue.

Cole shrugs. "Now that we're in the Cold War, the game has changed. There's a lot of behind-the-scenes human psychology to factor in. That's not my strength."

I choke down a laugh. "No kidding. Maybe Lucy can help you," I joke. Lucy would never help. She hates *Evolution*. But Cole thinks I'm serious.

"Maybe," he says. "She can be annoying, but she's really good with rallying troops." Cole shoots me a side glance. "On the Paleo Planet—"

"Shhh!" I say, scanning the alleyway again. "I know what you're talking about! You don't need to say it." I press my back against the stone wall and slide down until my butt hits the ground. Cole crouches beside me.

I close my eyes as my brain takes me back to the battle. Lucy rallies the Bounders while Cole issues the marching orders. Marco takes off in his blast pack, charging the Youli on the cliff. His body goes rigid as the alien seizes control of his atoms. For a second, Marco hangs suspended in space, then the Youli flings him across the valley directly into the herd of mammoths. Next thing I know, I'm tackling the alien on top of his ship as his words slip inside my brain. Then Mira bounds amidst the herd of charging wildeboars.

"I'm scared." I wouldn't tell most people, but I know Cole understands. All my pod mates understand.

"Earth Force has a huge incentive to protect its military assets," he says.

Cole offers this factual nugget to make me feel better. It kind of does. But by *military assets*, he means me. Us. The Bounders. The soldiers they bred to fight their war with the Youli. The next evolution of combat.

"That's something, I guess." I stand and brush off the back

of my jeans. "Let's get back. My mom will be worried."

And Addy will be mad.

And we'll still be soldiers.

At least we're shipping out tomorrow for our second tour. And when we return in the spring for our third, Addy will be twelve and coming with us. She'll find out the truth soon enough. She'll learn what it really means to be a Bounder.

· E_F ·

Cole and I beeline for my room as soon as we get back to my apartment. I slam the door and sink into the beanbag I begged my parents for after my first tour. If I close my eyes, it's almost like I'm in our pod room at the Academy with its green grass carpet, starry ceiling, and groovy light sticks. Unfortunately the hum of Addy's violin is blowing a hole straight through my imagination. Her sad song is proof that I'm in my bedroom and not in space, and a vivid reminder that I'm the world's meanest brother.

Cole lays his tablet on my bed and the projection for *Evolution of Combat* fills the air space above my blanket. "Let's mess around on some old levels. How about the Middle Ages?"

"Sure, as long as we can joust." I toss my tablet on the bed, activate, and sync up.

I select my armor, weapon, and horse for my avatar, but Addy's music won't let me go. Her notes drift through the walls and down my throat where they take shape as one of those close-to-crying lumps.

I don't know why I haven't told her the truth. Like Cole said, she's a Bounder, and she'll find out soon enough. But when I got home from the Academy, everything was shaken up, including me. I didn't know how to be Jasper who fought the Youli while being Jasper, Addy's brother, background boy, klutz. Plus, Mom was so sure that everything would go back to normal with me at home that I didn't want to disappoint her. So I left the new Jasper at the space station and went back to my old self. I keep my mouth shut and say *Huh?* and *Oops!* and *Sorry* all the time like I used to. It's as if I'm in a perpetual holding mode, hovering like a passenger craft waiting for clearance to land, but in my case, I'm waiting to get back to the Academy.

"Hey!" Cole says. "I thought you wanted to joust!"

"Huh?"

"The game, Jasper."

In the *Evolution* projection, my very dead knight stays upright on his horse only because he's skewered by Cole's lance at the tournament of champions.

"Oops! Sorry." At least I won't be in a holding pattern much longer. "Do you mind playing on your own for a few minutes? I'll be right back."

Cole doesn't respond, but I know he'll be fine. I grab

my clarinet from the top of my duffel bag and head into the hall.

When I knock at Addy's room, the music stops, but she doesn't answer. I crack open her door.

She shoves her violin into its case and pushes back her chair. "What do you want?"

I open the door the rest of the way and lift my clarinet. "How about a duet?" Her poster of Maximilian Sheek, the celebrity aeronaut, still hangs above her desk. She probably would've taken it down if I'd told her what a coward Sheek was on the Paleo Planet.

"No." The word's a dismissal. She steps to her closet and ducks inside. "Things have changed, Jasper."

She's right. Things *have* changed. I've changed. And even though I've tried to hide it, Addy knows.

"Can we talk, then?" I walk into her room and sit at the foot of her bed.

Addy emerges from her closet, arms crossed tightly against her chest. "What? You've finally decided to tell me all your secrets?"

This isn't going to be easy. "Look, Addy, I get it. You're mad. You have a right to be mad. But I'm in a tough spot. The admiral was crystal clear about one thing: confidentiality. We're under strict orders not to talk about certain things, even with our families."

"But I'm not just family. I'm a Bounder. Isn't Earth Force going to share these secrets with me, too?"

"Yes, but not until next spring, when you go to the Academy."

She throws her hands in the air. "I don't get it. If they're going to tell me anyway, why can't you tell me now? Am I not important to you anymore? How come you're choosing them over me?"

Huh? "That's not what I'm doing! You'll always be important to me, Addy."

"Maybe. But you're loyal to them. To Earth Force. Not to me." Addy's voice grows quiet. She climbs onto her bed—careful to keep a meter between us—and snuggles with a purple elephant Dad won at the fair a few summers back.

This is not going well. How do I make her understand without unloading everything I know about Earth Force? "Look, Addy, it's stuff you need to experience for yourself. And most of it's pretty amazing! As for the other stuff . . . well . . . I'll be there to help you through it."

Addy huffs. "What's that supposed to mean? What other stuff?"

"I told you about the confidentiality order, Ads. And I'm really not trying to be cryptic, it's just . . . there was this girl at the Academy. Mira. There was so much to take in, and she helped me. I want you to know that I'll be there for you, like Mira was for me."

Addy's face is all crumpled. I can't tell if she's thinking, or fuming, or about to burst out laughing. She squeezes her elephant so tight I'm sure the stuffing is going to explode all over her bed.

"I'm not happy you're keeping secrets," she finally says, "but I'm glad you talked to me. It's hard enough that you're leaving again. I don't want the night before you go to be filled with fighting."

I relax a little. "Good." I push up from the bed, and my mind jumps ahead to my jousting match with Cole.

"Not so fast," Addy says with a sneaky grin on her face. "Let's hear more about this girl. Mira."

Oh no. I should have seen that coming a mile away.

"She's just a friend," I say.

"Sure." Addy's clearly not buying it.

"No, really. She plays the piano, and we played this duet together once, and . . ."

Addy jumps to her feet. All the anger and frustration of moments before, now long gone. "I can't believe you didn't tell me you had a girlfriend! That's the biggest secret of all!"

"Shut up!" I grab a pillow from her bed and deck her with it. "She's not my girlfriend. But maybe this will give you a clue about why I don't tell you everything."

"Fine. She's not your girlfriend." The smirk on Addy's face tells me she doesn't believe it for a second. "Can I meet her tomorrow at the launch?"

Oh geez. No way. The last thing I need is my sister steamrolling quiet Mira. "No. She's . . . she's not what you'd expect. You can meet her next spring when you come to the Academy."

"Uh-uh, Jasper. I'm meeting her tomorrow, whether you like it or—"

The doorbell rings.

"Who's that?" she says.

"Let's find out!" Saved by the bell, I leap off the bed and dash out of the room.

An Earth Force officer stands at the open door. Mom blocks his way into our apartment. Her hands are on her hips, and she's shaking her head.

"I'm sorry, ma'am," he says. "Those are the orders."

"What's going on, Mom?" I ask.

Mom reluctantly steps aside to let the officer enter. She turns to face me. "It seems you and Cole are departing a bit early for your second tour. Make sure your bags are packed. You're leaving tonight."

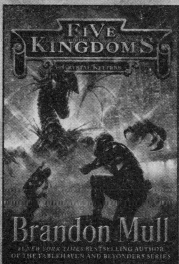 

Looking for another great book?
Find it
IN THE MIDDLE.

Fun, fantastic books for kids
in the in-be**TWEEN** age.

IntheMiddleBooks.com